The
Holy Lance

The English Templars Series

Book One

The
Holy Lance

Book One of the English Templars Series

A Novel

Andrew Latham

KNOX ROBINSON
PUBLISHING
London & New York

KNOX ROBINSON
PUBLISHING

34 New House
67-68 Hatton Garden
London, EC1N 8JY
&
244 5th Avenue, Suite 1861
New York, New York 10001

First published in Great Britain and the United States in 2014 by Knox Robinson Publishing

A CIP catalogue record for this book is available from the British Library.

ISBN HC 978-1-910282-41-0

ISBN PB 978-1-910282-52-6

Typeset in Adobe Caslon Pro

Printed in the United States of America and the United Kingdom

www.knoxrobinsonpublishing.com

Cast of Characters

The English Templars

MICHAEL FITZ ALAN, English Templar Knight

ARNALDUS DE FONTE, Gascon Templar Knight, Fitz Alan's friend

WILLIAM TURCAULT, commander of Fitz Alan's turcopole contingent

THOMAS WYTHEBERD, squire to Michael Fitz Alan

Outremer

ROBERT DE SABLÉ, Grand Master of the Knights Templar

FATHER RAIMUNDUS DE RAMLA, Hospitaller priest

CONRAD DE MONTFERRAT, Lord of Tyre, cousin of the King of France, pretender to the throne of Jerusalem

ALBERTO FANO CANOVESE (The Sinister One, Il Sinistro), Lord of Montegrosso d'Asti, vassal of Conrad of Montferrat

EMMANUELE VOLPIANO, Il Sinistro's henchman

GUY DE LUSIGNAN, King of Jerusalem

HUGO LE GRANT, Templar Knight, Armorer of the Kingdom of Jerusalem

The Crusaders

RICHARD, Duke of Aquitaine, Count of Poitou, crowned King of England in 1189

HUBERT WALTER, Bishop of Salisbury and Richard's chancellor

PHILIP II, King of France

ROBERT, Count of Dreux, cousin of Philip

PHILIP, Bishop of Beauvais, brother of Robert

FATHER BENEDICT ARKWRIGHT, Templar Chaplain and mentor to Fitz Alan

ALIAZARS D'UZEST, Occitan crossbowman and secret Cathar heretic, serving with Richard's host

The Saracens

SALĀH AD-DĪN YŪSUF IBN AYYŪB, known to the Franks as Saladin, Sultan of Egypt

AL-MALIK AL-ADIL SAYF AL-DIN ABU-BAKR IBN AYYUB, known to the Franks as Saphadin, Saladin's brother and "minister of war"

The
Holy Lance

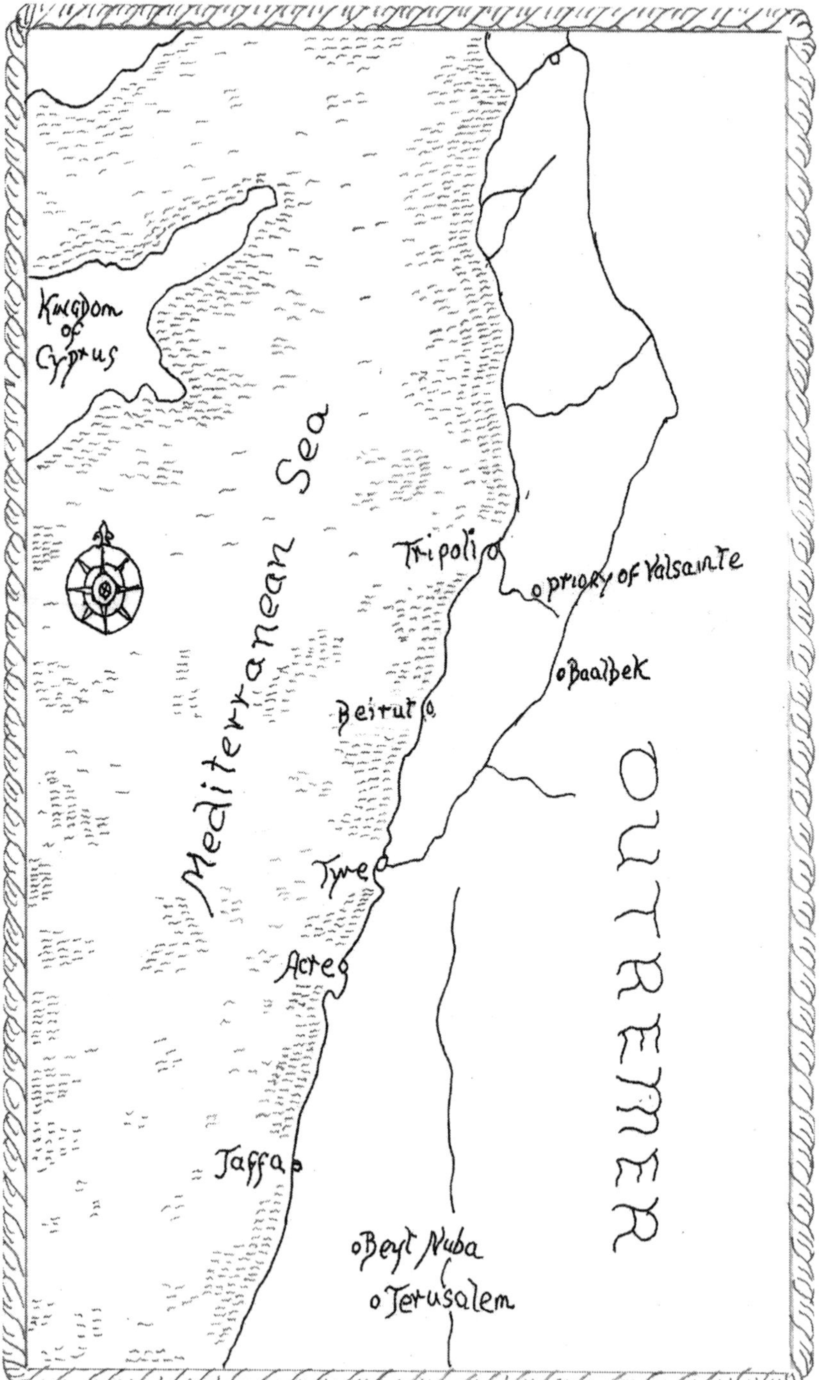
Kingdom of Cyprus
Mediterranean Sea
Tripoli
priory of Valsainte
Baalbek
Beirut
Tyre
Acre
Jaffa
Beyt Nuba
Jerusalem
OUTREMER

II

11 July 1191

Brother Michael Fitz Alan could not see the Saracen army, but he could hear both the rhythmic beating of its massive war drums and the unmistakable clamor of its warriors assembling in anticipation of the day's slaughter. He knew they were out there, the heathen bastards, gathering just out of sight in the folds and shadows of the broken and wooded country that lay beyond the Christian line; salivating, he was sure, at the thought of fighting and dying in the service of their false god. He raised himself higher in the saddle of his warhorse, straining to catch sight of the Turkish devils, but could see nothing other than a few brightly colored enemy tents and banners on hilltops in the far distance. Settling back in his saddle, he turned his attention away from the audible but unseen foe and back to his own men. To his front were two lines of dismounted fighters, each clad in kettle-hats and black tunics displaying either a simple red cross or a cross *patée*. The first line, the one closest to the Great Trench, was made up of three squadrons of sergeant-brothers, each about a hundred strong. Within each squadron, the men knelt side-by-side, shields and lances for the moment resting on the ground, but ready to be raised in an instant to form a dense and deadly defensive wall. As there were not enough men to form an unbroken line behind the trench, the spaces between the squadrons had been filled with rows of sharpened stakes firmly planted in the ground inclined toward the enemy. The second line was composed of pairs of *turcopoles*, native Christian troops. In dress, they were more similar to the Turks than the Christians, but each wore a kettle-hat like the sergeant-brothers to their front in order to distinguish them from the hated foe. The *turcopoles* were armed not with lances but with crossbows and were arrayed behind a wall of shields spiked into the earth to provide cover from the inevitable torrent of enemy arrows that would rain down on them once the battle was joined. Fitz Alan knew from experience that when the battle began, these men would work together

1

– one loading, the other shooting – to deliver volley after volley of deadly missiles into the ranks of the oncoming enemy. Experience also taught him that these weapons would wreak bloody havoc on those heathens brave or foolish enough to come within range. Having seen them at work in the months since he'd arrived, he thought it no wonder the Holy Father had forbidden the use of these weapons against Christians. Their only proper employment, he thought, was to slaughter the filthy heathen defilers of the Holy places that even now were amassing just beyond the rise to his front.

Behind these dismounted fighters was Fitz Alan's *eschielle* of knights, each of whom wore a white *cappa* or long-sleeved robe over his chainmail hauberk and a one-rounded iron helmet over the chainmail hood covering his head and chin. Each knight carried a lance, sword and shield, though as they had not yet been called to readiness these were at the moment either sheathed, slung or at rest. The mounted knight-brothers were on the far right of the Templar line, their formation anchored by an elongated tree-covered hillock that provided protection from Turkish encirclement, even as it concealed the next stretch of the trench line from their view. To their left, close to the low cliff that fell away to the sea below, a dismounted squadron of sergeant-brothers was deploying. Fitz Alan noted with approval the disciplined way in which these brothers were moving into their battle formation.

"May God and all His saints stand with us, brothers," said Fitz Alan, "for it sounds like those Turkish demons are working themselves up to fight the Devil's own fight today."

"If those heathens try to cross that ditch this morning, Brother Michael," replied Arnaldus de Fonte, second-in-command of the *eschielle*, "they'll find themselves in hell long before they can do the Evil One much good." In his early thirties, de Fonte was a bear of a man – big, muscular, and fierce. His hair and skin were as dark as a Saracen's, and along the left side of his face, only partly concealed by his closely cropped beard, he bore a long, thin scar earned in close quarters combat with a French-Gascon knight. Until a few years back, both he and Fitz Alan had served in the armies of England's Prince Richard, fighting together to assert their lord's rights against the aging and insipid Henry II. Once Richard had become king, however, each for his own reasons had decided to quit his service and enter the Order. After a year learning the basics of monastic life at the Temple Ewell commandery in England, they had sailed with Archbishop Baldwin of Canterbury for the Holy Land, arriving at Tyre in October in the year of our Lord 1190. For the last nine months, they had been here, fighting in the Christian armies besieging Acre.

"It's a good position, right enough, Arnaldus, but the Saracens know that if they don't break the siege now Acre'll fall for certain." Fitz Alan raised himself up again, straining to catch sight of the enemy horse-archers he knew were out there. "And don't forget," he continued, "they smashed through our defenses once before." That had been a near-run thing, he recalled. Only a few months after his draft of English Templars had arrived with the archbishop, that Saracen demon Saladin had launched a surprise attack that had broken through both the outer ring of Christian defenses and the inner ring of siege-works. This had allowed the heathens to bring fresh fighters, much-needed supplies and even a new commander into the city, enabling the defenders to hold out even to this very day.

"In any case, drums are getting louder. They'll be upon us presently," said de Fonte, who was already pulling the chain mail ventilator of his coif across his mouth and chin. "Will you give the command?" he continued as he fastened the laces over his left ear.

Before Fitz Alan could reply, the turopole commander of the sergeant-brothers barked out a single word: "Shields!" In an instant the front line of brothers pulled their shields up to form three tightly packed walls of wood, metal and leather. Each then moved as close as he could to the man on his right. "No gaps!" the *turcopolier* bellowed. "Get as close to the man on your right as the Rule allows!" As each man sought the protection of the man to his right, each of the dismounted squadrons shuffled a few yards to the right. Fitz Alan was impressed that the *turcopolier* had anticipated this when initially deploying the sergeant-brothers so that once the shuffling had ended each squadron was arrayed precisely between the clumps of sharpened stakes that filled and protected the unmanned parts of the trench line.

"Lances!" the *turcopolier* shouted. With that, each of the sergeant-brothers jammed the butt of his lance into the earth with the shaft inclined upwards and the point toward the enemy. "Bows!" he barked at the *turcopoles* in the second line. Each of these native fighters then placed the stirrups at the fore-end of the bow on the ground, put both feet in them, drew the string upward to catch the lock, and placed a bolt in the firing trough. Once spanned in this way, the crossbows were placed flat on the ground, and would remain there until the command was given to load the quarrels and prepare to shoot.

Now it was Fitz Allan's turn. "Squadron! Prepare!" he shouted. The knight-brothers of his *eschielle* responded to the command as they had countless times before, both in training and on the field of battle, quickly completing a final few pre-battle preparations such as fastening ventilators, securing helmets to coifs, drawing the chain mail hand-coverings of their hauberks over their hands, and unslinging their shields. These preparations complete, the knight-brothers, like the sergeants before them, fell into total silence. Then the *gonfanier*, a man chosen for his courage, discipline and piety, raised the distinctive black-and-while banner of the Knights Templar. Like the ancient Roman *Vexillum*, this was a small rectangular flag attached vertically to a crossbar so that it could be seen even on a windless day. Templars followed the *vexillum belli* or *Beauseant* into battle and rallied to it after a charge so that they could re-form and continue the attack. As all Templars knew, for it had been drilled into them from the moment they were admitted to the Order, as long as the *Beauseant* flew no Templar was to leave the field of battle. The banner was thus key to the discipline that almost always gave them the advantage over friend and foe alike.

Fitz Alan surveyed the scene one more time. He'd have liked to have more men in the front line, and maybe even a few more crossbowmen, but given what he had he was satisfied that the Templar division was now both properly arrayed and well-prepared to do its sworn duty – to fight and kill the enemies of Christ and His Church. He turned to his old friend, Brother Arnaldus, and was about to comment on the skill with which the *turcopolier* had deployed the front ranks of sergeant-brothers.

And then the arrows began to fly.

"Magnificent!" exclaimed Richard, King of England, Duke of Normandy, Duke of Aquitaine, Duke of Gascony, Lord of Cyprus, Count of Anjou, Count of Maine, Count of Nantes, and Overlord of Brittany. "Absolutely brilliant!"

"Yes, my Lord," replied Hubert Walter, Bishop of Salisbury, the king's chancellor, confidante and right arm.

"Those Templars move as if they are God's own sword arm. Who could possibly stand against them? Had I a hundred such men in France, things would have been very different, very different indeed."

"None can bear up against fighters such as these, my Lord. Their discipline and dedication makes them nearly unbeatable. And I dare say fifty would have been all you would have needed to press your case in France."

"Quite so, Walter, quite so. But what do you make of the way we are arrayed today? Have we the advantage, or do you give that bastard Saladin and his ungodly host the edge?"

"You are the warrior, my lord, and I a mere cleric, but to my unschooled eye, our forces seem well disposed. Indeed, I cannot see how we can lose."

"Oh, we can lose alright," replied Richard, "once the battle is joined anything can happen. But we do seem to be well arrayed. See how our various divisions are anchored against the possibility of being turned by Saracen enveloping attacks. The Templars on the left between the sea and that hillock; *les frères Dreux* between the two hillocks; and on and on right 'round the town to the sea on the other side. Saladin'll have a devil of a time trying to break through that line."

"Indeed my lord."

"But he'll try – he has to. If he can't break through and relieve the garrison soon, a day or two at the most, the fortress will fall. He'll have a hard time holding his army together if he suffers a defeat on that scale." The king looked over his shoulder toward the besieged town, even now suffering bombardment from the half-dozen or so trebuchets and other siege engines that continually rained massive stones on the town and its defenses. These great machines had already smashed huge gaps in the town walls and there was little doubt that the garrison would have to surrender soon if Saladin failed to relieve it. "Once the town falls, we'll have a base from which to strike south along the coast to Jaffa. And once there we'll be in a good position to move inland toward Jerusalem. But we'll also have hostages – bargaining chips to use to pry the True Cross from the grasping hands of that infidel bastard. And I'll have shown once and for all that Saladin can be beaten and beaten well. That'll make things difficult for him – very difficult indeed."

"My lord," the bishop interrupted, "the battle begins." From their elevated vantage point on a low hill behind the trench, the king's party could clearly see the Turks advancing all along the crusader line. They could also see that the main line of advance was on the Christian left, toward the Templar division, a route that offered them the shortest route to the town should they break through.

"Indeed it does. Looks like the Templar division will take the brunt of the attack. Who's in charge down there, Grand Master?"

"Brother Michael Fitz Alan, Sire. Relatively new to the order, but a ferocious fighter, a natural leader of men and a true servant of God."

The king looked quizzically at his chancellor. "Is that....?"

"One and the same, Your Grace, one and the same."

"Then I pity the poor damned Saracen swine leading the attack – he has no idea who he's tangled with."

"No, my lord, he does not," but then, thought Bishop Walter, neither did you, my lord, neither did you.

The Saracen horse-archers had been attacking for half the morning now, dashing forward, loosing their arrows at the Templar line, and then quickly retreating out of range. De Fonte turned to Fitz Alan, "You'd think after all these years, the heathen would know that the Knights of the Temple never fall for this nonsense." He was referring, of course, to the Saracen tactic of using horse-archers to wear down and infuriate the Christian forces in order both to weaken them and draw them into precipitous attack. If they succeeded in this, he knew from bitter experience, they would disperse the Christian knights, leaving them vulnerable to counterattack by Saracen heavy cavalry.

"Works well enough against the pilgrims," Fitz Alan replied contemptuously, referring to the crusaders, who were technically on an "armed pilgrimage" to the Holy Places, "especially those glory-seeking bastards who take the cross just to make a name for themselves. An hour or two of this sort of stinging and the intemperate and vain always break formation and give chase." He left unsaid the consequences of such vainglory, which rarely turned to the advantage of the crusader knights. Fitz

Alan subconsciously rotated his right shoulder, which was already beginning to ache in anticipation of the pains that always afflicted him when he went into battle. "In any case, they'll soon tire of losing men to no good purpose. Then we'll see what we're really in for."

Just then a knot of twenty or thirty Turcoman horse-archers closed to within about a hundred yards of the Templar line, pulled up and prepared to loose a volley. The ground was littered with a score or more of their comrades and perhaps a half-dozen dead horses, all victims of earlier efforts to sting the Templars into a precipitous attack. Fitz Alan watched as the man on the far right of the group dropped a short dart into the firing trough of his crossbow. At this distance, he could clearly see the man's double-breasted coat, his fur-lined hat, the ornate quiver suspended from his belt, the small round shield strapped to his left forearm, and even, when the Saracen's horse unexpectedly shifted sideways, the plait of long, black hair that hung down his back. Then, just as the Turcoman raised his crossbow and prepared to shoot his missile toward the Templar line, Fitz Alan saw a crossbow quarrel embed itself in the horse-archer's forehead, knocking him backwards with such force that the back of his skull crashed into his horse's croup. The animal, panicked, reared and then galloped toward the Templar lines, the lifeless rider still tangled in the stirrups, blood spurting skyward from the fatal wound. The *turcopolier* shouted a command and the horse was brought down just shy of the Templar trench, where it, like its rider, spent its last few moments frothing and twitching on the ground.

"By my count, that's about two dozen of the bastards dead," said de Fonte, "and what do they have to show for it? Three of our brothers wounded, and none badly enough to be pulled from the line. Damned fools!"

"Never mind that now, Arnaldus, the drums are back." Fitz Alan had only realized the drums had been silent for the duration of the horse-archers' attack when he heard them start up again, louder than ever, and mingled now with bellowed commands, the sound of horns, fifes and the clangor that could only be made by a very large number of warriors moving rapidly. He could still see nothing – the hillock to his right and the low rise to his front concealed everything – but the sound of masses of men moving to battle was unmistakable.

And then, over the crest, the Saracen host appeared.

"Walter," called the king, "do you have any idea how much I loathe that contumacious dog Robert of Dreux and his treacherous brother Philip, the Bishop of Beauvais?"

"My lord may have mentioned his distaste for *les frères* Dreux once or twice in the past," the bishop replied, "and, if I may, I can't say that they've ever impressed me much either." The bishop reflected briefly on the role played by these two vassals of the French king as they had worked against the Angevins over the past decade or so. "And yet…"

"And yet… there they are, anchoring the right flank of the Templar division, the whole line dependent on the resolution and competence of two of the most irresolute and incompetent vermin in all of Christendom."

"The Lord moves in mysterious ways, your Grace."

"Indeed He does, or so I am reliably informed by men such as yourself, but truly I fear that these incontinent swine will cost us the battle this day. They are able to contain neither themselves nor the knights under their command. How can I depend upon men such as this?"

The bishop mused at the irony of such of question. His king was undeniably a great warrior, and without a doubt a great leader of men. But he was just as surely a man given to great excesses of passion and great surfeits of self-discipline. To be speaking of the brothers Dreux in this way, the bishop thought, was akin to the kettle calling the pot black. "Your Grace," he replied, "the brothers Dreux are arrayed between the hillock that secures the Templar right and the wooded rise that secures the Count of Savoy's left. All they have to do is stay behind the trench and resist the pinprick raids the Turks will launch to draw them out. If my lord will but survey their line he will see a wooded knoll just behind the bridge that transects the trench. It is packed with crossbowmen. If the Turks try to send men across the trench, they'll be slaughtered. And yet, because we have maintained a causeway across the trench at precisely that point, it remains open to our horse should the opportunity arise to pursue that Saracen devil and smash his army. All that *les frères* Dreux need do is hold the line and await your command to attack if the chance presents itself."

"You've more faith in those cousins of France than I do, to be sure. Mark me, Walter, they'll fail us this day. My only hope is that they won't live to fail us again tomorrow."

"Your Grace," said the bishop, uttering a short, private prayer that his king was wrong and that the Count of Dreux and his division would indeed be able to hold their position and prevent the Turks from crossing the trench and turning the whole Christian line.

Fitz Alan surveyed the field with the practiced eye of a warrior who had seen too much battle. On the Christian side, no more than three hundred sergeant-brothers in the first line, another hundred or so dismounted *turcopoles* in the supporting crossbow line and a further hundred or so mounted knight-brothers in reserve. Good fighters, a well-prepared position, and God, as always, on their side – Fitz Alan felt guardedly optimistic. But opposite, he confessed to himself, was a truly terrifying sight. By the time they were formed up for battle, he guessed the Saracens had deployed three or four thousand infantry and, behind them, at least five hundred horsemen. And those were only the ones he could see.

"Brother Arnaldus," said Fitz Alan to his friend, "the Devil arrays his demonic host. What do you make of it?" De Fonte had an uncanny understanding of the Saracen armies and could read an enemy force as well as he could read scripture. Fitz Alan had come to rely on his friend's assessment of the enemy.

"The usual rabble, mostly. There on the right I see Bedouin tribal levies. In the center, Nubian archers. As they arrayed themselves, I saw Kurdish foot, too, though I can't see them now. Probably in the second line. Egyptian militia. Our friends, the Turcoman horse-archers, of course. Mostly useless – certainly no match for us. However,…"

"Go on, brother."

"On the left, I saw dismounted Mamluks – lots of them." Mamluks, called *ghulams* by the Saracens, were Turkish slave soldiers noted for their discipline, skill and ferocious loyalty to their comrades and commanders. They were worthy enemies, whether fighting on horseback or on foot.

"And?"

"On the crest, I saw Kurdish heavy cavalry. They're gone now, but they've been appearing and disappearing ever since the host began to assemble." Fitz Alan knew from experience the capabilities of the Kurdish heavy horse, along with mounted Mamluks the only cavalry in all of heathendom capable of besting a Christian knight in close-quarters combat.

"So the Lord will make us labor in the fields today after all," he said.

"The harvest truly *is* plenteous, but the laborers are few," quoted de Fonte from the Gospels, though he could not remember which one.

The drums and battle cries were growing to a crescendo now, and Fitz Alan knew that the host would be upon them very soon. He watched the *turcopolier* walk up and down the second line calmly reminding the crossbowmen to focus their attentions upon the Saracen leaders and standard-bearers. "If he rides a horse, shoot him," he said. "If he carries a banner, shoot him. If he looks like he's giving commands, shoot him. And, for the love of God, if you see any of those Saracen devils carrying a fire-pot, shoot him before he can even think about delivering his little measure of hellfire to us!" Fire-pots, Fitz Alan thought, only the devil himself could have dreamt up such an evil weapon. Then the *turcopolier* went silent, staring in the direction of the Saracen host. Fitz Alan followed his gaze and realized that the vast shoal of demons confronting them was quickly forming up just beyond crossbow range.

The battle was about to begin.

"Are we ready?" asked the Count of Dreux and Braine.

"Yes my lord," answered his brother, the Bishop of Beauvais. "We've two hundred knights ready to strike as soon as the heathen present themselves for battle."

"Good. I'll not have those Templar bastards claiming all the glory this time, not like at *Mons Gisardi*. Not this time, by the five wounds of Christ. As soon as the opportunity presents itself, we'll smash those Saracen swine ourselves, and then the glory will be ours and ours alone. God's teeth, but I loathe those sanctimonious Templar swine." He spat into the dry earth, raising a little cloud of dust, and then, realizing that he had wasted precious moisture, took a large draught of wine from the skin that always hung from the saddle of his mount. "Brother?" he asked, proffering the skin to his sibling.

"*Bien sûr*," answered the bishop, quaffing a generous mouthful of the warm but satisfying liquid.

The Count of Dreux looked over his shoulder in the direction of the besieged town of Acre. "Lord, how I wish we were fighting there, with the king, pushing our men forward against the Saracens, finally claiming the victory that is ours by right. Instead, here we are, fighting a mere holding action while others ready themselves for glory." His voice was thick with disgust for the situation in which he found himself.

"Is the bridge over the trench ready?" asked the bishop.

"Of course. We've a band of those contemptible little crossbowmen positioned just this side of the bridge – should be enough if those Saracen barbarians try to cross. But it'll never come to that. We're ready to strike the moment those savages present themselves and we've a good, solid bridge, four mounts wide, that will allow us to do so. Once we've unleashed our squadron of French horse the Turks will never know what hit them."

"My lord," answered the bishop. "But what of Richard's command to hold fast?"

"As you know, brother bishop, if there is one man on God's earth I loathe and despise more than all others, more even that those Templar eunuchs, it is that parricide Richard Angevin. I care not a jot for his commands. I serve Philip of France, and I serve him best when I kill the heathen and bring glory to his name. No. I'll not heed that Angevin bastard's commands." He loosed another contemptuous spit, and followed it with another generous draught of wine. "I serve my cousin France and his interests – and, of course, myself and the interests of our house. Everything else is dross."

"Brother," said the bishop, "the enemy presents himself!"

"Knights!" bellowed the count. "Ready yourselves to strike!"

Although he was anticipating it, Fitz Alan was more than a little startled when the Saracen drums finally began beating the signal to attack. "Hell calls to hell," said de Fonte, not for the first time misquoting the Psalm. Then the air was rent with a sudden terrible roar, and the entire Saracen horde charged toward the Templar line. The Templar crossbowmen got to work quickly, the foremost man shooting, while his mate wound and loaded. By exchanging weapons, they were able to keep a steady hail of death raining on the enemy. Fitz Alan watched as the *turcopoles'* crossbow bolts struck the Saracen mass, slicing through shields and armor, spraying blood and flesh and in all directions, wounding or killing masses of the howling, screaming men as they surged toward the Templar line. He wondered briefly which was worse, the wounding or the killing; for even the slightly wounded, if they staggered and fell, were being trampled to death beneath the thousands of feet that propelled the horde toward the Templar line. Probably irrelevant how they died, he decided, given the eternity of hellfire they would endure in the next life as a result of their unredeemed sins in this one.

"They're almost to the trench," said de Fonte.

"Thank God it's there," replied Fitz Alan, "without that Trench, the sheer force of that many demons crashing into our line would carry them straight through Acre and into the sea. As it is, they'll be slowed to a crawl by the ditch."

"I worry about the gaps, though" said de Fonte, referring to the spaces between the three squadrons in the front line.

"Whatever devils the crossbows don't kill," replied Fitz Alan, "the sergeant-brothers in reserve will make short work of."

The crossbow pairs were working feverishly now, shooting at almost point blank range, the steel heads of their bolts tearing through shield, mail and flesh. But the Saracens were in the ditch, the foremost pressed by those behind to find some way through the obstructions the Templars had placed at its bottom and up the sides. The first line of Templar sergeant-brothers were using their lances and swords to great effect, stabbing and hacking at any Saracen who made it to the lip. And several of the crossbow pairs had moved forward now, firing directly into the trench. Turks, Egyptians, Bedouins, every manner of Saracen lay down there now, writhing and dying, mixing in death as they seldom did in life. But still the Saracen horde came on.

"Shields!" bellowed the *turcopolier*, who had spotted a knot of Nubian archers moving up to try to get a better angle to shoot into the front line Templars. He was not heard over the din, however, and the enemy shafts struck home with the sound of cleavers slicing through meat. The *turcopolier* quickly directed the closest half-dozen crossbow pairs to focus their attentions on the dark-skinned enemy archers. Within a few seconds, a half-dozen of the Nubians were dead or dying and the others had melted back into the Saracen host.

The Templar crossbowmen had been butchering those enemy fighters trying to advance through the gaps between the squadrons since the horde had reached the trench, but they were running short of quarrels now and many had already discarded their bows and moved forward to fight with their swords. Hacking and slashing, all along the line the Templars were filling the trench with dead and dying Saracens. Indeed, to Fitz Alan's practiced eye it seemed as if the pressure on the Templar line might be easing a bit. Not surprising, he thought, given the sight and stench of slaughter that now greeted each successive Saracen wave as it approached. Here and there, Fitz Alan saw men fleeing back up the rise or over toward the hillock on the Templar right, presumably seeking refuge there among the rocks and thickets with which it was covered. If the sergeant-brothers and *turcopoles* could hold on just a little longer, he thought, the whole assault might be broken, and that bastard Saladin sent packing back to Damascus and his unholy horde with him.

"Firepots!" the *turcopolier* bellowed. "To the left. Firepots!"

But there were precious few crossbowmen still firing now and most of those were toward the right end of the line, unable to respond quickly enough to the new danger. "Jesus wept," blasphemed de Fonte, as a small group of Saracen grenadiers approached the line and hurled their flaming naphtha bombs toward the Templars. In a flash, the line was engulfed in smoke and flame, Templars and Turks alike screaming as fire scorched their clothes, hair and flesh. Another volley of naphtha bombs and the entire Templar left wing collapsed, the sergeant-brothers dying where they stood or fleeing to the relative safety of the squadron to their right or the one to their rear.

"What's that?' inquired one of the knight-brothers in a momentary lapse of discipline, pointing in the direction of a large number of unarmed men making their way down the slope carrying what looked like rough bundles of brushwood.

"Fascines," answered de Fonte, "they'll use them to fill the trench. Once they do, the gates of Hell will be opened and the demons will be upon us in their thousands." He'd have to charge that man for violating the rule of silence once the battle was over, he thought, assuming of course that either of them lived that long.

The Saracen sappers threw the fascines into the trench and even before it was filled enemy foot soldiers were clambering over them and forming up for battle. Fitz Alan could also see a large contingent of Mamluks on the far side of the trench waiting for the brushwood bridge to be completed. If they lodged themselves on this side of the trench, he thought, the Kurdish heavy horse would be in amongst the Templars in no time at all. And that might well mean that Saladin would again be able to relieve the garrison, or perhaps do even worse.

"Brother Matthew," he said to the standard bearer, "when those Mamluk devils are almost formed up, we are going to strike them – hard and fast. Then we're going to re-form back here and let the sergeant-brothers in the reserve squadron move up and retake the trench. Do you understand?"

"Aye, Master, I do," said the Yorkshireman.

Turning to his friend, he added, "prepare yourself, Arnaldus."

The Mamluks were almost formed up now, preparing to roll up the Templar line and create an opening through which the Saracen heavy horse would pour in their hundreds.

"Now, Brother Arnaldus, the Psalm, if you please!"

Fitz Alan was completely focused on the squadron now, the din of battle and even the hammering of blood in his own ears drowned out by the absolute silence observed by the knight-brothers. He was vaguely aware of a horse whinnying in the ranks, and in the far distance he heard what might have been a man screaming. But otherwise, in the tunnel that was Fitz Alan's inner world, as in the squadron he led, all was silent.

"*Non Nobis Domine, Domine!*" sang de Fonte, his mellifluous voice holding the first "*Domine*", before finishing abruptly with the second. The song pierced Fitz Alan's silence, bringing him back to the moment and the battle. Not unto us, O Lord. A heartbeat later, one hundred throaty voices sounded the refrain: "*SED NOMINE, SED NOMINE. TUO DA GLORIAM!*" But unto thy name, unto *thy* name, give glory! And with that, the *gonfanier* tilted the *Beauseant* slightly forward and a hundred Templar knights thundered into battle.

The Saracen horse-archers had been attacking for most of the morning now, riding forward, losing a few shafts and then withdrawing again beyond the range of the Christian defenders. The Bishop of Beauvais turned to his brother the Count of Dreux, "I'm not sure we can contain the squadron much longer, my lord. These pinpricks are driving them mad."

"I've no desire to contain them. I came here to fight the enemies of God and the king of France and I'll be damned if that usurping Angevin swine will keep me and my knights from doing precisely that." He turned to his trumpeter, "Prepare to sound the charge." Then he addressed his brother again, "The next time the cowardly dogs advance to sting us with their vile arrows, we'll surprise them with a charge the likes of which they've never even dreamt of. By the time we're done we'll have scattered the Saracen swine to the wind and put flight to Saladin and his horde once and for all. It'll be like *Mons Gisard* all over again, I tell you, save that this time the glory'll be ours. I'll tell you this, brother: those Saracen dogs'll never forget the day they tangled with the Count of Dreux."

"As you say, my lord. But I've seen the Turks in action before. They do like to provoke such charges and then counter-charge to great effect. Caution might be advised, especially with such limited visibility and...."

"Bah!" the count interrupted, "these savages have never encountered the likes of me and my knights. We'll teach them the true meaning of humility."

"My lord," called the knight nearest the count, "the horse-archers are back."

Robert looked toward the trench and, quickly sizing up the situation, turned to his trumpeter. "Sound the charge, by God, and let's have at the Saracen dogs."

And with that, the trumpet blared and two hundred of France's best knights charged confidently in the direction of the fifty or so Saracen horsemen scattered on the slope just beyond the trench.

The Templars covered the first hundred yards or so at the canter. Tightly packed, almost knee-to-knee, eight across and twelve deep, they formed a fearsome wedge of flesh, spirit and steel. As they approached the enemy, Fitz Alan knew that it was a simple matter of courage and discipline. If the Mamluk devils were well-led and brave, they'd quickly form up into a bristling line of shields and lances. If they braced hard and stood their ground, no cavalry charge in the world could break them. No horse, not even a Templar warhorse, would gallop into an obstacle it could neither jump over nor see through; nor would it charge headlong into a wall of deadly lances. It would shy away, rear up or retreat, no matter what its rider tried to force it to do. The charge would be broken and that would be that; the day would be carried by the defenders. If, on the other hand, the dismounted defenders believed that nothing in this world would stop the mounted warriors bearing down on them, that those attacking them actually welcomed martyrdom and would stop at nothing to ride down their enemies, and that they were done for, then in all likelihood those on foot would run away and the battle would be won by the attackers. As they closed to within a hundred yards or so, Fitz Alan could see the Mamluk commanders desperately trying to press their men into a defensive formation, shouting and shoving all along the line. He was not sure which way things would go until he was close enough to see the fear on their faces as they realized they were facing a Templar charge. Then he saw men begin to bolt. Gaps began to open up in the line. That was all he needed. "*Beauseant!*" he cried and the entire squadron spurred their horses to a ferocious gallop. Thundering now toward the Saracens, Fitz Alan gripped his lance tightly. The thing would be useless after the initial collision, he knew, but it would be devastating to the man who received it as he first crashed into the enemy line. Directly in front, he picked out his target. A swarthy man, wearing a helmet and mail, and heavily armed with a sword, lance and shield. Fifty yards now. The blood pounded in his ears and he felt as if his heart was about to explode. Twenty yards. He stood in his stirrups and leaned forward in his saddle. The Mamluk first raised his lance, but quickly thought better of it and lifted his shield up to cover his head and chest. Fitz Alan was so close now that he could almost read the script on the man's shield. Then the Templar's lance crashed into the long, triangular board, sending a shock shuddering up his arm and nearly driving him out of his saddle. He felt a sharp bolt of pain in his right shoulder, and dropped the splintered lance. Vaguely aware of the screams and cries all around him, though completely unaware of the fate of his victim, he allowed the force of the charge to carry him ever deeper into the Mamluk formation. Fitz Alan drew his sword and began hacking and chopping at the mass of heathens, first to his left and then his right, all the time keeping his *destrier* moving forward. He could sense it now: the demons were running. *Resist the Devil and he shall flee*, he thought. To his left Fitz Alan saw de Fonte ride down a Saracen who had dropped his banner and turned to run. De Fonte's sword caught the man where his neck met his shoulder, sending a thick mist of cloth and blood and bone spraying into the air. The man shot forward, face first into the ground, writhing and frothing as he lay dying. And then de Fonte was slashing at another Mamluk who was trying to pull him from his saddle.

Fitz Alan was through the Mamluk formation now, nearly to the fascine over which Saracens were no longer advancing but retreating. "*Beauseant!*" he called and the standard bearer quickly rallied to his side. "*Beauseant!*" he called again. Within heartbeats, the Templar squadron was forming up around him as they had so many times in practice and on the battlefield. The Saracens were running everywhere now, desperate to escape the Templar knights. They slid down into the trench, scurried over the low cliff that led down to the sea, even ran in the direction of Acre – anywhere rather than remain in the vicinity of the Christian knights. All except one small knot of Mamluks who, under the leadership of their gigantic, fair-skinned, red-haired commander, were trying to form up into some sort of hedgehog formation. That was all Fitz Alan needed. "Templars!" he yelled, pointing to the half-formed Saracen mass. "*Beauseant!*" This time, he spurred his horse to the gallop right away, sixty or seventy knights packed tightly behind him. His blood was up now and he could barely think straight. Kill the bastards, he thought, kill them all. And then he was moving through them, hacking with all his might against anything on foot, a pitiless, brutal killer at work in the fields of the Lord, all the while pressing forward, slashing as many of the Saracen demons as he could before emerging from their obliterated formation. The devils were in general retreat now, fleeing back up the slope and over the crest where de Fonte had seen the Kurdish horse earlier that morning. Those poor few who found themselves on the wrong side of the trench were quickly dispatched by the *turcopoles*, who showed exactly the degree of mercy they knew they would be shown if the circumstances were to be reversed. Fitz Alan began to feel the elation of the battle ebb and had to remind himself that their work was not done yet.

"Brothers," he called, "to me! Form up on me!" And Fitz Alan's remaining seventy knight-brothers began to array themselves once again into the massive butcher's cleaver that was a well-led Templar squadron.

King Richard could not believe what was happening, even though the whole sordid affair was unfolding right before his eyes. That fool the Count of Dreux had not only deliberately disobeyed his command not to venture beyond the trench line, but had fallen for perhaps the oldest ruse in the Saracen repertory. Stung repeatedly by the Saracen horse-archers, the count had ordered his squadron to charge across the bridge over the trench, to close with their tormentors and to kill as many of the heathen as they could. Initially, of course, the count's knights had delivered a thunderously devastating charge against the Turcomen, sending their tormentors fleeing in all directions. As the swarm of Saracen horsemen scattered and fled, however, the count's squadron became increasingly disorganized, spread out over the field, its energy dissipated and focus lost. When all was confusion, the Saracen heavy cavalry then launched a counter-strike, smashing into the count's disorganized mass of horse with devastating effect, first sending it reeling and then into panicked flight. Having driven the Christians from the field, they were now assembling into battle formation, preparing themselves to exploit the opening they had created in the crusader line.

The king shook his fist in the direction of the fleeing count and bishop, vowing before God that he would crucify the both of them before the day was done. Then he turned to Walter. "Send word to my cousin Philip that we have need of knights, at least one squadron, maybe two. Tell him to pull them off the assault if he has to; we're in dire straits here and we need to plug up the breech."

"Your Grace knows that this is not possible. We've never had enough men both to lay siege to the town and hold this line. We simply can't do both. That's why we built the trench in the first place and that's why no one was meant to venture beyond it. Everything depended on holding the trench while assaulting the walls. There is no reserve."

"Do you think I don't know this, you impudent dog!" yelled Richard, tempted in the rage of the moment to cut down the bishop where he stood. "Nothing matters now except sealing that breach. Even if it means that the assault on the town will fail, we need France to pull troops from the siege and send them here now. If he doesn't, and if we don't plug this hole quickly, not only will the siege be undone, but the entire expedition might be defeated. I can't speak for you, but I have no desire to spend the rest of my life as a guest of that swine Saladin."

"Yes, my lord," said the bishop, already composing in his mind the message he would have to deliver personally to the King of France. "I'll make it so."

"God's teeth!" exclaimed de Fonte, immediately penitent for his blasphemy. He was looking back toward Acre, the siege engines and Christian attackers in the near distance and the town itself a bit farther off. The tree-topped hillock that had been to the Templar right when they were facing the Saracens was now to his left, and the low rise upon which King Richard had assembled the leaders of the crusader host, was almost directly ahead. He had expected that once they had reached the designated point they would execute a standard Templar *volte face* and array themselves again to face the Saracen horde beyond the trench. As they approached that point, however, he saw scores of men, mounted and dismounted, fleeing in the direction of the Christian siege lines. The Devil, he thought, was clearly at work on the other side of that wooded hillock, though he could see nothing of what was happening over there.

"Brother Arnaldus," Fitz Alan called, his mouth now bone dry from the exertions of the day. "Seems those incontinent pilgrim bastards have failed us once again," he croaked.

"Who was arrayed to our right?" de Fonte asked.

"Robert, Count of Dreux, his half-wit brother, Philip, Bishop of Beauvais, and, I've no doubt, a pack of French glory-hounds only too willing to oblige the heathen and charge them at the slightest prospect of vainglory."

"What shall we do?"

"The only thing we can do, attack the bloody Saracens and push 'em back over the trench before they break the whole line. If they manage that, *nous sommes tous finis.*"

"Templars!" Fitz Alan called, "We're going 'round that hillock. If we see a knot of Saracen horse or foot this side of the trench, we're going to ride 'em down. Follow the *Beauseant* and kill every damned Turk you see! As always, brethren, God be with you!"

The *eschielle* maintained its silence, though Fitz Alan detected a grim and determined stiffening in the saddles.

"*Non Nobis Domine!*" he bellowed, not even pretending to sing the ancient Psalm.

"*SED NOMINE!*" came the shortened, shouted response. And with that the Templars spurred their tired warhorses to the charge once again.

Aliazars d'Uzest had always thought himself a good husband to his wife, Ermessenda, and a good father to his little daughter Bonassias. He was a faithful *credente*, a Good Christian, and a respected servant of the local *bonhomme*. He had long ago dedicated himself to the true faith of the Lord Jesus Christ and His gospel as taught by the apostles, rejecting the false authority and the corrupt teachings of the Roman Church. So how, he wondered, did he now find himself so far from home and in such grave danger? And, how, despite his beliefs, had he come to be engaged not only in killing, but in the killing of men on such a massive scale? How had his life come to this point, where all he had to look forward to was certain death on a battlefield far from home in the service of the hated Roman Church? He had pondered these questions for no more than a minute or two when a crossbow bolt embedded itself in the chest of the man standing next to him, sending blood spurting upward as his comrade fell backward. Focused again on the situation at hand, he finished spanning his crossbow and dropped one of his few remaining quarrels into the firing trough. He then sighted the weapon, taking aim at what appeared to be a leader of the horsemen trying to form up on the far side of the trench. He released the lock and watched with cold satisfaction as the bolt slammed into his target's face, throwing the man from his mount in a mist of blood, flesh and bone. Only a half-dozen or so quarrels left now, he thought, and once they were gone he and his men would be finished. Either the Saracen foot would close on their position and kill them where they stood or they'd be forced to flee and would be ridden down by the mass of heavy cavalry even now trying to force its way over the bridge. He stole a quick glance backward over his left shoulder and saw the last of the surviving Christian horse fleeing toward Acre. Useless bastards, he cursed, useless bloody *maudits batards*. God save me from the likes of these Roman cowards. Deliver me, lord, he prayed silently, placing the stirrups at the fore-end of the bow on the ground, from every evil. He put his feet into the stirrups and drew the string upward to catch the lock.

Deliver your poor servant from the minions of the Evil One, he prayed, and let me see my wife and daughter again. He placed a quarrel in the firing trough, and raised the weapon, looking for another target. This time he ignored the enemy horse, looking instead toward the more immediately threatening mass of Saracen infantry who had already crossed the bridge and were even now advancing on the hillock where he and his few remaining Occitan brethren were holding out. Lord, he prayed, why hast thou forsaken me? He pointed his crossbow at the mass of advancing Turks, and had fixed his aim on a particularly large Egyptian wielding a massive curved sword, when all of a sudden the enemy began to scatter. He looked backward over his shoulder again, half-expecting, despite himself, to see the Norman horse who had earlier been driven from the field returning to redeem themselves. What he saw instead astounded him. A wave of Christian knights, clad in white surcoats bearing red crosses, was closing on the Saracen horde. I called on you, O God, and you answered me, he prayed. Then, remembering the gravity of the moment, he turned back to the Saracen foot, some of whom continued to advance on his position. He thought of his wife and daughter back home and vowed, not for the first time, that if he survived just one more battle he would return to them without delay. Thank you, Lord, for delivering me from these demons, and, I pray thee, keep me safe that I may see my family again. And with that he took careful aim and fired a missile into the throat of one of the Egyptians trying to clamber up the slope in front of him.

He could see them now, beyond the shoal of Saracen devils closing in on the hillock ahead and to their right. A half-formed mass of Kurdish horse, their silk-covered aventails, festooned lances and round shields recognizable even to Fitz Alan. There were lots of them, he noticed, a few hundred at least, though no more than half had yet managed to cross the trench. "*Beauseant!*" cried Fitz Alan, and the Templar wedge thundered even harder toward the foe. As the foot rabble scattered in all directions before them, he could see the Kurds desperately trying to spur their mounts into some sort of formation. He wished he had his lance, though he was confident his bloodied sword would make short work of any heathen devil that got in his way. As always, the last few score yards were the hardest, but then he was amongst them, hacking and slashing, his mount rearing and biting as it sought to find a way through the loosely packed Saracens. He spurred his horse forward, looking, as he had been trained, for a way through the writhing mass of enemy horsemen. A mounted Saracen appeared to Fitz Alan's right, half-heartedly tilting his lance in the direction of the Templar's chest. He parried the lance with ease, drawing his sword across the Saracen's throat as he rode past the horseman and on through the mass of enemy fighters. "Christ!" he exclaimed, a bolt of pain shooting through his always-aching shoulder as his sword slashed easily through the flesh of the enemy horseman's throat only to meet the stiffer resistance of his neck bone. He reminded himself, however, that in the mortification of the flesh lay deliverance from the temptations of the flesh, and he rode on, reveling in the pain. He could see the trench now and the hundreds of Saracen foot and horse milling about beyond it. He had but a split second to decide what to do. He could re-form the squadron once it was through the Kurdish cavalry. Or he could press on and smash the next line of Turks forming up along the road to Acre. Either way, he knew the knights who had charged with him would be with him still, though, he was also sure, there numbers were even fewer now.

"Shall we press on?" his friend shouted as he rode up beside him. The right side of de Fonte's once-white woolen *cappa* was drenched in blood and gore, giving him the appearance more of a butcher than a man of God. He was glad to see him nonetheless.

"*Deus Vult!*" exclaimed Fitz Alan, his voice thick with blood-lust, and the two spurred their sweaty, panting, blood-soaked mounts forward once again. Stealing a quick glance over his left shoulder, Fitz Alan guessed that forty, maybe fifty knights were behind them now, hacking and killing as they rode, but still in something approximating formation. And then they were over the trench and galloping up the rise that had blinded them to the Saracens' movements for most of the day.

The Kurdish cavalry were fleeing now, a panicked mass of men and mounts desperately seeking to escape the certain death that was bearing down on them. Some of the horsemen had managed to spur their mounts to a gallop and even now were disappearing over the crest of the rise. The less fortunate, however, the ones who couldn't quite manage to get their horses to move quickly enough, were caught by the Templars and speared or hacked to death. Fitz Alan pressed on, not bothering with the melee behind him. I must see what's on the other side of the crest, he thought, half-expecting the kind of ambush that the Turks were so adept at inflicting on undisciplined Christian knights. Once over the crest, however, Fitz Alan could hardly believe his eyes. He pulled up his horse and motioned to the remnants of his squadron to do the same. There in front of him, in the valley below, was a sea of Saracens. In the near distance, fleeing horse and foot of all sorts. Arrayed beyond them, though, untold thousands of Egyptians, Bedouins, Kurds, Turcomen, and every sort of heathen imaginable, all arrayed for battle. He could see tents and banners, all the detritus of an encamped host, and even in the far distance a figure that might well have been the Saracen emir himself, perched on a hill with all manner of colorful grandee surrounding him, though at this range he couldn't be quite sure. They were neither advancing nor retreating, just sitting there, a great demonic horde waiting to see which way the initial assault went before deciding what to do next. Well, Fitz Alan thought, they had just witnessed their best fighters bloodied and beaten by the Templars. Perhaps that would convince Saladin once and for all that Acre was beyond salvation and that he should withdraw his host.

"We've given them something to think about, this morning," panted de Fonte, "maybe it'll be enough to send them packing."

"Pray God that it is, brother," said Fitz Alan, taking his hand from the gloved sleeve-end of his hauberk and wiping some of the sweat, blood and grime from his face, "pray God that it is."

II

13 July 1191

In the near distance he could hear the familiar words of the *Salve Regina*, sung antiphonally by hundreds of brethren assembled to give thanks for the fall of Acre. *Salve, Regina, mater misericordiae, vita, dulcedo et spes nostra, salve.* Hail, holy Queen, Mother of Mercy, our life, our sweetness and our hope. *Ad te clamamus, exules filii Hevae. Ad te suspiramus gementes et flentes in hac lacrimarum valle.* To thee do we cry, poor banished children of Eve; to thee do we send up our sighs, mourning and weeping in this valley of tears.

The words, and the voices singing them, gave him comfort, as they always did. Now, though, all he wanted was sleep. He pulled off the torn, stained and stinking *cappa* and threw it to the far corner of his tent. "Thomas," he called tiredly, "help me get out of this thing, will you?" Thomas Wytheberd, his squire since he had left England all those long months ago, obliged him, pulling the heavy mail hauberk over his head. Although most Templar squires were engaged by the order for a short period of time, Thomas had committed himself to the Temple for life as an act of religious devotion. Fitz Alan had thus far been pleased with his work, though he thought the food he cooked in the field a bit bland, even by English standards.

"I'll have it sanded and ready before you wake, sire." Thomas was referring to the common practice of rolling mail armor in a barrel of sand to clean it.

"Good. And while you're at it, see if you can get the Draper to give me another *cappa*." He said wearily. "That one," he gestured with his forefinger in the direction of the bloodied and discarded garment, "is beyond redemption – and the other is so stained and brown that it makes me look more like a sergeant-brother than a knight of the Temple."

"Sir." Thomas responded simply, knowing that Templar knights in general, and this one in particular, disdained idle chatter.

Fitz Alan proceeded to pull off his mail leggings or *chausses*, and then, clad only in his linen breeches and shirt, fell onto his palliasse. The heat was appalling, he thought, though nothing, he was sure, compared to the heat those dead Saracen demons were enduring in the fiery pit at this very moment. And his shoulder was paining him again, reminding him as it always did of the weakness of the flesh and the need for a strong spirit. His eyes closed and he prayed. *Pater noster, qui es in caelis, sanctificetur Nomen tuum....* Feeling himself drifting off, he continued with difficulty.... *Adveniat regnum tuum. Fiat voluntas tua, sicut in caelo et in terra...*

He was on the verge of unconsciousness when the flap of his tent opened and a man called his name, startling him to wakefulness.

"Fitz Alan? Is this the tent of Brother Michael Fitz Alan? I'm here on the king's business."

"I'm Fitz Alan," he said, raising himself wearily and pulling his white mantle over his shoulders. "And I serve no king, but Christ Jesus. What do you want of me?"

The man standing before him was tall and thin, with pinched features and long black hair that gave him a more-than-vaguely feral appearance. He was wearing mail and a sword and otherwise had an air of supercilious authority about him.

"I want to deliver this summons to you. Can you read?"

"Latin, French and English. And even a bit of the tongue those Saracen devils speak. And you?"

"French well enough to know that your king has summoned you!"

"My king is Christ Jesus, and I doubt very much either that he writes in French or that he has elected you as his emissary."

"It is the king of England, Richard, who commands your presence." And with that he flung the scroll at Fitz Alan's feet. "And I am told that the Master of the Temple, Robert de Sablé, also requests the honor of your presence. You have been summoned; my duty is discharged. Decline at your own peril." And with that he turned and departed the Templar's tent.

Typical bloody knight of the Earthly City, Fitz Alan thought. All vanity, hubris and indifference-to-the-will-of-God. He stooped, picked up the scroll and then, realizing the light was hopeless in the tent, walked outside to read it. Even at this early hour, this sun was oppressive, another welcome mortification and reminder of the fires of hell that awaited all this world's sinners.

He read the document aloud. "You are hereby requested and required to attend His Grace this day, during the hour following sext. The matter is of utmost importance. You are enjoined to discuss it with no one." Then, in Latin, "*Ricardus, Dei gratia rex anglorum, dux Normannorum et Aquitanorum, comes Andegavorum.*" So that puffed up popinjay of a knight had been speaking the truth after all – the king did wish to speak with him. Given all that he had seen of Richard in France, he had no desire to be caught up in whatever schemes he might be brewing. The man was the antithesis of St. Bernard's new knight: a vain, selfish, quick-to-anger killer who cared for nothing but battle and the glory and wealth it might bring him and his family. A formidable warrior, to be sure, and even a great leader of men, but one afflicted with all the vices and corruptions of every other grasping knight, low born or noble. Yet to refuse the summons would be unwise, Fitz Alan knew, especially since the ferret-faced knight who had delivered it had mentioned that the Master of the Temple wished him to be there also. *De par Dieu*, he thought to himself, "for God!" though the thought was the product more of habit and duty than any real conviction.

"Thomas!" he called to his squire who was over by the sergeant-brothers' tents stuffing Fitz Alan's hauberk into an old sand-filled wine barrel.

"Sir?" replied the squire. "Just sanding your hauberk, sir. Won't be long, now."

"I am expected to attend his…. I am expected to join some of the king's men for the midday meal. Please have my tunic, mantle and cap ready. And wake me in time for sext, will you?" He slipped off his white mantle and handed it to his squire.

"Yes sir." replied Thomas, taking the garment and making his way back to the barrel.

Having arranged all he could, and feeling weary beyond weary, the English Templar returned to his tent and fell into his palliasse, asleep almost before his head met the pillow.

Fitz Alan was greeted outside the royal compound by a minor chancery official who could barely conceal his disdain for the lowly Templar knight standing before him. The thought occurred to Fitz Alan that he should gut this insolent swine here and now, just to teach the presumptuous toad a little of the Christian virtue of humility, but he quickly banished the impulse as unworthy of a knight of Christ. "Here is my summons," he said, shoving the parchment just a little too forcefully into the lawyer's chest. "Honor it or not, I care little either way."

"It's alright," said the Ferret, coming out of the nearest tent, "he's with me."

"We meet again, sir," said Fitz Alan.

"*Bien sûr*. Now follow me if you please. The king and his counselors await."

Fitz Alan followed the knight along a packed-earth path that wound through a cluster of large tents. The king's campaign chancery, he assumed, given the din of self-important prattle in the air. Finally, they approached a tent guarded by half a dozen heavily armed knights and festooned with a dozen or so banners bearing King Richard's new royal device, three golden lions on a blood-red field.

"Here we are," said the Ferret. "And now, a few instructions. His Grace will be present, but you are not to address him unless he calls upon you directly. Your audience is with the chancellor, Hubert Walter and the new Grand Master of your order, Robert de Sablé. I will also be in attendance, as will a priest who is a native of the Kingdom of Jerusalem. You will not speak until spoken to. When you are dismissed, you will bow to His Grace and then follow me out the way we came in." Before Fitz Alan could say anything, and he had already formed a few choice comments for this arrogant swine, the flap opened and they were ushered into the royal presence.

Fitz Alan had half-expected the king's campaign tent to be sumptuously furnished in the manner of the great manors and palaces he had known during his life before joining the Order. King Richard's field accommodations, however, were almost as ascetic as his own. As he looked around the tent, he saw a few simple desks and chairs, a palliasse somewhat larger, though not much, than his own, a small table with water for washing, and another with wine and a few fruits and dried meats. That was it, save for the large campaign table in the middle of the tent, covered in maps and documents. As the Ferret had suggested would be the case, the King and Grand Master, de Sablé, were there, sitting around the campaign table. The chancellor,

Bishop Walter, was standing at the wine table, helping himself to a drink and some food. On a seat off to one side was the priest, Hospitaller by the look of his dress, and behind him at a small table what looked to be a scribe or lawyer, armed with quill and ink.

"Brother Michael," said the Grand Master, motioning him forward, "please be seated." A servant appeared out of nowhere and pulled out a chair at the opposite end of the table.

"By your leave, my lord," he responded, removing his black cap and taking his seat at the table.

"A drink, Michael?" called the chancellor from where he was standing.

"It would be intemperate of me at this hour, my lord, and a violation of the rule by which I live."

"Come now, Michael. I've known you a very long time and have always found you partial to a little wine, often more than a little. And this one's quite good."

"Thank you, no, my lord bishop."

"As you wish," said Walter, walking back with a full cup to take his seat at the right hand of the king.

"Brother Michael," began the Grand Master, "I suppose you are wondering why you have been summoned in this way."

"No, my lord. I have learned to trust in the Lord and lean not on my own understanding."

"Quite so, quite so," replied de Sablé, not quite sure if that was insolence he detected in the knight's voice. "Well, in any case, it seems that by your actions yesterday you have brought considerable glory...."

"The glory is not mine, but the Lord's."

"...to the *Order*, and considerable attention to yourself. The king informs me that he is well pleased by your exertions on the field of battle. Had you not acted so decisively in your twin charges, that minion of the Antichrist and his demonic host may well have broken our line and relieved Acre. I shudder to think of the fate of our pilgrimage had that happened."

"I did what any knight of the Temple would have done, my lord."

"The King is impressed; the Grand Master is impressed; God's Wounds, even I'm impressed," interjected Bishop Walter, "let's leave it at that, shall we. The details of how you have come to our attention are less relevant than those of the *mandatum* which we are about to bestow upon you."

"My lord?"

"We have a delicate task for you, Michael, er, *Brother* Michael, one that will require not just the courage and fighting spirit we saw on the field of battle yesterday, but the intelligence and resourcefulness both His Grace and I have come to know you possess in abundance."

Curious now, Fitz Alan was eager to hear more about this great *mandatum* and, despite his misgivings about being involved again with Richard Angevin and that murderous bastard Hubert Walter, found himself leaning slightly forward in anticipation.

"The king believes," continued the bishop "that the success or failure of this expedition to the Holy City turns to a considerable degree on whether we can recover two powerful relics: the Holy Spear and the True Cross." Hubert paused, finishing his cup of wine and then motioning a servant to bring more. "The first of these, as you may know, was the lance used by the Roman centurion Longinus to pierce our Lord's side as He hung upon the Cross. It was discovered in St. Peter's Cathedral in Antioch during the original pilgrimage to Jerusalem and is credited with delivering several miraculous victories during and after that expedition. It was lost about fifty years back, though no one seems quite sure how. The second is a piece of the Cross upon which Our Lord was crucified. It, too, has been credited with delivering miraculous victories, including the great defeat inflicted by your order on that devil Saladin at Montgisard. It was lost, however, as ultimately was the Holy City itself, at the Horns of Hattin."

Hattin. Fitz Alan, like all Templars, knew of that terrible defeat and the mass slaughter of the Templar and Hospitaller brethren in its aftermath. Twenty thousand men, including over two thousand knights, had marched on Saladin's forces besieging Tiberias; fewer than three thousand survived to tell the tale. None of the Templars or Hospitallers captured that day had survived the day's battle, for the sultan himself had ordered them beheaded. Stripped of its fighting men, and especially of its warrior monks, the Christian kingdoms were left with no means of defending themselves against the victorious Saladin. In the aftermath of the battle, the Sultan had rolled up town after town, fortress after fortress. By October of 1187, he had captured the Holy City itself.

Sensing a long peroration in the offing, the king interrupted his chancellor. "Brother Michael, let me be more direct than is the good bishop's habit: I want those relics. We face staggering odds here in *Outremer* and if we are to overcome those odds and take back what is ours by right – Jerusalem and the Holy Sites – we need the advantage they will confer upon us. The Holy Lance has proven its worth in battle time and again. I need it in hand before we lay siege to Jerusalem. As to the True Cross, the advantages associated with prising it from the covetous hands of Saladin are obvious. In addition to the blessings that it will confer upon us, the simple act of taking it from the Saracen will demonstrate both that he can be beaten and that God smiles on our cause. If we are to do God's work here and liberate the Holy city I must have those relics."

Fitz Alan felt his heart racing at the prospect of the battles that he was sure would attend whatever role he was going to be asked to play in this venture – battles fought for God in the hopes of earning His forgiveness.

Now it was the Grand Master's turn. "His Grace and I are in complete agreement on this issue. The relics must be recovered. Can we count on you to do your duty and help in this regard?"

"*De par Dieu*! But what would you have me do, my lord?"

"We need you to recover the Holy Lance," de Sablé responded. "It has been conveyed to us that it might be found at the lazarette de Valsainte, which is some miles south and inland from Tripoli, near the Forest of the Cedars of God. It is a secluded hospital of the Order of Saint Lazarus, built to treat those poor Templars and Hospitallers afflicted with leprosy. If you choose to accept this commission you will proceed there with a small detachment of Templars and *turcopoles*, you may decide its precise composition yourself, and determine if in fact the relic has been secreted there. If it has, you are to retrieve it and bring it back to King Richard. Simple."

"The saying of it may indeed be simple, my lord. I wonder, though, if the doing of it will be quite so... uncomplicated."

"Doubtless it will not," said Bishop Walter, "we know for certain that that grasping whoreson Conrad of Montferrat also has his minions out searching for various relics. And, who knows, perhaps Philip of France and that Saracen devil have their lackeys out looking as well. Besides which, you'll have to travel close by Sidon and Beirut, both of which are now in

Saladin's hands, or through the Beqaa valley, which is crawling with the heretics. Then there are the Assassins. The monastery is close by their lands, and you never know what the Old Man of the Mountain and his pack of murderers are up to. Other than that, though, it should be as simple as the Grand Master suggests."

"My lord."

"Two additional items, Michael," said the bishop of Salisbury, "First, although the Master here could command you to do this, for reasons that need not concern you we'd prefer a more…" he searched for the right word, "*willing* leader. So, this mandatum is entirely voluntary. You may accept or decline as the Holy Spirit moves you. We have need, however, of your answer no later than compline tomorrow."

"And second, my lord?"

"If you decide to take this on you'll be accompanied by this good man, Father Raimundus de Ramla. He is a native of these parts, speaks many local languages and has, let us say, a rather… *developed* understanding of the political complexities of in this part of the world. He also knows something of relics in general and the Lance in particular. And don't let his Hospitaller mantle put you off – I guaranty that he'll be a great asset to you on this holy pilgrimage."

More likely he'll be your damned spy, thought Fitz Alan, uncharitably. Nevertheless, he rose to meet the priest and extended his hand to grab the other man's forearm. "God be with you, Father," he said.

"And with your spirit," came the strangely accented reply of the *poulain* priest. "I look forward to serving with such an esteemed knight of the Temple to recover the Holy Lance and restore it to the Lord's people. In the past, the relic has proven to be a source of great power on the field of battle."

"Surely, Father, if it is in a house of the Order of Saint Lazarus, it is already with God's people." There were two views of lepers prevalent in Christendom. The first was that the affliction was a punishment for moral failing; the second, that it was a reflection of Christ's suffering and thus of holiness. Fitz Alan subscribed to the latter view.

The Hospitaller looked slightly perplexed. "My son, we have no idea who controls the house these days. It is on land nominally subject to the Count of Tripoli and through him to the King of Jerusalem, but following the catastrophe of Hattin their writ no longer runs that far inland. Neither, though, do we think the Saracens have imposed their rule that close to the coast. In any case, since the Catastrophe, no one has heard from the Master of the house nor any of his knights. No, my son, we have no idea in whose hands the lazar-house lies. We have reason to believe, however, that the relic is still secreted at Valsainte. And we have no reason to doubt it."

Simple, thought Fitz Alan, is that what he called it? Not bloody likely.

"My lords," he said, "you do a humble servant of God an undeserved honor by offering such a great commission. As you have asked, I will reflect upon the matter and report my answer back to you tomorrow."

With that, the Grand Master rose and all but the king followed suit.

"Brother Michael," said de Sablé, "Think hard upon what has been said here today. We look forward to seeing you again tomorrow evening after compline. Until then, go in peace, glorifying the Lord by your life."

Although the Psalms and *Kyrie* of compline usually helped him banish his night-demons and attain at least a degree of serenity before sleep, today the intrusion of that godless bastard Hubert Walter left him troubled. "Thomas," he called out to his squire as he approached his tent.

"Sir."

"Should I assume that you've tended to the horses and that my arms and armor are ready should I need them?"

"Yes, sir. Everything's right as rain… well, the palfroi's a bit colicky, but I don't reckon it's anything to worry about. I'll keep an eye on it, though."

"Please do," he said, "I'm going to visit Father Arkwright now. As you know he's quite ill and, seeing as how it's after compline, I'd like to share a drop of wine with him to raise his spirits. Can you go to the dining tent and have the sergeant-brother in charge give you two cups and a small flagon of wine. If he gives you any trouble, just let him know that it's for a squadron master and a very ill priest-brother. That should make it easier for him to do the Lord's will."

"Yes, sir. I'll see to it straight away."

"And then get your head down for a bit of sleep. I've a notion we're going to be busy in the next few days."

"Sir," the squire said, just a hint of weariness in his voice, and with that he was off on his errand.

Fitz Alan made his way in the opposite direction, past the massive chapel tent where a dozen or so knights were still singing the *Kyrie* and toward the Infirmarer's small compound. He made a quick detour to visit the latrine pits on the edge of the Templar encampment, then he hurried on to see his friend and confessor before darkness and the Rule forced him to his bed.

"Come in, Michael, my boy" coughed Father Arkwright, "sit with me for a bit before the light leaves us entirely." Arkwright was a Templar chaplain, very old now, who'd had much experience in the Holy Land. He had retired from active service in the East to the Temple Ewell Preceptory, and that was where he had met Fitz Alan, whom he had counseled ever since. Despite his age, he had returned to the Holy Land with Fitz Alan for one last pilgrimage. Somewhere along the way, though, he had contracted one of the many terrible wasting illnesses common to the region. The Infirmarer was convinced that he was dying, though Fitz Alan was not entirely persuaded.

"It would be my pleasure, Father," said Fitz Alan, "I've asked Thomas to bring us a drop of wine to finish off the day."

"You're a good man, Michael. A drop of wine before bed always helps," he coughed again, spitting up an ungodly red and yellow-green mass, which he quickly wiped away with a stained and filthy cloth, "especially when one's old and ailing." He smiled ruefully, the light of the candle at his bedside amplifying the sallowness of his complexion.

They sat in silence for a few moments before Thomas arrived and poured the libation into the two cups.

"That'll be all, Thomas. Off to bed with you now, man."

"I'll just have a little look in on the *palfroi*, first, sir. Then I'll turn in, so I will." And then he was gone.

"How are you, Father?"

"Been better, my boy. Afraid my Earthly pilgrimage is drawing to a close." His voice sounded frail to Fitz Alan, and perhaps even a bit resigned.

"We are all in God's hands, my friend, but I think your time has not yet come."

Another lung-wretching cough, followed by more bloody phlegm and another half-wipe of the filthy cloth and Fitz Alan was almost ready to change his mind.

33

"Father, this may not be the best time...."

"'In the time of my favor I heard you, and in the day of salvation I helped you,' saith the prophet Isaiah. Ask what you will." He sipped on the wine, and seemed momentarily soothed by it's warmth.

"Today I met with that devil Richard Angevin, now King of England, and his minion Walter, false bishop and bastard offspring of the Evil One himself. They have given me a great charge, but I am not sure whether it is a *mandatum* from heaven or hell."

"Surely you need say no more, my son. Forgive the bishop all his offences against you, it is your soul that is damned if you don't, but otherwise reject his imprecations. Whatever he and the Angevin would have you do will doubtless prove more malediction than benediction."

Fitz Alan raised his hand. "Afraid it's not that simple, Father. The new Grand Master, Robert de Sablé, was also in attendance. He clearly wished me to accept the commission. While a Templar knight is subject to no temporal power, and might refuse the commands of even a king of England, disobeying the Grand Master is simply unthinkable." He sipped his wine, but after sampling the king's wares, found it bitter to the taste.

"Look," said Arkwright, struggling only half-successfully to contain another fit of coughing, "when you first sought entry into the Order, I asked myself the question I always ask of postulants: why is he seeking to become a Templar? As you now know, men seek to join the Order for all sorts of reasons. Some are sentenced to serve with us as punishment imposed for a crime; some seek to join for what they perceive is the glory of fighting in defense of the Holy Sites and Christian pilgrims; and some seek to join to atone for their sins and earn their salvation by fighting and dying for Christ and His Church. In your case, the reason you approached us was obvious. The unholy life of a worldly knight – a knight motivated solely by love of self and the riches of this world; a knight indifferent to the will of God – had taken its toll on you. Burdened by sin and a life of selfishness, pride and vainglory, your soul was nearly crushed. Your wound, though you thought it well concealed, was plainly visible – at least to me." He paused to take another sip of the soothing wine.

Taking advantage of this opening, Fitz Alan interjected: "I know why I joined the Order, Father. I was doing nothing but destroying and being destroyed, polluting and being polluted. Had I continued along the path I was on, all that was in store for me was unbearable suffering in this world and eternal damnation in the next. But, mercifully, God intervened and diverted me from the path of wickedness; bade me place my sword in the service of the City of God rather than the Earthly City."

"Yes, Michael, like many, many knights in recent decades you needed to find a home where you could find salvation without being untrue to your martial nature, where you could atone for your sins without abandoning your sword. And like many others, by the grace of our Lord Jesus Christ, you found your way to the Order, a place where the disciplines of the Rule could burn away your sinful nature, transfiguring you into a New Knight, a true *miles Christi*."

"Father, I do know all this."

"Yes, Michael, I'm certain you do, though it doesn't help to be reminded of it." Another spasm of coughing was followed by another deep draught of wine.

"What you do seem to have forgotten, though," he continued, "is that your entrance into the life of the Order did not complete your conversion, but only marked its beginning. There are many battles of temptation ahead, battles that you must win if you hope to attain *perfectio* and truly taste the sweetness of God's divine love. The question I have been asking myself since we left England is this: will the trail of trials he has now embarked on transform Brother Michael into a true knight of Christ or will it confirm him as a worldy knight, perhaps one who is superficially a Templar, but a knight whose first love remains himself and the things of this world?"

"And have you formed an answer?" Fitz Alan didn't really want to hear his friend's judgment, but steeled himself for the worst by draining his cup of wine.

"Indeed, I have." He paused, feeling another bout of coughing coming on. When it had passed, he continued. "Indeed I have. You have come a long way this past year, my son. You have mastered the forms and rhythms of Templar life. You have submitted to the spiritual disciplines of the Order and her Rule, all of which are designed to purge you of the values of the worldly knight and order your entire being to God. You have learned much about the virtues and dispositions of the New Knighthood from the writings of Augustine and of Bernard of Clairveaux, from the *vitae* of accomplished, if sinful, warriors who preceded you on the path of salvation and, of course, from the Holy Scriptures. And you have even developed a passable mastery of the hymns and chants that imbricate our liturgical life." The priest smiled wryly as he uttered this last judgment, for in truth Fitz Alan's singing was awful.

"Why do I sense you are about to qualify this litany of praise, Father?"

"I imagine because I am. Despite all the progress you have made, Michael, you are only at the beginning of your trail of trials. Precisely because this land has been sanctified by the incarnate presence of our Savior, the Devil sees it as a crucial battleground in his eternal war on God. He and his minions are everywhere. And by this I do not simply mean Saladin and his horde, though those usurping brutes are certainly to be counted among the demonic host. No, I mean all those citizens of the Earthly City, whether Christian, Muslim or Jew, who have succumbed to the temptations of the Evil One or the blandishments of the Earthly City and now labor on behalf of evil here in the vineyards of the Lord. The longer you are here, Michael, the more you will be confronted by these enemies of Christ, and the more they will test and tempt you. And each time they do, you will be forced to decide which is your first love: yourself and the things of this world or God and the things of the next; pride and vengeance -- or humility and justice. If you choose prudently, of course, these tests will only strengthen you, indeed will help you become a true *miles Christi*. But if you are unwise, if you give way to temptation, if you lose sight of the true enemy and fail to conquer him in the theatre of your heart, then the worldly knight whom you have not yet fully cast out will grow strong once again. And the more trials you fail, the stronger he will grow until at last it is the new knight who has been cast out and the Earthly City will have regained a sword." Arkwright slumped back now, drained by the effort it had taken to bring this warning to his young friend.

"As always, there is much wisdom in what you say, Father. But what has any of this to do with the commission I have been offered?"

"My son, you have eyes, but cannot see. The Devil in his terrible wisdom clearly fears the new knight that is growing within you. So what does he do? First, he strikes *me* down to deprive you of what little advice and guidance I might have to offer. Then he draws you into the desert, as he drew Our Lord long ago, to ensnare you in his deadly traps. My fear, Michael, is that unlike Our Savior, you are not ready for the trials and temptations the Evil One is laying out before you."

"Don't worry about me, Father...."

"But I do, my young friend, I do. I worry that if you fall in again with that false apostle, or if you follow the path of vengeance which you have labored so mightily to depart, bitterness in this world and damnation in the next are all that you can hope for."

Fitz Alan slumped back into the campaign chair arranged beside his friend's sickbed, and tasted the bitter wine once again. "I've no wish either to fall in with the bishop or wreak vengeance on him, though avenging his many injuries against God and man would be right and just. But I do wish to see us in Jerusalem again. And recovering the Holy Lance might just help bring about that noble end."

"The Holy Lance? Do you speak of the Lance of Longinus?" Arkwright half-raised himself, before a frightful coughing fit forced him to recline once again. "Is that the great commission you've been speaking of? Recovering the Lance that pierced Our Lord's side as He hung dying on the Cross?"

"Yes," he said, proceeding quickly to recount the story of his meeting in the king's campaign tent, leaving out only what he thought the more insignificant details.

When he was finished, Arkwright struggled for a moment and, with Fitz Alan's help, managed to sit himself upright. He coughed, fetching up another bloody discharge that he wiped away with a fresh, though still only half-clean, rag. Composing himself, the old priest looked into Fitz Alan's eyes with an intensity that the younger Templar had never seen in his friend before. "Now you listen closely, lad," he rasped, his cloudy gray eyes suddenly full of fire and purpose, "for I'll say this once and only once. Don't let yourself get caught up in this unholy business. Do not be seduced by the Lance and do not let Hubert Walter and that contumacious Angevin brute ensnare you with talk of honor or duty or Jerusalem. They are impious men, concerned only with power and glory and wealth. They care nothing for Christ and His Church, and even less for Jerusalem, save the worldly rewards they will reap if they can liberate it from the heathen." He hacked up another diseased clot from his lungs and slumped back onto his palliasse. "And for the love of God do not seek the Lance. Nothing good can come of any effort to recover that relic or to place it in the hands of such malicious souls."

"They are prideful and self-serving bastards, to be sure, Father, and utterly indifferent to the will of God. But what do their motives matter?" Fitz Alan asked. "If the Lord chooses to use evil men to further His divine cause, who are we to stand in His way? Surely, any advantage we can gain in the struggle to liberate Jerusalem from those heathen devils can only serve God's purpose."

"I wasn't finished, Michael," the old priest said, his voice barely a rasping whisper now. Fitz Alan leaned over to hear the rest of what his friend had to say, then stiffened slightly, staggered by the odor of mortal corruption rising up from the dying man. "It's not just the dangers posed by Richard and his bishop-lackey. They're bad enough. But it's the Lance itself – that's the real curse. I've never told you this, no reason I should have, but I have some knowledge of this relic. Many years back, I too was asked to perform a duty related to the Spear of Destiny, though not," he coughed viciously, "though not to recover it. No, my task was to conceal it, to lodge it somewhere neither Christian nor Turk would ever be able to find it, to place it beyond the mailed and grasping fists of godless knights and heathen savages alike."

"But why? Why conceal a relic that has served the cause of Christ so well in the past?"

"Because the relic is a two-edged blade, my son. On the one hand, it can bring great victories, as it did during the First Crusade when Peter Bartholomew discovered it in St. Peter's Cathedral in Antioch and the Christian host subsequently scattered the besieging heathen army to the winds. But it can also sow great division and dissent, as it did in the aftermath of the siege." The old priest coughed and sputtered, though this time he brought forth nothing. "The Christian nobles fell out among themselves, some believing the Lance to be real and others believing it a fraud," he continued, "indeed, so great was the discord caused by the relic that the great expedition was almost lost. Peter himself was forced to submit to trial by fire to prove that he really had been visited by Saint Andrew and that the Lance was an authentic relic. When he failed to survive the ordeal, God's judgment seemed obvious and the matter was considered closed." He paused to catch his breath and take a sip of wine, but the coughing returned and most of the wine ended up staining his kerchief even further. "The Lance itself then disappeared and was considered lost; it played no role in the affairs of the East until the 1130s. Then it reappeared and served to rally the Christian forces in Edessa as they sought to resist the heathen emir Zengi. After the initial victories, however, the count of Edessa, Joscelin, fell out with his erstwhile ally the Count of Tripoli and the heretics captured the capitol on Christmas Eve 1144 – Christmas Eve, mark you. Again the Lance was implicated, many believing that it poisoned the relationship between the two counts and led directly to the fall of Edessa to the infidels." Fitz Alan's friend coughed and sputtered again. "The relic then disappeared again for a few decades until it reappeared and, along with the True Cross, inspired King Baldwin to attack that devil Saladin at Montgisard. What a victory – five hundred Templars and a few thousand foot against the assembled hordes of Hell. We bested them that day, by God, slaughtering thousands upon thousands of the Evil One's minions and securing all of *Outremer* for decades to come -- or so it seemed to us at the time. In the end, however, it was all for naught, for the Lance worked its evil yet again, and Christian was pitted against Christian, and the fruits of the battle were ultimately lost. It was then that I was commanded to assemble a small band to dispose of the relic; to secrete it where it would never be found, where it would never again tempt a Christian prince, where it would never again be able to sow discord among God's people and place the Holy Sites in jeopardy."

"And who gave this command? Who bid you conceal the relic, Father?"

"Odo de Saint Amand, the Grand Master of the Order himself. It was he who finally grasped the terrible power of the Lance; and it was he who finally ordered it concealed – not destroyed, mind you, that would be sacrilege – but placed beyond the grasp of those who saw its power but were blind to the evil it always wrought." The old priest closed his graying eyes and uttered a string of sounds that Fitz Alan found utterly incomprehensible.

"Father!" said Fitz Alan, shaking the his friend back to his senses, "Where did you hide the Lance, Father?"

"A small monastery, a then-new lazar house, built on an old Byzantine site in the county of Tripoli. It was in the highlands, not very far from the Forest of the Cedars of God." The fire and purpose were gone from the priest's eyes now, leaving only a foggy grayness that suggested that the man's spirit was slipping away. "I have no idea now what the place was called." Arkwright thought for several moments, trying to dredge up the long submerged memory of the place where the terrible thing had been secreted. "No, wait… Valsainte perhaps. Yes, I think that was it, the priory of Valsainte. It was so long ago, though, so long ago – I… I'm just not sure." Now even the grayness seemed to fade. His eyes closed, and for a moment Fitz Alan thought the old priest dead. Leaning closer once again he heard a rattling in his friend's chest and throat that reassured him that the old man had succumbed only to sleep.

Fitz Alan gently shook the old man back to part-consciousness once again. Arkright was babbling now, bloody spittle gurgling in the back of his throat. Then, clarity: "'No one comes to the Father except through the Son…'"

"Father?"

"'I am Alpha and Omega, the beginning and the end, the first and the last.' Remember that, Michael. If you must do this terrible thing, remember that."

Fitz Alan dismissed his friend's confused plea. "Of course, Father. But tell me, why there?" he asked, "Why conceal the Lance in such a godforsaken nothing of a place?"

"Because, Michael," he wheezed, the bloody spittle dripping down the side of his mouth, dabbed slowly by his faltering hand, "because no one would ever dream of looking for it there."

Apparently, though, Fitz Alan thought, someone had.

Hubert Walter, Bishop of Salisbury, King Richard's chancellor and right-hand man, was busy combing through various reports from the network of spies and turncoats in Saladin's army when his clerk announced that the dark-skinned Hospitaller priest had finally arrived. He motioned for the man to take a seat and then pointedly continued to review the reports before him, noting with satisfaction the rumors that the Saracen demon was having great difficulty keeping his coalition happy and intact. Plenty of his allies, or so these reports seemed to indicate, were either lukewarm towards him or were pre-occupied with struggles for power in other parts of heathendom and had no great investment in the goings on in this little corner of *Dar al-Islam*. Promising, he thought, very promising indeed, though he reminded himself that even the best paid spies were at best unreliable and at worst self-serving liars. He'd have to do a bit more digging to verify these encouraging reports. But still....

Looking up from the pile of parchment on his table and called for his clerk to bring two cups and a flagon of wine. Once the wine had been poured, he finally addressed the priest.

"Thank you for coming, Father de Ramla. What news have you?"

"I have heard from our friend," he said in the peculiar accent of those Christians, the *poulains*, who had been born and bred in *Outremer*, "and he assures me that the relic remains at the monastery." Although of Breton ancestry, Raimundus de Ramla was a true son of the Latin East. He had been born into a lordly family in the Kingdom of Jerusalem and had been weaned on the politics of the Christian realms in Syria and Palestine. But he had also spent some time in captivity with the heathens, and before he was ransomed had learned something of both their ways and their tongue. His insight into the Saracen mind, and his ability to communicate with them, discreetly, had proven useful to more than one Christian prince. And now he was in the service of Bishop Walter.

"Excellent!" said the bishop, "then we can proceed as planned."

The priest said nothing, taking the opportunity to empty his cup of wine and pour himself a second. He thought the bishop a fool, a powerful and dangerous fool to be sure, but like all these tedious pilgrims, and especially the English, a fool nonetheless. His wine, however, was both good and plentiful. As was his money.

"You will accompany that sanctimonious bastard Fitz Alan to the Priory of Valsainte. There you will contact your spy and endeavor to recover the relic with a minimum of bother. But if it cannot be recovered peacefully, you are authorized to recover it by whatever means you deem necessary. I sincerely hope that it can be recovered without bloodshed, but I rather suspect that the lazars now possessing it will not surrender the relic without at least baring their fangs. That is why I chose Fitz Alan for this expedition. He's a holier-than-thou jackanapes these days, but beneath that he's a clever and resourceful man and he'll not only get you to your destination, but if it comes to a fight he's the man you want at your side."

The bishop finished a date and washed it down with a mouthful of wine.

"Mark me, de Ramla," he continued, "this is serious business indeed; much hangs in the balance here. Whatever it takes, you must recover the Holy Lance."

If only you knew how much actually hung in the balance, or the real purpose of what you have called this "serious business", thought de Ramla.

"I am familiar with the plan, my lord, and with the stakes. And I've no doubt that all this can be accomplished, with the right resources and resolve. What more can you tell me of this Templar, though? If I am to depend on him I'll need to know all I can."

The bishop paused for a moment, wondering how much – or, more properly, what version – of the story of his association with Fitz Alan he should share with the Hospitaller priest. "Well now," he proceeded at length, "there's much I *could* tell you, but here's what I choose to. I first met Fitz Alan when we were both in the service of Richard's father, the late king Henry, God rest his soul. In the service of that great king, I had many occasions to observe him in action, and I must say, neither before nor since have I ever encountered a more accomplished knight. He was and is a truly formidable warrior, the like of which one encounters only once or twice in a lifetime. On Henry's death, both Fitz Alan and I transferred our allegiance to his son, the present king Richard. Again, I had numerous occasions to observe our friend in battle and again was I struck by his fearlessness, physical prowess, intelligence and, above all, his insatiable lust for killing. He has always impressed me as an ambitious man, one for whom glory and wealth are the wages of the warrior vocation."

"And yet now," de Ramla interrupted, "he has turned his back on all that and is pledged to fight and die solely for the glory of Christ."

The bishop had wandered off to the sideboard as he had begun telling his tale, and was pouring himself a cup of wine when de Ramla had broken into his narrative. He spun around, losing for just a moment his famous self-control, and glowered at the priest. He composed himself before speaking. "My dear Father de Ramla," he said slowly, concealing as best he could his impatience – nay, loathing – for this irritating fool. "He has done no such thing. It is true that Fitz Alan left the king's service and entered the

Templar Order, though I know not why." This, of course, was a lie – the bishop knew precisely why his former friend had left the king's service. "But this does not signal any great conversion. Fitz Alan may have experienced a temporary lapse of prudence or fortitude when he joined the Templars. And now that he's in the only way out is via the grave. But what conclusion should we draw from this? Bearing in mind that he could have joined any non-martial order – the Benedictines, the Cistercians, the Carthusians and so on – the fact that he entered the Templar order suggests to me that, whatever momentary madness afflicted him, it was not sufficient to drive him to give up his great loves: fighting, killing and living for the glory that can only come from victory in battle. No, he had his chance to turn his back on temporal warfare and become a simple spiritual warrior; he had his chance to put the life of the worldly knight definitively behind him. This, though, he did not do. Instead, he entered the most murderous of all the monastic orders, the Templars; an order where a man of ability could still be a warrior, could still rise in glory, could still lead the life of a knight."

"Perhaps, my lord, perhaps. For it is true that many a repentant warrior seeks refuge in the more pacific orders. For others, though, this is not enough. As repentant as they are, they cannot give up the life of temporal battles for those of the spiritual world. For them the only path to salvation is one of both spiritual warfare and temporal warfare in the service of Christ and His Church. For these men, both forms of warfare are acts of devotion and *caritas* – and, indeed, taken together they are doubly salvific. In any case, and whatever you chose to believe, my lord, I have always found men like this, accomplished warriors driven by powerful spiritual needs, to be formidable allies. He sounds like an excellent choice for the task at hand."

"He is. Let me caution you, though, de Ramla – whatever else this knight of Christ may be, and whatever nonsense *you* choose to believe, Fitz Alan's no saint. His hands are as steeped in blood as any knight I've ever served with. I've seen him in action – he's a brutal, merciless butcher. No, he's no saint, that one, regardless of his newfound self-righteousness. You're badly mistaken if you think he is."

"You have not been here long, my lord, so I don't expect you to understand the ways of these Templars. That Fitz Alan's a ruthless killer I don't doubt. They all are. That's why those Saracen devils murder them without mercy whenever they lay hands on them. But it's their motives that both make them formidable in the eyes of the enemy and justified in the eyes of God. Unlike worldly knights, who kill only out of greed, lust for glory or the desire to avenge injuries against themselves or their families, Templars kill for one purpose and one purpose only: love of Christ. They are dead to those things that move the knights of this world, my lord, utterly dead. They kill only those who would injure the Crucified One and His Church. They seek not glory for themselves, nor their families, nor even their order, but for God, and they are happy to die in that cause. The only reward they seek for themselves is salvation, achieved through the redemptive power of penitential violence. What's more, and I believe you have witnessed the fruits of this yourself, they submit to the most brutal martial and spiritual discipline, designed to prepare them body and soul to fight for God. When they charge, it is as one; controlled, fearless, and thirsty for the blood of Christ's enemies. They strike with a single mind and a single terrifying purpose. Such men are not to be trifled with, my lord, as I believe that heretic Saladin discovered again only yesterday."

"Bah! You make them out to be gods, but these *knights of Christ*," he almost spat the words out, "like all knights, are mere mortals. Templars, I am quite certain, are capable killers, as well they should be given that the order is full of bandits, homicides and other felons, not to mention those warriors of lowly birth who seek to make a name for themselves in the glorious battles of the East, or those who join simply because they love battle and killing. But they are no more holy than you or I. And I can certainly assure you that that bastard Fitz Alan is not. I have known him a very long time. Like all men, he has weaknesses. He keeps his better hidden than most, to be sure – though not as well as he thinks. But beneath that precious white mantle, he is what he's always been – an ambitious, prideful, glory-seeking and merciless killer. The only difference now is that instead of killing for the Duke of Aquitaine or the King of England he kills for the Bishop of Rome."

"Perhaps, my lord, perhaps," replied the priest, taking yet another gulp of the bishop's wine, "but on a mission like this, with great peril and the legions of hell waiting at every turn, I'd rather ride with a man like Fitz Alan and a few true Templars than with Saint Michael and the heavenly host itself."

"Suit yourself," replied Walter, thinking the man a pitiable, if useful, fool.

"Just make certain you recover the relic. If you don't, I swear to you by the bowels of Christ that neither Fitz Alan, nor Saint Michael, nor all the angels and archangels in heaven will save you from my tender mercies."

"*Deus Vult*, my lord!" de Ramla said, more than a hint of irony in his voice. God wills it! And with that he drained his cup, rose from his chair and departed the bishop's tent.

Father Benedict had told Fitz Alan when they departed England that, when the time came, he wanted his funeral mass to be said in Jerusalem. It pained Fitz Alan deeply that he could not honor his friend's final wish, but had to settle instead for a simple service in the Templar chapel compound just outside the recently liberated city of Acre. There were dead Templars arranged row upon row before the altar, scores of them, all carefully dressed in either their white or brown mantles, their swords gripped in dead hands crossed on their tunics. All except Father Benedict who, being a priest and therefore forbidden to bear arms, held a simple wooden crucifix on his lifeless chest. Knights and sergeants alike wept as they mourned their departed brethren. The sounds of the *paternoster*, chanted by hundreds of assembled Templars, almost brought Fitz Alan to tears as well – almost, for he had no tears left now, not after the long night he had spent with Arkwright, first watching the life ebb from him and then, when the old man was gone, pouring out the proof of his grief. He took cold solace from the heap of heathen war-banners piled high on the altar, evidence of the great victory the Order had won both outside the city and in the course of its capture. Great victories, he thought yet again, always seemed to come at such terrible expense.

"He was a good man, Michael, a good Christian man and a faithful servant of Our Lord. We'd be nothing without him, you and I," said de Fonte, kneeling beside Fitz Alan as the mass ended and the assembled brethren began to depart. "The world's a better place for him having been in it." He crossed himself. "And it'll be a poorer place with him having departed."

"A lot of good men died today, Arnaldus. And a lot more will die of their wounds over the next day or two. I grieve for all of them."

"Grieve not, my friend, for the Lord knows his own. By God's grace they are home now, at peace in the arms of the Redeemer. We should not mourn them overly much." As they hurried past the bodies of their fallen brothers, de Fonte glimpsed the young knight-brother who had spoken out of turn on the field of battle a few days earlier. He was lying lifeless on his palliasse, now, his face horribly disfigured by a gaping wound that stretched from above his left eye to the right side of his chin. De Fonte crossed himself again, absolving the knight-brother in death of the offence he hadn't the opportunity to punish or forgive in life.

The two knights rose and left the compound, each deep in prayer for the brothers they had lost over the last few terrible days.

"I have news," Fitz Alan confided at length, pulling off his cap and scratching his head through his close-cropped hair.

"Go on, brother."

"Seems we are to serve Richard Angevin yet again, though this time as king of England and one of the leaders of the Christian host."

"God save us," he blurted, instantly remorseful, as he always was, for his ill-disciplined and blasphemous tongue.

"It gets worse. That fatherless swine Hubert Walter is also involved. He's a bishop now, and Richard's chancellor."

"God save us," said de Fonte again, though on this second occasion without remorse, for this time it was a genuine prayer.

Fitz Alan quickly apprised de Fonte of the mission, omitting the voluntary nature of the assignment. He's already decided to accept the *mandatum* and didn't want to rehearse again all the arguments against doing so. Besides, if Arkwright had been unable to persuade him to decline the commission it was unlikely that de Fonte could.

The two walked some distance in silence, each pondering the implications of the mission. When they had reached the empty refectory tent, Fitz Alan took a seat at one of the tables and motioned that his comrade should do the same.

"What do you think our old friend the bishop is really playing at?" Fitz Alan asked.

"No idea, Michael," replied de Fonte. "I doubt, though, that it has much to do with retrieving a relic. He may be a bishop now, but Hubert Walter is no man of God, and I've never known him to put much stock in holy things."

"He's a godless swine, true enough, though if he thought a relic would give him or his master even the slightest advantage over their enemies he'd not be above sending men to their deaths to acquire it. No, I think the relic has something to do with this commission, I just suspect there's more to it than that. And then there's the matter of the Hospitaller priest that he's assigned to guide us. Native of these parts, speaks many tongues, an imposing man destined for great things. So why has the bishop assigned him to this lowly commission? Why would Walter send such a man with us when any *turcopole* man-at-arms would do just as well? No, there's more to this than meets the eye, Arnaldus. We'll have to keep a close eye on the Hospitaller and be ready for whatever surprise he has in store for us."

"As you say, brother, as you say," replied de Fonte. The two knights drifted into silence again, privately contemplating the known and unknown dangers before them.

"Right then, old friend," said Fitz Alan at length, "there's work to be done if we're going to achieve our purpose and survive whatever dish the bishop is preparing for us." Rising from the bench, he continued: "Here's what I need you to do. Find that *turcopolier* who stood with us at the trench the other day and recruit him to our cause. Be discreet, but let him know that it's King Richard and the Templar Grand Master himself who're asking for his aid. Tell him too we'll need a half-dozen of his best fighters, men who know Tripoli and Antioch, if possible. We'll also need another half-dozen sergeant-brothers, good both on a *chevauchée* and in a *mêlée*. You know the type. Tell him we'll travel in the manner of the sergeant-brothers, one warhorse apiece with a few packhorses for the provisions. You and I and the *turcopolier* will bring our squires. That'll be it."

"Anything else?"

"No – wait, yes. Ask him to assemble the troupe after sext tomorrow on the field where we bested Saladin's horde the other day. That'll give us a chance to take the measure of the men and to poll them regarding their needs for the expedition. It'll also give us a chance to let them know what's expected of them. God willing, they'll all prove worthy and we'll be on the road to Tripoli before prime the following day."

"*De par Dieu!*" replied de Fonte. And with that he turned and went to find the *turcopolier*.

As he looked around the great hall, Hubert Walter felt a great sense of satisfaction. Not only had a terrible siege finally been won by the pilgrim host, but in the aftermath of the great victory, Richard had successfully asserted his superiority over Philip by taking Acre's royal citadel for himself and forcing the French king to take up residence in the Templars' house. Not for the first time, the bishop marveled at the unparalleled regal qualities of his liege lord: he was a fearless warrior, a great leader of men and a fierce champion of his empire and family dynasty. To be certain, his romantic life was... unorthodox, but the bishop put this down to his outsized appetite for the rewards of this world rather than those of the next. Not for Richard the hand-wringing that afflicted so many lesser mortals in this age of rising piety. No, if he was concerned about his immortal soul, Walter had never seen even the slightest evidence of it. He loved life, was generous to his friends, ruthless with his enemies, and utterly unafraid of death. A great man and a great king – someone whom Hubert Walter was willing to follow to the very ends of the earth.

"My lord bishop," said Richard, rousing Walter from his meditations. "Come sit with me and tell me what news have you from Saladin?"

"My liege," responded the bishop, crossing the length of the great hall and sitting himself down at the small table where Richard had until a moment before been conversing with his wife Berengaria. A servant appeared out of the shadows, offering Walter a cup of what he suspected was warm, stale water. "Thank you, no," he said, peremptorily, waving his hand dismissively, "wine instead."

"Hubert," said the king impatiently, "tell me, what's the news?"

"The news, my lord king, is very encouraging indeed. The heretic has agreed to your terms."

Richard banged the table with such force that the two Sicilian hounds belonging to his sister Joanna rose with a start and left the hall. "By God, we have him," he exclaimed. "Tell me more."

"The sultan will deliver to us 200,000 *dinars*, the relic of the True Cross captured at Hattin, and sixteen hundred Christians in his captivity. In return we will release, unharmed, the remnants of the Acre garrison and the city's other inhabitants." A look of almost boyish pleasure spread across Richard's face. "Everything? Are you saying he agreed to everything?"

The look and the question gave the bishop pause.

"My liege," Walter responded, "he did indeed agree to everything, and there are reasons to believe that he will keep his word, but…"

"But what?"

"He's a Saracen; the cost to him of keeping this promise is staggering; he may not have the money or the captives or the True Cross; he may simply be playing us for time," responded the bishop, half-afraid of the king's response to his gloomy litany of possibilities.

Richard considered Walter's words for a few moments, the confidence and joy of a moment earlier suddenly draining from his face. Then his countenance was restored. "My lord bishop," said the king, "I appreciate your frank counsel, but really – what choice does he have? If he doesn't fulfill the terms, he knows I'll slaughter every last one of those devils. And I swear to you Walter, as sure as God is in his heaven and Christ is seated at his right hand, if that heathen prince does not keep his word, I *will* slaughter them, in plain sight, and make Saladin and all of heathendom weep for the loss of so many mothers and children. If that happens, if he allows the hostages to die, when it's within his gift to save them, he'll sow such bitterness and resentment among his allies that not even he will be able to hold his coalition together. No, my lord bishop, he'll pay the full ransom; for whatever it costs him to do so, it'll cost him many times more not to."

"As you say, my liege, but…," he hesitated, "we must at least consider the possibility. We must at least be *prepared* for any potential perfidy on his part." The king reached down to stroke his sister's hounds, which had returned from their self-imposed exile. After a few moments, he spoke. "Quite right, my friend, quite right. Let us prepare then for two scenarios: if Saladin keeps his word, we will hand over the Acre captives; if, however, he fails to deliver the ransom, in full and on time, we will slaughter every last one of them in full view of Saladin's camp."

"As you command, your grace. I shall make contact with my counterpart in King Philip's court and apprise him of our intentions."

"Good, good. My cousin France does not like surprises. And I cannot treat with Saladin for only half the prisoners."

"No, my liege, you certainly cannot," said the bishop, rising and bowing to his king. "I will see to it immediately."

ℑℑℑ

15 July 1191

Like his former lord, Arnaldus de Fonte had taken quickly to the rhythms and disciplines of the Order. He liked the routines of prayer and work, of singing and training. And he especially liked that he could fight and serve God at the same time, for he could not imagine a life without either God or battle. And while he could not gainsay the fact that he missed some elements of his former life – especially the women – he had to admit that, on balance, the sacrifice was well worth it. Since entering the Order he had known a kind of peace that he had not known before; a feeling of fulfillment that he had never experienced in his previous life. No, de Fonte thought to himself, however much the lack of women was an ongoing trial for him, he wouldn't exchange his life in the Order for anything, save of course eternal life in the presence of Almighty God. Luckily for him, he thought, the two were not mutually exclusive.

"Brother Arnaldus," said William Turcault, the *turcopole* leader, "the men have been gathered together as you requested."

"Very good, *Turcopolier*. You may begin."

Arnaldus, charged by Fitz Alan with assessing the battle worthiness of the hastily assembled troupe, watched as the *Turcopolier* assembled the eight sergeant-brothers and ten *turcopoles* into a standard Templar battle formation. As they had just completed the Office of Terce, the sun was already quite high in the sky, and the heat was beating down on them with its typical ferocity. Warm work today, thought de Fonte, shifting his horse sideways until he was in the shade of a tall cedar on the edge of the field. He watched as the *Turcopolier* led the troupe at a slow canter or lope until they were about a mile distant from the row of effigies arranged on poles twenty or thirty yards to his right. After executing an always-difficult *volte face*, Turcault then led the men in a well-controlled charge against the row makeshift infidels. De Fonte noted the tight discipline of the sergeant-brothers in particular. Knee-to-knee, they held their formation, advancing slowly toward the enemy until within striking distance and then breaking into a thundering gallop. The *turcopoles* in the second row were somewhat looser in formation, but that was how they always fought. Very impressive, thought de Fonte as they crashed into and demolished the row of effigies. He noted with approval the way in which Turcault quickly reassembled the men and led them back down the field in tight formation. Once there, they executed another about-face and repeated the evolution, though not before the effigies had been hastily reassembled by a small group of sergeant-brothers engaged for precisely this purpose.

Turcault kept the men at the exercise for most of the morning, allowing de Fonte more-than-adequate opportunity to judge the individual and collective mounted fighting skills of the members of the troupe. As the hour of noon approached, the exercise was suspended for the prayers and psalms of the midday Office and for a quick meal of salted fish, bread and dates, all washed down with a little water and wine. After the men had eaten, and tired mounts had been exchanged for fresh ones, Turcault separated the sergeant-brothers from the *turcopoles*. The former he put to work assembling the butts that they would use to demonstrate their mastery of the crossbow. Once they had assembled the targets, they arranged themselves into pairs and began shooting as they had on the day that Saladin's horde had been repulsed, one spanning the bow and the other firing at the target. While this was going on the *turcopoles* were set to demonstrating their ability to shoot their bows while riding, by turns galloping past a large cypress tree and shooting their quarrels into it from distances of fifty and one hundred paces. De Fonte moved between parties, observing both in detail. He was impressed once again with the skill and discipline of these warriors. They all seemed very well-suited to the task at hand and he was pleased that he would be able to make a positive report to Fitz Alan.

"*Turcopolier*," he called out to the *turcopole* commander, still busy putting the men through their paces. "That'll be enough for today; I've seen all I need to see. You've chosen your men well and I'll report as much to Brother Michael. What I need you to do now is canvass the men regarding their needs and have the armorer and draper see that they have everything necessary for a lengthy *chevauchée*. We will assemble here at Prime tomorrow and depart shortly thereafter."

"*De par Dieu!*" the *Turcopolier* replied. "The men are fit and in good spirits, Brother Arnaldus; I am confident that they are ready for whatever trials the Evil One has in store for us."

I pray so, thought de Fonte as he spurred his horse in the direction of Fitz Alan's tent. In his heart, however, he knew full well that they could never be fully prepared for all the snares and traps the Devil had laid up for them. And after seeing these fine Templars perform so magnificently on the practice field this day he was saddened by a thought he simply couldn't shake: that many of these brave *milites Christi*, good Christians one and all, would probably not survive the expedition. It was ever thus, he knew; good men fell as readily as those who were evil on the field of battle. That was the only real law of war – and it was a law that neither he, nor Fitz Alan nor even God himself could undo. De Fonte, of course, had long ago steeled himself to this divinely ordained truth. On this day, however, his equanimity failed him. And as he rode toward his friend Fitz Alan he prayed, in vain he knew full well, that at the end of the mission all these wonderful warriors would return safely home.

15 July 1191

Saphadin, lord of Egypt and brother of the great and noble Saladin, believed his brother to be a fool and, worse, a powerful and charismatic fool. If the sultan had any strategic or political sense whatsoever it would have been different, but the old bastard was simply incompetent as a military commander and even less capable as a political leader. That Saladin had enjoyed great success in recent years was beyond dispute. His armies had smashed the Christians at Hattin and he now presided over a great Islamic empire that stretched from Libya to the *Jazira*. The claim that any of this was attributable to the Sultan's martial prowess or political acumen, however, Saphadin knew to be nonsense. For was it not he, Saphadin, who had counseled and prodded his elder brother both to victory on the battlefield and to success in the political arena. Was it not he who stiffened his brother's spine in times of adversity. And was it not he, Saphadin, who had liberated the holy city of Jerusalem and reduced the Christian presence in Syria to Tyre and a few isolated inland fortresses. No, the younger brother thought,

Saladin might be sultan and might even enjoy a reputation for military and political genius. In truth, though, it was he, Saphadin, who was the cunning leader and inspired general.

"What shall we do now, my brother?" the elder Kurd asked. "What shall we do now that the Christians have taken Acre? The Christian kings have bested us on the field of battle and taken dozens of our noble friends as hostages. I fear, my brother, that all is lost. Tell me I am wrong."

Saphadin held his tongue for a moment or two before responding. You are not wrong, you incompetent fool, he thought, but for the sake of the empire I cannot let you believe that you are right. "All is not lost, my lord; for if Allah wills it, we may yet prevail over the unbelievers. But the situation is dire, my lord. The Christians are firmly lodged at Tyre and now Acre. They have destroyed our fleet and seized control of the seas. And now they have seized the initiative on land. Jerusalem is in jeopardy as, indeed, is Ascalon, perhaps even Egypt. Your reputation as the unbeatable emir, the hammer of the Christians, has been dealt a severe blow. And, as a result of all this, for the first time in many years the unity of the empire has been called into question. No, my lord, if Allah wills it we may yet prevail. But absent His divine intervention, I do not see how we can hold Jerusalem. Alternatively, should the Christian host make for Ascalon and then press on to Damietta and Alexandria...."

"Then we would be finished, for without the riches of Egypt first the army and then the empire would disintegrate."

Saphadin picked up a date from the campaign table near where he and the sultan were seated and turned it between his fingers before popping it into his mouth. Once he had finished it and discarded the pit, he replied simply "As you say, my lord. Without Egypt we are finished"

"And the terms those cowardly dogs defending Acre agreed. Two hundred thousand *dinars*, the relic of the True Cross captured at Hattin, and sixteen hundred Christians in our captivity. I can't deliver on those promises. Even if I could raise the money and deliver the Christian prisoners, returning the relic is simply inconceivable. Its capture at Hattin was symbolic of the turning of the tide in Syria; it signaled that their false gods had abandoned them. Returning it now would similarly signal a turning of the tide, only this time not in our favor. No, I cannot return the relic to them. To do so would be suicide."

"My lord," said Saphadin, plucking another date from the bowl before him. "Although the situation might appear hopeless, there are steps we can take that might strengthen our position."

"Such as?"

"Such as, do everything in our power to drag out the settlement of the surrender terms. Every day we can keep the Christians tied down at Acre is a day we get stronger and they get weaker. Even as we speak, troops flow in to your army from every corner of the empire; with each passing day, however, their forces are whittled away by disease, dissolution and disaffection. And if we can hold them until the winter, then the rains will sap their strength even further." He paused as he finished another date. "Promise the Christians everything they want, then, when the hour we are to deliver the goods arrives, beg them for more time. Any excuse will do. My spies tell me that the Christians are, as always, divided amongst themselves. The *poulains* have in mind the long term goal of building a defensible Christian kingdom in Syria; the so-called pilgrims see only the short term goals of discharging their oaths and earning whatever glory they can while here. The two factions do not mix well, disagreeing about both ends and means. The longer we can prevaricate, the greater the chance that the tensions among them will erupt into open conflict."

"Eventually, though, they will want the terms fulfilled. What then?"

"I for one doubt that the Christians will go so far as to butcher the captives. They surely will not kill the nobles among them. The ransoms are too tempting. And then there are the sixteen hundred of their people that we hold. Would they be willing to see so many of their people slaughtered in retaliation? No. The Christian host and the Christian captives are too intertwined by family and feudal relations. The former would never put the latter in jeopardy."

"Nevertheless...."

"Nevertheless, brother, as we know these *Faranji* dogs are not particularly given to reason. My advice would be to have the money, the relic and the captives ready to exchange should they appear to be willing to actually go through with their threat. I don't think it will come to that, but we can't afford to have the captives murdered in full view of our army. There are many emirs who would abandon our cause should such an eventuality come to pass."

"And then what? Even if they don't murder the captives, what if they march on Jaffa, as they surely will? And what if they then strike for Jerusalem or Ascalon? The captives are only the first of our problems."

Saphadin offered a silent prayer, not for the first time, that Allah might finally grant his brother just the smallest measure of strategic sense. "My brother, if the Christian kings are united and bold, there is nothing we can do to salvage the situation. Jerusalem will fall, Egypt will be severed from Syria and the empire will collapse. But if they are not, then we have a chance. We can harass them as they move down the coast. Perhaps they will commit another blunder of the magnitude of Hattin, perhaps their internal conflict will sap their strength. If they take Jaffa, we can destroy Ascalon, thus eliminating the possibility that they might seize it and so command the road to Egypt."

"Destroy Ascalon?"

"The lesser of several evils, my lord. And though it might be enough to drive several emirs to abandon us, it will keep the route to Egypt open. In any case, what choice do we have? If we lose contact with Egypt, we are finished. Finally, my lord, if the infidels do take Jaffa and then strike inland toward Jerusalem, we can deploy the field army to threaten their lines of communication. If Allah smiles on us, the lesson that we administered at Hattin will have been well learned by at least some of their commanders. If so, they will not advance too far inland without securing the road to Jaffa and thus their supply lines to Christendom. If we can field a sizable army north or south of the Jaffa-Jerusalem road we can give them pause, maybe even force them to withdraw."

"So there is hope?"

"Yes, brother, there is hope. But we must make preparations now if that hope is to be realized. First, we must prepare to make good on the terms agreed by the Acre garrison. If it is the will of Allah, we will not have to deliver on them; if not, however…. Second, we must reconnoiter the route to Jaffa and identify a suitable battleground, one where we might bring the infidels to battle and defeat them. Some place where their impetuous cavalry will feel that they might carry the day. If we can tempt them to precipitous action, as we have so many times before, we might defeat them before they even approach Jerusalem. Finally, we must strengthen the defenses at *al Quds*. I doubt that we can defend it if the Christians are able to do there what they did at Acre, but we shouldn't make it easy for them."

Saladin did not know whether to be reassured or further disheartened by what his brother had just said. The situation was dire and the prospect of holding the Holy City seemed poor indeed. Still, there was a glimmer of hope now where a moment ago there had been none.

"There is one other matter I wish to bring to your attention, my lord."

"Yes."

"My spies inform me that the *Faranji* seek a relic – a relic they believe to have such great power that it will guaranty victory over us."

"What of it?" replied Saladin. "Surely the capture of the Cross at Hattin has demonstrated that their relics are powerless in the face of Islam."

"No, my lord, it did not. They are a very superstitious people and their faith in the powers of these objects seems both blind and bottomless. But while the relics are indeed powerless, their faith in them is not. And that faith, even though without foundation, can inspire them to acts of boldness that they would otherwise never consider. No, my lord, the relics that they prize so highly may have no power, but they fire the infidels nonetheless. And, as my spies assure me, they attach great significance to recovering this particular relic. If that is the case, then we must do all in our power to keep them from doing so."

Saladin nodded in agreement. "And what, precisely, is this relic?"

"They call it the Holy Spear. It is the remains of the lance that pierced the body of their false god as he hung on the Cross."

Not for the first time, Saladin wondered how anyone could believe that God could be killed on a cross. Or emerge from a woman's nether parts. Or be at once three and one. Now he wondered how these people of the Book – people who professed monotheism – could also elevate a mere prophet into a false idol.

"When the *Faranji* first came to Syria a century ago," Sapahdin continued, puncturing his brother's reverie, "the relic played an important role in their conquest of Antakiya – indeed, they believe that absent that relic they would neither have held that city nor proceeded to conquer al Quds. They have come to invest it with near miraculous powers. If they get their hand on it now, when all hangs so precariously in the balance…," his voice trailed off, leaving the sentence, though not the sentiment, uncompleted.

Saladin assembled the pieces. "We must prevent that, my brother. We must send forces to acquire this relic before the *Faranji* do. I assume you know where it is to be found?

"Indeed I do, my lord: a monastery called Valsainte, near *Horsh Arz el-Rab*, the Cedars of God. We must act quickly, though – the infidels, I am told, have already sent men to recover the relic. It will be some days yet before they arrive, so we have time. But given the difficulty of communicating with our holdings on the coast we must set our plan in motion now if the garrison at Bayrūt is to have any chance of sending a detachment to arrive there ahead of the infidels."

And that was all that the sultan needed hear. "Scribe," he called.

"Sire," a man replied, emerging from the shadows.

"Record this command and make it so."

It was the hour of Terce and Fitz Alan could just make out the strains of *Crucem sanctam subiit* coming from the Templar chapel tent in the middle-distance. *Crucem sanctam subiit, qui infernum confregit, accintus est potentia, surrexit die tertia. Alleluia. He bore the Holy Cross, who shattered hell, He was girded with power, He rose on the third day. Alleluia.* As he continued on his way to the armorer's compound, Fitz Alan was stirred, as he always was, by the sound of scores of pious knights and sergeant-brothers singing this distinctively Templar chant. Arnaldus will be putting the chosen men through their paces by now, he thought. He had considerable confidence in the ability of the *Turcopolier* to assemble a formidable troupe of Templars for his *mandatum* to retrieve the Holy Lance. Still, it never hurt to have a man like de Fonte, a man he had fought beside for many years now and whose martial prowess he respected without qualification, judge them and pronounce them worthy.

"There you are, Brother Michael," said the armorer, wiping copious amounts of what appeared to be soot and animal fat from his massive hands. "I'd heard you were stopping by this morning. What service can I do for you this day?" Hugo Le Grant, Armorer of the Kingdom of Jerusalem, was a huge man, a full head taller than Fitz Alan. Of middle years, his dark hair and beard were threaded now with gray, though both were so short-cropped that this was noticeable only on close inspection. Like Fitz Alan, the armorer was from Shropshire. He had entered the Order over twenty years earlier and had spent almost all of the last two decades serving in the East. Since the terrible defeat at Hattin, where his predecessor had perished, he had served under the Marshal of the Order as the knight in charge of procuring, manufacturing, repairing and distributing all the weapons used by Templars throughout the Holy Land. From the moment he had first met him, Fitz Alan had found the massive Shropshireman to be possessed of a kind of jovial serenity that made him approachable and easy to converse with. In his relatively brief time in the East, Fitz Alan had come to know and respect Hugo Le Grant as both a competent officer of the Order and a font of knowledge regarding all things related to the Holy Land. Indeed, the two had become close friends. Now, on the eve of his great *mandatum*, he wanted from the armorer not only weapons, but the benefit of his many years of experience in the East.

"I have need of weapons, my friend," said Fitz Alan, "after that last battle, all I have left is my sword, and even that is looking decidedly worse for the wear."

"Always happy to accommodate a Poor Knight such as yourself," the armorer replied, leading him to a well-guarded tent in the middle of the compound. Le Grant pushed aside the flap and the two Shropshiremen entered the massive pavilion.

"Right then," he said, "what exactly do you have need of?"

Fitz Alan was already poring over a stand of shields. "I'll need one of these, to start," he said, pulling one off its peg. Like all Templar shields this one was roughly triangular in shape and curved to fit around a knight's body. It bore the Order's colors, black for the worldly city they had left behind upon entering the Order and white for the City of God they now inhabited. Made of wood and leather, it provided a good yet lightweight defense against Saracen arrows, spears and swords. He slipped his left forearm into the *enarmes* or arm straps and pronounced it acceptable.

"Lances, too?" asked the armorer. Fitz Alan nodded and Le Grant led him to another part of the massive tent where bundles of the twelve-foot long weapons were lashed upright to poles sunk into the ground and resting on large flat stones. They were stored this way to prevent them from warping. He cut the cord lashing one bundle to the pole and then pulled two lances from the bale. He inspected them both with a practiced eye, then passed them to Fitz Alan who did the same.

"These'll do," he said.

"A mace?" asked the armorer.

"Yes. I left the last one embedded in the face of a Kurdish horseman."

"This way," said Le Grant, leading Fitz Alan all the way to the far side of the tent. There, arrayed on a long table, were dozens of Turkish maces, their flanged iron heads coated in animal fat to keep them from rusting. The armorer picked one up, quickly and expertly judged its balance and handed it to Fitz Alan.

"Excellent," he exclaimed. It was a weapon he found very useful in close quarters fighting.

The two men left the storage tent and walked to another where a clerk carefully noted what weapons had been issued and to whom. The weapons were then given to a servant who was charged with delivering them to Fitz Alan's squire. The two Templars then proceeded to the workshop where Fitz Alan had first been greeted.

"My friend, I have need of your counsel," said Fitz Alan.

"Of course you do, otherwise you would have sent your squire to draw your weapons."

The two sat at a small table in the shade of a large olive tree.

"I cannot divulge much regarding the nature or purpose of the expedition, but suffice it to say that I must lead a small banner of Templars deep into Saracen territory to a place in the County of Tripoli. We are to be accompanied by a *poulain* who, I am assured, has knowledge of the country thereabouts, but..."

"But you want a more, er... *reliable* perspective. Natural enough. What do you need to know."

"First off, what is the general situation in the County of Tripoli? Are we likely to travel unmolested or will we find swarms of Saracens on the roads and the towns?"

"Just a moment," said Le Grant, rising from his bench and disappearing into his tent. When he returned to the table he had a large map, which he proceeded to spread out before Fitz Alan.

"This is a map of the main fortresses, towns, roads and pilgrimage sites in *Outremer*. We are here," he said, pointing to Acre, "and your destination is somewhere near here." He pointed to Tripoli. "The pilgrim host," he continued, "will likely proceed southward along the coast to Jaffa, shadowed all the way by the greater part of Saladin's horde. At the moment, though, the bulk of the Sultan's fighters are in this area." He pointed to the town of al-Kharruba, half-way between Acre and Nazareth.

The armorer paused long enough to summon a servant and have some water brought to them. "What this means for you, my friend, is that if you avoid the larger towns, you will likely encounter few Saracens on your journey, for you will be going north and the greater part of them will be going south."

Fitz Alan looked at the map. Such things were not entirely unfamiliar to him, but he had seen relatively few of them in his life and he always found them more than a bit confusing. "I see that Tyre is on our route. What sort of reception are we likely to find there?"

"The count of Montferrat is no friend of King Richard. If he gets wind that you are in the service of the Lionheart, he is likely to try to impede you, perhaps even detain you. Probably best to take the more inland route and avoid Tyre and Montferrat's men altogether." He pointed in the direction of the town of Tiberias. "Follow the inland road toward the fortress of Safad, then head north. That'll put you in the Beqaa valley, which you can then follow until you reach here," he stabbed a finger at the map, "at which point you follow this road toward Tripoli. Once there you can follow the coast road to Tripoli."

"Anything else?"

"Sidon, Beirut and much of the highlands to the west of the Beqaa valley are in the possession of the Saracens. The town of Tripoli remains in Christian hands, as do the Hospitaller fortresses of Margat and Krak des Chevaliers. Seems that in his desire to sustain the pace of his campaign, and to avoid any setbacks that might tarnish his reputation as an unbeatable leader, the great Saladin decided not to attack these two impregnable fortresses. You should know also that with his attention focused on Acre and much farther north on Antioch, he has not invested much time or effort in imposing his rule – or even consolidating his hold on – the lands he has captured. He has taken important but weakened strongholds like Kerak, Beaufort, Saone and Belvoir, but he has avoided well-garrisoned fortresses like Margat and ignored many minor fortifications and Christian religious houses that he thinks pose no threat to him."

Fitz Alan's gaze shifted to a point on the map north and east of where he guessed their destination to be. "How far is that from Tripoli?" he said, stabbing a finger toward a territory labeled "Lands of the Assassins."

"No more than forty miles from the city, though the county abuts it. What do you know of them?"

"What everyone knows, I suppose. They're Saracens, but of a different stripe than Saladin and his followers. Indeed, there is considerable bad blood between the two factions. I've even heard it said that the Assassins have tried to murder the sultan once or twice. Their king is referred to as the Old Man of the Mountain, or some such nonsense. Not much else. Is there more you think I need to know of them? Do you think I'll have to worry about these devils on my journey?"

"No. That just about sums them up. You shouldn't encounter any unless you are planning on entering their kingdom, in which case…."

"Not to worry. I've no intention of going anywhere near that particular hornets' nest. It is said they are unpredictable and untrustworthy and I'd just as soon not have anything to do with them." Fitz Alan straightened himself and adjusted his mantle. "Anything else I need to know?"

The armorer paused for a moment to finish off the water in his cup.

"That, I fear, is the limit of my wisdom in this regard – I have no more knowledge to share with you. I do, however, have something a bit more…. *tangible* for you to take on your expedition, something that may prove even more helpful than the knowledge I have imparted." The armorer rose from his chair and ducked into a nearby tent. When he emerged he was carrying two objects. The first, a tubular leather case, he placed on the table in front of Fitz Alan.

"For the map. I daresay you'll have more need of it than I."

"Thank you, my friend. Your generosity is much appreciated."

The second object, loosely wrapped in a dark oilcloth, was longer and narrower than the first.

"I've been saving this for a worthy soul about to set out on a difficult path, Michael. Seems I need save it no longer." Le Grant held it out for Fitz Alan to take.

"What is it, my friend?" he asked. "From the shape of it, it's clearly not an impenetrable shield. An unstoppable sword, perhaps."

The armorer smiled. "As a pious Christian, you surely know that faith and righteousness should be your impenetrable shield and the word of God your unstoppable sword."

"I do indeed, and they are my preferred weapons when I am waging spiritual war against the devil and his demonic horde. I have found, though, that when the fighting is of a more worldly nature, a sturdy shield and a well-balanced sword are of somewhat more immediate use."

"Then you'll be well pleased with this gift, my friend. Go ahead and unwrap it."

Fitz Alan did as the armorer bade him, carefully uncovering the object.

"Behold," said Le Grant as the object became visible, "an unstoppable sword."

"Unstoppable?" said, Fitz Alan, instinctively testing the balance and feel of the weapon.

"Unstoppable!" replied the armorer. "Behold," he continued, taking the sword back from Fitz Alan. He walked over to a pile of gore-spattered Saracen helmets that had been recovered from the field of battle, pulled one bashed and crumpled specimen out and placed it on the ground. He then lifted the sword over his head and brought it crashing down on the battered-but-formidable looking helm. The sword passed though it as if though butter.

"Unbelievable!" exclaimed Fitz Alan.

"And yet your eyes bear witness to the truth of it. What's more, I've tried it out against *our* helmets – mail armor, too; even a few of our swords. Same result. Unstoppable!" The armorer was clearly awestruck by the sheer beauty of the weapon and the *perfectio* that allowed it to do so perfectly that which it was created to do.

"Whence came this unstoppable blade?"

"We recovered it from a dead Saracen knight on the field of battle outside Acre. Felled by an arrow, he was, before he was able even to draw the weapon. Had he got in amongst our men with that thing he might have single-handedly turned the tide of battle. I shudder at the thought"

"Are there any more?"

"No. Of all the arms recovered, this is the only one that bears this peculiar pattern." Le Grant pointed to the sword's blade. "See. Like running water. Doesn't look like an inscription. Probably something to do with the way it's forged. Never seen anything like it before and I certainly hope I do not see it again – at least not amongst the Saracen horde."

Taking the weapon back from the Shropshireman, Fitz Alan asked "Is it truly unstoppable?"

"No, not really. It possesses no magical or supernatural qualities, if that's what you're asking. It's just a damn sight better than anything we have – and nothing we have is proof against it. God help us if the infidels manage to make swords like this in any quantity." He trembled at the thought of the Saracen horde armed with such weapons – the prospect of it was truly horrifying to him. "In any case, I'd like you to have it. I've a sense that you've a difficult path ahead of you. The *verbum Dei* here might just be the difference between success or failure."

"*Verbum Dei?*"

"Oh, that's what I've been calling it. You know, from Ephesians: 'And take the helmet of salvation, and the sword of the Spirit, which is the word of God,' *verbum Dei.*"

"*Verbum Dei*. Fitting indeed. I shall wield it in that spirit. Thank you, again, my friend."

"Not at all," replied Le Grant. "Now, I have business to attend as I'm sure do you. May Our Lady keep you and your band of English Templars in Her prayers, Michael; I certainly shall."

English Templars? Fitz Alan thought. Only he and a handful of others in the banner hailed from Richard's English possessions, and none would have thought of themselves as *English* Templars. What a curious thing to call his small detachment. He half-considered correcting his friend, but then thought better of it. They were, after all, his men; and he was from Temple Ewell preceptory; and that preceptory was in England. Maybe that was all it took to make his band of holy warriors English Templars. He decided he'd have to give the matter a bit more thought.

"And I you, my friend," was all he finally said. "And I you."

17 July 1191

He had a hard face, savagely tanned by the Eastern sun and brutally battered by the hardships of two decades of politics, diplomacy and war. It was no longer a youthful face, but it was handsome nonetheless – sharply featured, square-jawed, framed by a brown-black head of hair and close-cropped beard, neither of which were yet corrupted by the grey threads of wisdom that his hard life had earned him. It was the kind of face that usually angered Alberto Forno Canovese, Lord of Montegrosso d'Asti, his own both tragically deficient from birth and considerably worsened over the years by battle and the pox. But this face, the face of Conrad de Montferrat, was the face of his lord, king and earthly savior. This was the face of the man whom he loved and served without reservation; the face of the lord for whom he had forsaken all other lords. This was the face of the man for whom Alberto Forno Canovese would do anything.

"You summoned me, my lord?"

"Indeed I did, Alberto. Come. Join me in a cup of wine." He gestured to the servant hovering nearby, and two cups of wine instantly appeared on the thick cedar table at which he was seated. The Lord of Montegrosso d'Asti, better known among Conrad's inner circle as the Sinister One, sat on one of the cushioned seats across from his liege, uncomfortable at once with the comfort it provided. He waited impatiently for Conrad to drink first and then eagerly quaffed the wine in a single gulp. The Angevin spy whom he'd been questioning since dawn had proven a tougher nut to crack than he'd expected and, despite the pleasure and gratification that the interrogation had provided, it had been a draining day – a very a draining day, indeed. He was tired, hungry, and above all, thirsty. Given the hour and all he had been through since the dawn, he felt no compunction whatsoever about prevailing upon his lord's servant for another cup of blessed, blessed relief.

"I sense you have been about your lord's work. Anything you'd like to tell me?"

The Sinister One put his empty cup on the table, savoring for just a moment the soothing warmth he felt spreading outward from his belly. "Not much, my lord. The man had not been in the pay of the Angevin for long and so appears not have had the opportunity to do us much harm. Between his screams and pleas for mercy, he did suggest that there were others in the pay of Richard, but if he knew who they were he died before he could reveal their names."

"You really could not extract the full truth from the miscreant?"

"Given what that poor bastard suffered, my lord, I truly doubt he knew much more than he revealed. He'd gotten to the point where he was suggesting that even his aged mother was somehow in the pay of our foes. As my lord knows only too well, subjected to the Pear of Anguish, in the end a man will tell you anything he thinks you want to hear." He was referring to an extremely effective torture device made up of a pear-shaped metal body divided into spoon-like segments. The device was inserted into a victim's mouth, vagina or anus, and the segments spread open through the use of a screw mechanism. As the screw was turned, the pain grew progressively worse until it became unbearable. "Ultimately, though, I truly believe that we drained this particular swamp. The traitor told us all he knew. And then he died."

"Not to worry, Alberto. If there are more of the Angevin's men amongst us I'm sure you'll ferret them out. More wine? Some food, perhaps? I know from experience that such days as this can test the limits of even the best of Christ's servants."

"Indeed, my lord, I would relish both. As you say, it can be a trying field in which to labor."

Conrad motioned the hovering servant to attend him and ordered him to fill his servant's cup and bring some food. Within a few minutes several large serving plates of cold meats, cheeses, bread, olives and dates were served. The Sinister One again waited impatiently for his lord to begin and then set upon the food as if he hadn't eaten for days.

When it seemed as if his vassal was nearly finished, the Marquis of Montferrat beckoned a servant to begin clearing the plates. A second man appeared with more wine and proceeded to refill the two cups. "I have need of your talents, Alberto," said the marquis.

The Sinister One looked up from his now-empty plate and wiped his mouth with the palm of his hand. "My lord has only to ask and it shall be done."

The marquis smiled, for he knew that his man would descend into hell itself if he but suggested that it would please him. "As you are doubtless aware, my position here in the East is precarious at best. My claim to the throne has never been widely accepted among the lords of *Outremer*. And I now realize that I seriously overrated Philip of France's ability to get those ungrateful bastards to accept that claim. Richard has stymied him at every turn, and support for the Angevin's vassal Guy de Lusignan," he almost spit the name out, "grows by the day." He recalled, not for the first time, the bitter tale of the crushing defeat at Hattin, a defeat attributable in his mind solely to de Lusignan's incompetent leadership and overweening pride. "And to make matters worse, he tells me that he will soon seek to be released from his vows so that he can return to France. Worried about enforcing his rights in the Artois now that that old sodomite the Count of Flanders is dead, or so he says. More like he smells an opportunity to try to prise some of the Angevin territories away from Richard while he is tied down here." He raised the cup of wine and took a long draught. "Once Philip is gone, I'll be totally isolated. Worse, the crown'll be placed back on the head of the bastard who would have lost all of *Outremer* had I not rallied the remnants of the Christian host and held Tyre against Saladin." The thought of Guy being decisively returned to the throne genuinely sickened the marquis.

"My lord, perhaps you have backed the wrong horse in supporting Philip, but surely it is not too late to back the right one. Any number of Philip's supporters have gone over to Henry's side in recent months. Why not you? There is no doubt that Richard wants one of his men on the throne. But why must it be Guy? Surely even Richard can see that you would make the superior king. And if you were to become his vassal…."

Conrad raised his hand peremptorily. "He'll never forgive me denying him entry into Tyre when he first arrived in the East. Never. No. Salvation does not lie in seeking Richard's favor – he'll never give it. The only hope is to secure the support of the major part of the council *despite* Richard's opposition. If I can do that, the crown'll be mine and there'll be nothing that that Angevin whoreson will be able to do about it."

"But how will you do that, my lord? How will you convince the majority of the council to back you rather than Guy?"

"That, my good friend Alberto, is where you come in. If I am to sway the council in my favor, I'll have to demonstrate that our good Lord Himself has ordained it. To achieve that, at the next gathering of the council, I propose to present the Templar Grand Master with a simple gift – the relic of the True Cross."

The Sinister One had been enjoying a mouthful of wine when his lord had uttered these words. On hearing them, he choked on the warm and soothing liquid. "My lord?" he sputtered, composing himself as best he could.

"You heard me correctly, Alberto. I'll have the lords of the pilgrimage confirm me as King of Jerusalem by restoring the relic of the True Cross to its rightful guardians, the Templars. In so doing, I will show them that God favors my candidacy. There'll be no way they could deny me the crown then."

"But…But, how?" All of Christendom knew that the relic had been lost to Saladin at Hattin and that the Sultan would never return it as long as Christian armies were present in the East. Greeks, Georgians, Armenians and sundry others had tried to purchase it, for all knew that to recover the relic would bring great glory. Knowing this, however, and fearing that any Christian in possession of the Cross would be emboldened to wage war against one who had so unjustly seized it, Saladin had refused every offer. He simply would not part with it, not for money, nor land nor rights. And now Conrad de Montferrat, the rock upon whom Alberto Forno Canovese, Lord of Montegrosso d'Asti, had built his entire world, was ranting about restoring the relic to Christendom. The usually unflappable Sinister One drained his cup, prayed for guidance, and called for more wine.

"No, my faithful friend, I have not gone mad. I am as sane as you. But I do know where the relic is, or rather where it soon will be… and I do have a plan for acquiring it."

His prayer apparently answered, the Sinister One felt his habitual sense of icy calm descend once again. Restored, he leaned forward and, speaking in his native Piedmontese rather than Latin the two men had been using, said simply, "Go on, my lord."

"My spies inform me," Conrad replied in the same tongue, "that Saladin has agreed to return the True Cross to Richard as part of the ransom for the Acre garrison." He sensed his vassal bristle in instinctive disbelief. The marquis smiled. "Like you, old friend, I don't for a minute believe that the Sultan will actually turn over the relic, at least not readily. But…."

"My lord?"

"But I do believe he will have it moved into closer proximity, just in case worst come to worst and the Sultan needs it on short notice – say if Richard actually appears ready to carry out his threat. And if I am right about this, if my spies are telling me the truth, then it is reasonable to deduce that the Holy Relic will cross the Jordan between Bethsaida and Capernaum sometime in the next week or so. It will then be carried along the road to Genesaret, thence to Magdala, and finally to Sepphoris where plans have been made to receive it and convey it to Saladin."

The Sinister One heard the next words out of Conrad's mouth almost before they were uttered.

"And that, my faithful friend, is where you come in. Should you be willing, I would have you proceed forthwith with a band of trusted men and conceal yourself somewhere along that route. When the Cross appears, I would then have you and your men seize it from the Saracen bastards and bring it directly to me." The marquis finished his wine as if he had not a care in the world. "Can I count on you to render me this service, old friend?"

"I serve you without question, my lord. You can count on me."

"Good. Then let us talk of details. You will need to have your men in place within the week. Depending on where you wish to lay your trap, it is only a three or four day march from here so you are not wanting for time. Whom do you wish to take with you?"

The Sinister One hesitated only a heartbeat before answering. "I'll take Jean de Maron. He's a *poulain*, and a prideful bastard at that, but he's dependable, and he knows how to hunt the Turk."

"Good, Alberto, good. Will you need anything else?"

"I think not, my lord. My men-at-arms plus de Maron's retainers should suffice. Two dozen good men, well-trained, well-provisioned and well-led. Should be all we'll need to deal with what is likely to be a small escort. With the benefit of surprise, I'm sure we'll have no difficulty dispatching the Saracen guard and securing the relic."

Montferrat smiled. "You always inspire confidence, my friend. I have no doubt the True Cross will be back in Christian hands again before long."

"Thank you, my lord. May I be about my work?

"Indeed, you may."

And with that the Sinister One was gone, off to do the will of his lord, the Marquis of Montferrat.

IV

18 July 1191

Fitz Alan surveyed the band of warriors assembled on the field before him. They were an impressive lot. From their bronzed and leathered faces he inferred that all of them had served in the East for a very long time. That meant that neither the climate nor the enemy were unknown to them. And he had been assured by de Fonte that they were as skilled a group of fighters as any in Christendom. Fitz Alan felt confident that God had given him precisely the instrument he needed to carry out his *mandatum*. Looking around, however, he realized that the assembled warriors were largely unknown to him – and he to them. To be certain, several of the sergeant-brothers had served with him for some time now. He was well acquainted with Brother John, Brother Diarmait and Brother Enyon. All good men whom he had known since he arrived in the East and assumed command of the *eschielle*; men who could be counted on in a fight. But the others, including one so massive he dwarfed even de Fonte, he knew not; nor, save the *Turcopolier*, did he have any acquaintances among the native fighters. Given the extent to which the Order these days comprised men whose first loves were neither Christ nor His Church – felons and other reprobates sentenced to serve; low-born strivers seeking advancement in the Earthly City – he felt it prudent to say a few words about discipline.

"Brother Arnaldus," Fitz Alan bellowed so that he would be overheard by the troupe, "these men doubtless know the Templar Rule, but have you instructed them in my Rule?" He was referring to his abbreviated version of the Templar Rule that governed the lives of all who fought with and for the Order.

"I have not, Brother Michael." Arnaldus bellowed back. "I thought it best they hear of it directly from you."

"Very well." Fitz Alan adjusted himself in his saddle and turned to face the assembled warriors. The sergeant-brothers of Fitz Alan's acquaintance, having heard this peroration before, were all grinning broadly. "Listen closely, you men, for I'm only going to say this once. Fitz Alan's Rule consists of only three canons, but if you violate any of these I'll see your souls in hell. First, you kill for one reason and one reason only – to protect Christ and His Church. You will not kill for honor, hatred, property or any of the other sinful lusts of this world. Second, you will obey me, Brother Arnaldus and the *turcopolier* without question. If any of us order you to ride into hell, you will do so without question or hesitation. And third, when in the presence of the enemy you will consider yourself in the presence of Satan himself – and you will fight accordingly. You will fight even the lowliest Saracen bastard, in other words, as if your immortal soul is at stake. Because it is. Where the infidel is concerned, my Rule is simple. Kill. Kill. Kill. That's it! Fight only for the glory of God, obey your superiors without question and, when you engage the heathen, fight as if you're fighting the Devil himself. Do you understand these canons as I have put them to you?" The sergeant-brothers immediately roared the traditional *de par Dieu* in assent, but there was a half-puzzled silence among the *turcopoles*. Once the *turcopolier* had translated, though, a half-hearted murmur of assent rippled quickly though the ranks of the native contingent. "Do you understand the Rule as I have put it to you?" Fitz Alan bellowed again, his intent now clear to one and all. This time the response was a loud cheer from Templar and *turcopole* alike. "Good," said Fitz Alan.

He turned to the *turcopolier*. "Form them up into a column of twos and get them ready to move."

"Bien sûr, Frère Michel!" replied the *turcopole* commander, who then set about organizing the troop as instructed.

Once assembled, Fitz Alan and de Fonte took their place at the head of the column, just in front of the *gonfanier* and Father de Ramla. The *turcopolier* took up position at the rear of the column. Satisfied that they were as prepared as they'd ever be, Fitz Alan gave de Fonte the signal and the huge Gascon ordered the Templar band to move out. Within a matter of minutes they had crossed the trench line that marked the limits of *Outremer* and the beginnings of heathendom. As they entered the wood just beyond the snaking scar in the earth, Fitz Alan turned to de Fonte and crossed himself. "Thus it begins," he said.

De Fonte swatted a fly from his horse's mane, and then, turning to his friend, he offered a simple prayer in response. "God be with us, Michael," he said, "God be with us."

Conrad de Montferrat was an angry man. A very angry man. First, he had been left hanging in the wind by his faithless cousin Philip of France who, though he had not yet departed the Holy Land, had made clear to the Lord of Tyre that he intended to do so in the very near future. Conrad had pinned his hopes for gaining the crown of Jerusalem on the support of the French king, and in furtherance of that aim had actively opposed King Richard when the Angevin had first arrived at Tyre. Now, for his own selfish reasons, Philip had abandoned him. As a result, the Lord of Tyre now found himself exposed to the tender mercies of the English king. And, as everyone knew, Richard was nothing if not vindictive.

And, then, as if that weren't enough, his right-hand man, *Il Sinistro*, was now reporting to him that someone had beaten him to the ambush site, killed the Saracens conveying the True Cross to Saladin, and then carried the relic off to God knows where. And all without leaving even the smallest clue as to their identity or destination. Conrad had come to believe that acquiring the relic would decisively seal his claim to the throne of Jerusalem. And now, when it was so nearly within his grasp, it was plucked away by malevolent phantoms of unknown provenance or purpose. Perhaps Richard now possessed it, he thought, shuddering at the prospect. No matter whose hands it had passed into, though, the loss of the relic was a terrible setback, for it left the disposition of the crown in the hands of a council that would unquestionably be dominated by Richard once that faithless coward Philip had departed *Outremer*. The betrayal of the French king; the loss of the greatest relic in Christendom; command of the pilgrimage passing indisputably into the hands of his most implacable adversary.... He shuddered to think what setback fate would deliver him next. But he resolved that nothing – not Richard, not Saladin, not even Christ on His holy throne – would come between him and what was his by right, the crown of the Kingdom of Jerusalem. It was his and he would have it, no matter the cost, no matter the sacrifices, no matter the deals he'd have to do, or with whom he'd have to do them.

"You, old friend," he could barely contain his rage, "have let me down." The final words were discharged like a bolt from a crossbow.

"My liege."

"The relic was my answer to that bastard Philip and his conniving cousin Richard. And you have let it slip through my fingers. What have you to say for yourself?"

Alberto D'Asti was himself a proud man, a man of ambition – indeed, a ruthless, brutally ruthless, man of ambition. He was accustomed to being addressed by his lord in this fashion, but he'd never liked it. He knew, though, that he had failed his liege; and he suspected, at least, the implications of his failure. "Nothing, my lord," were the only words he could muster in response.

"Nothing? Nothing? Christ on His holy cross, man. That is all you have to say to me? You've lost me the crown and that's all you've to say to your lord and master. I'll have your balls, you useless dog. Your balls, d'ye hear me?"

"My lord." D'Asti had learned long ago that on occasions such as this, it was best simply to let the waves of his lord's anger wash over him.

"You've one last chance, you useless bastard," Conrad frothed. "One last chance to redeem yourself."

"My liege," D'Asti seethed. Always one last chance, he thought, always one last bloody chance.

"Well?"

"There is a way forward, my lord."

Conrad, fully cognizant of all that his man had done for him, yet equally mindful that he might have to kill the miscreant simply to encourage the others in his employ, was in part intrigued and in part relieved.

"Tell me. Now!" he said, his voice betraying a struggle between hope and ambition on the one hand and deepening frustration and anger on the other.

"There's talk, my liege, of another relic. Not the True Cross, to be sure, but a relic of nearly equal worth."

His anger subsided slightly, allowing his ambition to begin to reassert itself. "Tell me."

"'Tis but a report, my lord."

At that, Conrad felt his anger rising again. "Spit it out, you bloody fool, or I truly will have the balls off you!"

D'Asti shuddered. He'd seen it done by one of Conrad's men before and knew full well that there were those in his lord's employ who would do it again – to him – if necessary. "My lord, there are those of my acquaintance in Richard's circle who tell me that a Templar named Fitz Alan and a small band of men are, even as we speak, on their way to a monastery somewhere in what's left of the County of Tripoli, a lazar house called Valsainte. Their goal, I am told, is the recovery of the Spear of Longinus and its return to the Angevin king."

"God's Wounds! Can this be true?" Conrad knew the legend of the Holy Spear as well as anyone. It was not the True Cross, to be sure, but recovery of the relic would be sufficient to tip the scales against Richard and his preferred candidate Guy de Lusignan. And then there were its reputed powers to bring victory on the field of glory. He was more than intrigued.

"According to the accounts I've received, my lord, there's little doubt it is. And..."

"And what?"

"And if we move quickly we can beat this band of Templars to the Spear's resting place and seize the relic from the monks who would keep it from us."

Conrad was calculating now, working out the odds of success, the consequences of failure and the details of what needed to be done if the scheme was to have any chance of bearing fruit. "Do your acquaintances know if they'll be taking coast road?"

"They know not the precise route, my lord. But if I were to place a wager, I'd place it on the inland route, through the Beqaa Valley. This Fitz Alan must be aware he can't move easily through Tyre or its environs and we control the seas between Acre and Tripoli. That being the case, what choice has he? In any case, it'll be simple enough to put patrols out on the coastal road to stymie him there. That'll add a few days to the Templars' journey. Meanwhile, with your permission, I'll head to Tyre by ship and assemble some of my warriors who remain there. We'll strike quickly for the lazar house. Depending on the winds and how quickly my men can be assembled, it may be a very close run thing. We've a reasonable chance of beating the Templars to the relic...." His voice trailed off, suggesting he had more to say.

"Spit it out, man."

"But if we don't, if we lose the race and this Fitz Alan manages to recover the relic, we'll have de Maron and his men follow the inland route the Templars will have to take and ambush them on their return journey. Unless they can fly, we'll catch these Templars at a narrow pass through the mountains just south west of Lake Tiberias. It's the only way through; they'll have to take it. And when they do, we'll have 'em."

Conrad could taste triumph now, the gall of his earlier setbacks receding from his memory. He grew hopeful once again. "My dear D'Asti, yet again you have turned defeat and failure into at least the possibility of victory. Your talents in this regard are…" he searched for the right word, "…unmatched – which is why you not only live, but live well. Well done. Now set de Maron and his men after this Templar. And get yourself aboard a ship bound for Tyre; once there, move quickly. I'll have the coast road blocked immediately, just in case they decide to risk that route. One way or another, we'll have the relic within the week. And once I have it, the crown will surely follow."

"Yes, my lord," said *Il Sinistro*, feeling relieved that, for now at least, his manhood was likely to remain safely attached to his body.

20 July 1191

Fitz Alan saw it first, a sight that would have been familiar enough in England or France, but one that struck him as utterly improbable here, two days ride inland from Acre in territory that had been in Saracen hands for several years now – what seemed to be a perfectly normal Christian village. To the left of the main road was a barn, a byre and a few cottages; to the right, a village green bordered by several more cottages, a bakery, winepress, and mill. And just a little way down a side road, more a track really, a church that was indistinguishable from most of the churches he had encountered in Aquitaine. Most astonishingly, Fitz Alan saw a priest leading a small procession through town parading what Fitz Alan surmised was a holy relic of some sort.

"Brother Arnaldus," he called, "take some of the sergeant-brothers and make sure there are no Saracens in the area."

"My lord," came de Fonte's reply, followed in rapid succession by a few barked commands and a storm of hoof beats.

Fitz Alan then turned to de Ramla. "What's going on here?" he asked. "I thought these lands were all in the hands of the damned Turks."

"My dear Brother Michael," de Ramla said, "you've much to learn about the complexities of life in *Outremer*."

"Instruct me, then. I've been here for nine months or so, but in all that time I've never been able to venture far from the siege positions at Acre. There, all was devastation. And the few villages and manors we've passed on the way here have been ravaged as I've seen so many ravaged in France. But now we enter this bloody valley and we come upon a little island of Christendom carrying on as if Saladin had never been born and Hattin had never happened. What's going on?"

"Well, the first thing you need to know is that Saladin's conquest is incomplete. He's conquered a vast territory, but he's not yet been able to impose his writ on all of it. Most of the folk hereabout are Christian, have always been Christian and will remain Christian as long as we are here fighting for their liberties."

"And if we lose? If the pilgrim host is defeated? Then he'll proceed to sweep up all these little towns and estates."

"Just so. Only when he's sent the host packing will he lay siege to the great fortresses that remain in our hands. Once he's taken those, he'll turn his attention to places like this. If that happens, life will become very unpleasant for these good Christian folk."

"Well, we'd best make sure he doesn't defeat the host then, hadn't we?"

"Brother Michael," said the *turcopolier* as he pulled up his mount beside the Templar's.

"What is it, Master Turcault?"

"Are we bedding down here for the night?"

"What do you think, de Ramla. Shall we stay here 'til morning?"

De Ramla surveyed the town with an experienced eye, then looked heavenward, not seeking any spiritual inspiration, but only to try to estimate how much time they had until sunset. "I'd say this is as good a spot as any. We've not much daylight left. Doesn't really make much sense to press on any further today."

"Right then, Master Turcault. Seems we'll be stopping here for the night."

"In that case, Brother Michael, I'd like your permission to send a few of my men to watch the approaches to the town. Wouldn't want to be surprised by a Saracen patrol, would we?"

"Are we likely to encounter any Saracens here, de Ramla?" Fitz Alan said, turning to the Hospitaller.

"It's possible," de Ramla conceded, "they have no permanent presence here, but the Saracen horde is always hungry. We may well encounter foraging parties and patrols the farther we proceed."

"Very well, Master Turcault. Post your men. Mind though, Brother Arnaldus is scouting the region with a few of the sergeant-brothers. Be sure your men know that and don't shoot them down as they return. Once you've done that, set the men to making camp. Remind them, too, that these are our people, not filthy Saracens. Tell the men to treat them right. If they don't, they'll answer to me." Fitz Alan reached into a bag that was fixed to his saddle and withdrew a fistful of coins, which he then handed to the *Turcopolier*. "Pay for what we take, William."

"*De par Dieu,*" responded the commander of the native auxiliaries, spurring his horse to action even before the words had left his mouth.

Fitz Alan admired the man's competence and felt, not for the first time, that Turcault had been the right choice for this expedition. He then turned to de Ramla, "We'll continue with the lesson after prayer, perhaps over a small cup of wine, if one can be procured."

"As you wish, Brother Michael. Until then, I'll see if I can learn anything from the priest we saw leading the procession. And I'll try to talk to the reeve, too, if these poor souls even have one."

"Good. Let me know what you learn, Father Raimundus."

"What is it you Templars say? *De Par Dieu?* I'll do it for God!" And with that, the Hospitaller priest spurred his horse and headed off in the direction of the largest building in the village, which was sure, he believed, to belong either to the village reeve or the local priest.

De Ramla had been questioning the reeve, the priest and a few other village notables for the better part of an hour when Fitz Alan rode up. The Hospitaller turned to his Templar commander. "The Lord be with you, Brother Michael."

"And with your spirit, Father de Ramla."

"I have much to report."

"I'd hoped you would. Get on with it, then. It'll be night soon and I've decisions to make."

"This town, I'm told, is the Ville d'Espérance. No one knows its original Christian name, but during the time of the Muslim usurpation it was called after the Arab potentate who ruled hereabouts. Shortly after the liberation of Jerusalem in 1099, the restored Christian authorities renamed it Ville d'Espérance. It has retained that name from then 'til today."

"Espérance, eh? Hopefulness. Seems fitting, somehow, now that the Christian host is on the march," said Fitz Alan, surveying the town in the fast fading light. He wondered, though, what had sustained their hope in the aftermath of Hattin and the Saracens' subsequent conquest of almost all of *Outremer*. The Templar turned abruptly to the two village leaders, the reeve and the priest. "So, tell me, what's been going on here these past several years, eh? You appear not to have heard of Hattin or the conquests of that heathen Saladin. A simple man might even think you've been cooperating with the heretics to purchase some peace and quiet. Have you?"

"We've heard of the conquests, my lord," the reeve replied, "they simply haven't afflicted us much – at least not as yet. And hopefully they never will. And, no, we haven't been cooperating with the Saracens. We haven't even seen them. Not a glimpse. God's truth!"

"What? You've been under the heel of the great and mighty Saladin for the past four years and you've not seen any Saracens. You must think me mad."

"Please, my lord. They simply haven't been here. Other than losing our lord and his knights at Hattin, and there was a terrible wailing and gnashing of teeth over that, our lives have changed little in the past four years. We sow and we reap. We are born and we die. It was ever thus, the Catastrophe has changed nothing for us."

"It's as I told you, Michael," de Ramla interjected, "out here, the rules are different. You'd think the Great Heathen would've mopped up everything straight away. Yet he hasn't. What was Christian before his conquests, at least outside of the great cities, remains Christian. And why shouldn't it? The Muslims arrived here six hundred years ago, and since then, despite all their depredations and oppressions, they have failed to convert the greater part of the people. In the four years or so since Hattin, this has not changed. And why should it be otherwise? The new Saracen overlords are spread thin and have other priorities."

Fitz Alan was wondering just how truthful the reeve was being when the thunder of approaching hoof beats caught his ear. Instinctively, he began to draw his sword in anticipation of a Saracen attack and was about to kick his *destrier* into action when he saw his friend de Fonte rounding the bend at the head of his patrol. He sheathed his partly drawn blade and calmed his mount.

"My lord," said the massive Templar as he reined his horse to a halt.

"Brother Arnaldus," Fitz Alan replied, "what news have you?"

"Nothing good, my lord, nothing good. We rode up the road three or four miles and found there at least a dozen of the Turkish bastards bedding down for the night."

"Did they see you?"

"No. Don't think so."

"Good! With the element of surprise I'm sure we can sort them out with a minimum of bother. Why so concerned, Arnuldus?"

"Not sure what to make of this, Michael, but they are travelling with a dozen or so carts…"

"And?"

"And they're full of women and children."

The reeve and priest gasped, looking at each other as if the second coming had just been proclaimed.

"Slavers!" exclaimed de Ramla.

"What?" said Fitz Alan.

"Slavers. The Saracens are ever on the hunt for slaves. The women and girls are enslaved as concubines for their emirs; the boys as fodder for their horde – or worse. Wherever they conquer, the slavers are not far behind." He crossed himself.

"You must stay here and protect us," begged the reeve, almost beside himself with fear. "If you don't, they'll enslave all these good Christian folk, folk whom I've known all my life and who look to me to keep them safe. You must stay and protect us from these devils, my lord."

"The good reeve speaks the truth, my lord, so he does," said the priest, his thick Ulster accent striking a dissonant note to Fitz Alan's ear. "It is your duty as Christians and knights of Christ to protect us from the heathen demons. You must stay and fight. You must save us."

"Brother Michael," said de Ramla, "may I remind you that we are charged by the king himself with recovering the relic. Nothing must be allowed to sway us from our mission. Nothing."

"Please, my lord," said the reeve. "Without you we are doomed. But if you stand with us, we have a chance. Even if you don't kill the heathen, but merely drive them off, they'll come to believe the village is garrisoned once again. If they believe that, they'll move east or west in search of easier pickings. Either way, they'll leave us be. Brother Michael, I pray thee, stay and fight for us. For pity's sake."

Fitz Alan's mind was reeling. The thought of Christian women and children being enslaved by the heathen enraged him almost beyond reason.

Seeing the look on Fitz Alan's face, de Ramla interjected. "Brother Michael, slavery is a fact here in the East. Though forbidden by holy scripture and natural law, the heathens have practiced it from the time of Mohammed – indeed, from time immemorial. It is part of their religion and folkways and they see nothing wrong with it. While we might recoil at the thought, it is part of the rhythm of life here in the lands conquered by the Saracens – along with the poll tax and all the other humiliations imposed upon subjugated Christians. We have a mission and we cannot be diverted from it by the prospect of a score or so Christians being subjected to what so many have had to endure since the Saracens first arrived."

"Arnaldus," Fitz Alan called, turning to his old and trusted comrade, "what d'ye think?"

"The good father speaks wisely, my lord," he said, slipping unconsciously into the language of their old relationship. "But the Church teaches that there's evil in this world, and surely this is proof of that teaching. We cannot make aright what the Fall of Man has made our lot. However, the Church also teaches that our calling as Templars is simple: fight for what is right and just – and kill the enemies of Christ and His holy Church. Seems to me our path is clear, Michael."

Fitz Alan turned to de Ramla. "Are you telling me that this mission exceeds my Templar vows – and the dictates of natural law and divine revelation? Surely, nothing exceeds my obligation to free these poor Christian women from a horrible life of eternal slavery and unending rape at the hand of these filthy heathens."

"In the Christian West, Brother Michael, many labor in the fields of the Lord," said de Ramla, "and many do so in conditions little better than slavery. Why should any of this distract us from our mission?"

"Damn you, de Ramla. This is worse, far worse, and you know it. What was it de Fonte said, women and children, concubines and worse? No, by the bowels of Christ, I'll not stand by and watch such infamy again. Neither for the king nor the Grand master nor anyone else. We're going to free those poor Christian souls, no matter the cost, and if you don't approve you can ride back to your lord and master, that murdering bastard and false bishop Hubert Walter, and kiss his poxy backside."

"Brother Michael, you misunderstand me. If you judge it to be right and just, I'll follow you into the fires of hell. But before you ask me to do so, please assure me that what you decide is, in fact, right and just."

"It is," he replied defiantly, though he doubted the Hospitaller priest actually believed it. Then, turning to de Fonte, he said, "What's our best course of action, Arnaldus?"

"There's a blind spot as the road down the hills bends into the valley," de Fonte replied. "If we place the *turcopoles* and Brother Enyon just this side of the turn they can slaughter the outriders and guards as they pass by. Then a well-timed attack by the sergeant-brothers and the caravan should be secured. Can't guarantee that all the prisoners will make it through alive, but it seems to me that this is the best way to proceed."

"Good man, Arnaldus. Make preparations for an attack at dawn, for there's no telling when these slaver swine will decide to move out."

"My lord!" came de Fonte's instinctive reply.

"And you two – reeve, priest – make sure my men have all they need this night. We'll pay you for what we take, but make no mistake, we'll take what we need. Best you cooperate."

"Rest assured," said the priest, whom Fitz Alan now saw clearly was the only real authority in the village, "you'll have our full cooperation, so you will."

"Make sure we do, Father, and none of your damned bog-Irish nonsense, d'ye hear? I've fought your people before and I know what you're all about."

Before the priest had a chance to reply, Fitz Alan kicked his horse in the flanks and rode off up the road to see what he could see of the ambush site before the fading light made it impossible for him to do so.

21 July 1191

The lead rider, a Tawashi cavalryman, rounded the bend in the main road that twisted into the valley, his bow tucked away in a large holster on his belt, his sword sheathed and his lance resting lazily across the withers of his mount. Behind him came several more horseman similarly attired and equipped, none of whom seemed particularly alert to the possibility of attack in this God-forsaken place so far from Acre and the Christian host. Behind them came a dozen horse-drawn carts, each filled with filthy and forlorn creatures that even at a distance appeared to be little more than broken and hopeless remnants of what had once been human beings. Bringing up the rear of the column was another half-dozen horsemen, accompanied by a well-armed and -armored man who rode slightly taller in his saddle than all the rest. This man had the unmistakable aura of authority about him and was obviously the man in charge of the slaver caravan.

Brother Enyon was fully concealed by a rock outcropping about half way up the slope that defined the eastern edge of the valley. He had his bow and several sheaves of arrows and, while not exactly comfortable, was satisfied that he was well placed to do what he had been called by the Lord to do. Looking backward from his vantage point, he could see where the other sergeant-brothers were concealed, though he could not actually see his *confrères*. He looked toward the far ridge, knowing that several of the *turcopoles* were similarly arrayed along the ridge that defined the western edge of the valley. He could see no sign of them. Enyon removed his gouged and battered white-on-black kettle hat and peered through a crack in the massive stones that concealed him, spying the caravan as it wound its way down the slope and onto the relatively flat plain that opened up between the two ridges. Once the last man in the column had passed by, he reminded himself, he was to rise up and smite him. Once he had loosed his first arrow, he and the other concealed Templar bowmen were to continue shooting until the entire rear guard had been destroyed. Won't be long now, he thought, settling back behind the rock separating him from the Saracens and placing his kettle hat back on his head. Won't be long now. Just enough time for a few *Pater Nosters*, he told himself, and then his bow would sing and the day's killing would begin. And then, unbidden, he heard his long-dead father, a bishop who had sired him out of wedlock, saying as if he were right there in the valley with him: *diabolus accipere extremos, Enyon*. The devil take the hindmost, Enyon, the devil take the hindmost!

"Brother Michael," whispered de Fonte quietly, riding left to right along the line of Templar horsemen to report to Fitz Alan.

"Yes," came the reply.

"The men are ready, my lord. Six sergeant-brothers in front, six *turcopoles* in the rear, Master Turcault and the two of us in the lead. Once we hear that the slaughter has begun, we'll ride the bloody Turks down and kill the lot before they have a chance to murder the captives. Shouldn't take but a moment or two."

"Always feels like much longer than that."

"Indeed it does, but this time it'll be over quickly. There's only a dozen or so of the infidels. They'll not last long…"

Fitz Alan raised his hand to silence his old friend. He could hear now the din of the Saracen caravan as it entered the valley and he knew the battle would begin soon. "No Psalm this time," he whispered, knowing that he needn't have said anything to his battle-hardened and experienced friend. "When I drop my lance, we'll charge these miscreants. Pass the word again to be sure everyone knows the signal."

"*De par Dieu*," said de Fonte as he wheeled his mount and began whispering instructions to the men as he rode back along the line.

Fitz Alan adjusted himself in his saddle and checked yet again that his sword moved freely in its scabbard. He could feel his heart beating in his chest now, and hear the familiar thumping in his ears. His blood was up and he wanted nothing more to be at the enemy's throat, slashing and hacking, killing, killing, killing. It was only with a supreme act of will that he was able to contain himself and wait for the sound of his bowmen killing the heathen bastards.

"The men are ready, Michael," de Fonte reported.

"Good," he said thickly, the prospect of battle already beginning to inebriate him, just as the prospect of women and the hunt once did. "Good." Fitz Alan strained now to hear what was going on just around the bend. The clatter and clanking of carts on the move. Hoof beats. A child sobbing. The occasional barked command. Nothing to suggest that the alarm had been sounded or that they were in any way concerned. What were Brother Enyon and the others waiting for, he thought, why have the quarrels not begun to fly? From the sound of it, the slavers would be at the bend soon, robbing his horsemen of the space they needed to spur their mounts to a full and fatal gallop. For the love of God, he thought, what are they waiting for? He raised himself in his saddle, straining yet again to hear the telltale signs that the bowmen had begun their day's lethal work. What are they bloody waiting for, he thought, his whole body pulsating now with the pent up energy of a man hungry for killing and not wanting to be kept from it. What in Christ's holy name are they waiting for, he asked himself again? He turned to de Fonte, a half-formed curse about to emerge from his parched mouth.

And then the screaming began.

Enyon ap Madoc had seen a great deal of action in the ten years or so since he had walked into the Templar preceptory at Newport in Gwent. A year of training in his native Wales; two years of fighting the Saracens in Hispania; another year training acolytes at Temple Ewell in England; and six years of near-continuous fighting in the Holy Land. He had been a hard man when he had entered the Order. He had grown up an orphan and survived for many years as an outlaw in the Royal Forest of Wentwood, and playing cat-and-mouse with the foresters who made life miserable for all those unfortunate souls reduced to scraping a living off the sheep and deer that roamed the vast royal hunting reserve. He had entered the Order to escape the hardness of that life, but the years since had made him harder still. There was, of course, no gainsaying the fact that the rhythms and disciplines of Templar life had transformed him from an insensate brute into a man of God. But the rigors of life as a Templar and the harsh realities of unrelenting war in the East had hardened him over the years as even his harsh life as an outlaw had not. He was a brutal and disciplined killer now. A man who killed only for Christ, to be sure, but a brutal and disciplined killer nonetheless. And a killer who no longer feared death. He didn't seek it, for as long as God and the Grand Master had plans for him while on his earthly pilgrimage, to deliberately court death would be a terrible sin. It was simply that he didn't fear it anymore; for he believed, as all Templars did, that death in the service of Christ and His Church would not only relieve a man of the nearly unbearable burdens of this life, but secure for him an eternal seat at God's holy banquet table in the next.

That he was a brutal and disciplined killer did not distinguish Brother Enyon within the Order. What *did* set him apart was the instrument of his lethality. Where Templar sergeant-brothers typically fought with lances, swords and crossbows, Enyon had been given special dispensation to fight with the deadly warbow of his native Wales. It was a big bow, as tall as the man who wielded it, and incredibly difficult to master. But he had spent his youth learning its ways, and had developed the powerful chest, shoulder and arms muscles necessary to draw it to its full extent and discharge its lethal missiles accurately time after time. Enyon ap Madoc could now shoot faster, farther and more accurately than any other member of the Order. While the crossbow was very effective at short ranges if used as the Templars used it, it was less accurate and had a lower rate of discharge. And the small Saracen bow, while it could be used quite effectively from horseback, had neither the range, the accuracy nor the penetrating power of the Welsh war bow. Enyon's superiors had recognized almost from the day he entered the preceptory at Newport that God had blessed this humble man with special talents and that those talents had to be put to proper use in the service of Christ. They had originally assigned him to try to train other sergeant-brothers in the ways of the bow, but after a year or so had realized that mastering the weapon required a lifetime of practice and that the crossbow, so deficient in other ways, had the advantage when it came to ease of use. Once he had come to appreciate the difficulties associated with teaching acolytes how to use the war bow, the Grand Master had terminated the training program and attached Enyon to his own personal command, using the Welsh archer's special talents wherever he thought they might tip the scales of battle in favor of Christ and His Church. When he learned of

King Richard's plan to recover the Holy Lance, he had naturally attached Enyon to Fitz Alan's banner. Accustomed to such assignments, upon being given his most recent charge, Brother Enyon had silently prayed the prayer he always prayed when receiving such commands: *Non mea voluntas sed Tua fiat*; Not my will, Lord, but Thine be done.

The Welsh sergeant-brother peered again through the crack in the stones and saw that the last of the Saracen horsemen had finally entered the killing field. He stood slowly, knocked an arrow and drew its grey goose feathers back to his right ear. Instinctively judging the range and movement of his target, he aimed for the point between the man's shoulder blades, shifted the bow to the left a bit to compensate for the wind, and loosed the cord. The arrow flashed from his bow in a flat trajectory, slicing through the air and penetrating the rearmost Saracen's mail armor just below his right shoulder, spinning the man around and throwing him forward with terrible force. The Saracen should have been thrown from his horse, but his feet were tangled in the stirrups so he was merely flung out of the saddle, hanging lifeless down the right side of his mount as it panicked and bolted back up the valley and into the hills. The second shaft, knocked before the first one had found its mark, flickered through the sky and struck the dead Saracen's companion in the small of the back, causing him to arch violently before he, too, fell lifeless from his saddle, staring skyward. Enyon could hear screaming now, the screams of wounded and dying men interspersed with those of panicked women and children. He coolly knocked his third arrow, this time taking aim at a particularly large Saracen who had somehow managed to wheel his mount in the direction of the Welshman and was attempting to unholster his short bow. The Templar's bolt found its mark, smashing into the man's face and sending a spray of blood, flesh, teeth and shattered bone skyward as the enormous Saracen's head was thrown back violently by the force of the arrow's impact. Enyon could see the Saracen column disintegrating into chaos now as crossbow quarrels tore into men and horses up and down the line. And then he saw Fitz Alan and the main Templar force thunder round the bend in the road and smash straight into the half-dozen or so Saracen warriors at the front of the column who, upon realizing what was happening, had begun to flee down the valley and out of harm's way. Within a few heartbeats the slaughter was complete. Enyon watched as the mounted

Templars cut and hacked the fleeing enemy horsemen to bits, showing, he thought, precious little of the mercy and clemency extolled in the Gospels – and exactly as much mercy and clemency as they might expect from the Saracens were the tables to be turned. He watched as the *Turcopolier* reigned in his men, took the Saracen wagon drivers prisoner and posted a picquet up the road that the slavers had followed down into the valley and to their deaths. And he watched as Fitz Alan, knight of the Temple, calmly rode up to one of the survivors, the owner of the slaver caravan by the dress and demeanor of him, and viciously smashed his flanged Turkish mace into the man's unarmored face.

The *Turcopolier* and his men moved quickly among the dead Saracens, thumping their eyes to see if they were still alive. The dead never responded to this simple test. Those who were merely pretending, however, always reacted with an involuntary gesture that gave the game away. Once discovered, they were either killed or taken captive – their fate determined as much by whim as anything else.

"Brother Arnaldus," Fitz Alan barked.

"My lord," came the instinctive reply.

"Secure those women and children. See that they're fed and watered and prepared for the return to Espérance. If you can, find out what the devil happened here. Don't upset them too much, mind. Looks to me like they've been through hell this past little while and we don't want to add to their suffering."

"*De par Dieu*," said the massive Gascon, wheeling his *destrier* about and trotting off in the direction of the slaver caravan.

Fitz Alan then proceeded to check on the picquet he had set up the road. Once he was certain that his men were well positioned, he rode a little farther into the hills to see what lay ahead. Having satisfied himself that the banner faced no immediate danger, he turned around and headed back to the ambush site.

As he approached the killing field he was intercepted by de Fonte and de Ramla, both of whom wore looks on their faces that foretold nothing but trouble.

Fitz Alan pulled up his mount. "What is it, de Fonte?" he said.

"Trouble, my lord."

"I can bloody see that from the look on your face, Arnaldus. What kind of trouble?"

"The worst kind, my lord" said de Ramla.

Fitz Alan looked back and forth between the two. "Are you pair going to tell me what the devil's going on here, or am I going to have to ride back to the caravan and find out for myself?"

"The women, and even some of the children, have been violated, my lord," said de Fonte

"What?"

"The women, including the aged abbess of the Convent of Saint Elizabeth, Abbess Cecile, and several of her young acolytes have been raped by these slavers, Brother Michael. And there are five or six young orphan girls in their charge who also seem to have been subjected to the same unspeakable abuse." Having made his report, Father de Ramla spit into the dry sand, disgusted that human beings could lower themselves to such bestial behavior.

"Are you telling me…?"

"Yes, my lord."

"Are the felons still alive? Are they among the survivors?"

"According to the women, my lord, the Tawashi horsemen were honorable men, mere escorts who, though implicated, conducted themselves relatively decently. It was the slavers themselves, those driving the carts, who perpetrated the evil. According to the women, the man you killed with the mace, the commander of the slavers, was the very worst of the devils when it came to the despoiling."

Fitz Alan could feel his blood rising now. He'd been regretting his act of vengeance against the slaver lord whose face he'd smashed in, but now he felt as if he hadn't quite exacted the full measure of justice this man deserved.

"Round the bastards up, Brother Arnaldus, and present them to me without delay! By the living God, I'll see that these animals pay for what they've done!"

"*De par Dieu*," came de Fonte's reply, spurring his mount in the direction of the prisoners.

Fitz Alan turned to de Ramla. "You know what I'm going to do, don't you?"

"I do."

"And you've no objections?"

"Of course I've objections. This is a distraction. We are risking our expedition and with it the entire pilgrimage in a vain attempt to avenge these poor women."

"And so you think we should forget what was done to them and get on with the king's business?"

"No."

"No? Why not?"

"Because, as it says in Proverbs, 'When justice is done, it brings joy to the righteous but terror to evildoers.' While it's a distraction today, at the end of days, I want it written that I always served the cause of justice and did not suffer demons such as these to escape the temporal punishment that is their proper lot."

"Good, we are in agreement then. Let justice be done and let us bring some terror to these evildoers."

"I believe we are, Brother Michael, and, yes, let us bring terror to these evildoers."

"*Levez vous, maudits batard,*" said de Fonte, grabbing the nearest of the Saracens by his long, greasy hair and pulling him out from under the wagon where this batch of the prisoners had been sequestered. The man, bound at the wrists and ankles, stumbled and fell, but eventually de Fonte hauled him out and stood him up in front of Fitz Alan.

"You have been accused," the Templar commander said, "of violating several of these young women, some of whom have been consecrated to God. How d'ye plead?"

He turned to de Ramla for a translation.

The Hospitaller priest duly rendered the words into Arabic.

Terrified, the wagon driver sputtered a few words – words unintelligible even to de Ramla, a man who knew more than a few of the Saracen tongues.

De Fonte took a couple of steps toward the man and kicked him savagely between the legs. The man doubled over and, gasping for breath, vomited on de Fonte's boots.

Wiping his soiled boots on the Saracen's robe, de Fonte kicked the groveling Saracen again, this time in the belly. "Perhaps now you'll tell us what happened."

The man whimpered, but when the Hospitaller threatened him with further violence he confessed that he and the other slavers had indeed committed depraved acts against the enslaved Christian women.

Hearing a horse approaching, de Fonte turned. It was Fitz Alan. "My lord," he said, "The heathen bastard has confessed. He and his accomplices are all guilty of despoiling these Christian women."

"There's no doubt?"

"Not according to this one. We can kick the shite out of him if needs be, but why bother? The swine's confessed."

"Let's beat the truth out of at least one more of the swine, Arnaldus, just be sure."

Arnaldus seized the next closest of the slavers and stood him up next to the wagon. He grabbed the man's right wrist and, before he could resist, smashed it up against the vehicle's wooden side. He then pulled out his arming dagger and thrust it through the man's palm and into the side of the wagon. The Saracen screamed as blood shot out of his hand and spilled down the inside of his forearm. De Fonte twisted it back and forth and then repeated the question he had posed to the man's comrade. When de Ramla translated the question, the man muttered something barely intelligible but unmistakably defiant. Not waiting for de Ramla to confirm the meaning of the man's words, de Fonte smashed him in the face with his mailed glove. Blood, flesh and teeth sprayed into the air.

"The next time it'll be worse, much worse," interjected Fitz Alan, "so tell me now, did you bastards violate these women? Yes or no? Put it to him, de Ramla." The Hospitaller priest complied instantly, translating Fitz Alan's words into a tongue the Saracen could understand. Despite the pain, the man remained defiant, spitting in de Ramla's face and unleashing a vicious barrage of invective. In response, de Fonte kicked the man's leg just below the knee, shattering his kneecap and sending waves of nauseating pain shooting through his body. The Saracen screamed, collapsing in a heap just as de Fonte delivered another kick, this one to the man's jaw. Coming finally to understand that this might not end well, the man began to plead with de

Ramla. De Fonte pulled his enormous Turkish mace from its loop on his belt and raised it menacingly. The man held up his one unpinioned hand and, looking to de Ramla, began speaking rapidly.

"What's he saying, de Ramla?" Fitz Alan inquired.

"He's confessing the most monstrous of sins, Michael. If he's to be believed, they all violated these women, he says. They always do. The violence of it helps break 'em. Once it's done, the victims are less trouble on the way to market and even less for their future masters."

"God's wounds!" Fitz Alan exclaimed.

"The bastard's sorry, though, so he says, and begs our forgiveness. He has gold, too, which will be ours if only we'll let him go."

Fitz Alan turned to de Fonte, "Perhaps God can forgive them, de Ramla, but I cannot."

"Are you sure?"

"I bloody am. Finish the bastard, Arnaldus."

That was all the massive Gascon needed to hear. Having received the command, he closed quickly with the Saracen, drawing his flanged mace backward and then swinging it in a massive arc into the side of the slaver's head. The man's skull exploded into a hundred bloody pieces, a clotted mist of blood and bone spurting into the air. His body fell to the ground in a quivering heap and de Fonte pulled his bloodied mace from the man's head.

"Good man, Arnaldus," Fitz Alan said. "Throw that pile of shite on the fire; then get the men ready to sort out the rest of these slaver bastards."

"*De par Dieu!*" came the reply. And with that de Fonte called the banner to his side and prepared for the killing.

"Line 'em up, Brother Arnaldus."

The Gascon Templar grabbed the nearest slaver by his collar and shoved him up against the largest slaver cart. "Happy to do so, brother Michael!"

"And bring me the women. I want them to witness this, but I also need them to attest to the crimes."

"*De par Dieu!*" came the reply.

Once the slavers had been lined up, Fitz Alan spoke to the assembled women. "Are these the Saracens who violated you?"

Silence.

"I ask you again: are these the heathens who violated you?"

The abbess stepped forward and spat on the nearest of the Saracens. "This man is guilty of the most abominable crimes. I have seen many deaths during the two score and five years of my earthly pilgrimage, but nothing like the horrors inflicted by this man. Poor Sister Mary, God rest her soul. What she suffered at his hands, none should ever have to endure."

In rapid succession, the other women stepped forward, identifying their rapists and those who had murdered the priests, monks and others whom the slavers had deemed worthless.

The abbess spoke up again. "And these two," she pointed to the smallest of the Saracen captives, "killed the orphaned babies in our charge. Three little girls barely out of their mother's bellies and a boy of not more than three. Took them by the ankles and dashed their heads on a rock." She spat again, then crossed herself. "God forgive me, Brother Michael, for I know that our Lord has enjoined us to forgive those who would trespass against us, but I've not room in my heart for that. Not given what I've witnessed these animals do. I want them dead. D'ye hear me? Dead." She was sobbing now, "I want justice! And I'm not particular about how it's done."

Nor am I, thought Fitz Alan. These dogs are guilty of the most heinous crimes imaginable and I'll see them roasting in hell before the day is done.

"De Fonte! Turn 'em 'round so they're facing the cart."

"My lord!"

De Fonte and the *turcopoles* shoved the Saracen captives up against the side of the cart.

"Sergeant-brothers! Take up positions now. Each of you, behind one the heathen bastards. Move!"

A dozen Templars moved into position.

"On the command of Brother de Fonte, you will draw your arming daggers and slit the throats of the animal before you. Any man who fails to carry out his duty will suffer at my hand. D'ye understand?

"*De par Dieu!*" came the unanimous reply.

"De Fonte, carry on."

"Draw daggers!" bellowed the massive Gascon.

A dozen arming daggers were drawn from their sheaths.

"Now!"

At the Gascon's command, a dozen daggers were drawn across as many throats. The side of the cart was instantly spattered red-brown as the blood of the slavers shot forth from their severed throats. A dozen bodies dropped lifeless in front of the vehicle.

Fitz Alan, satisfied that justice had been done, turned to de Fonte. "Get 'em buried, Raimundus. Even animals such as this deserve a proper burial. But get it done quickly. We need to be moving before Sext tomorrow."

"*De par Dieu*, my lord." And with that the Gascon Templar turned to his men and commanded them to dig a hole big enough to hold the dozen Saracen slavers who had just been killed in the name of justice.

21 July 1191

Madame Eloise Roquefeuil, wife of the reeve of Ville d'Espérance, surveyed the great hall with a sense of pride and satisfaction. In less than a day, she had managed to prepare a banquet that, in her own mind at least, was the equal of any she had attended before The Catastrophe. The linen tablecloths were old and overused, to be sure, and there was precious little wine. But looking around the table, she was struck by the enthusiasm with which even the notoriously disciplined Templars were devouring their food. From this, she judged that if the meal was not quite as sumptuous as she might have liked, it was nevertheless more than adequate for the occasion. The same with the table settings. As if to compensate for the faded-white tablecloths, the platters and bowls gleamed brightly even in the dim light cast by the too-few candles and torches arranged on the table and about the hall. And to add to the festive air, Madame Roquefeuil had even arranged for a harpist to entertain their valiant defenders, these holy warriors sent by God to aid them in their hour of need. For the first time since she and her husband had assumed the mantle of authority in the town of Espérance, Eloise Roquefeuil felt she was playing her proper role as the wife of the reeve. She was finally entertaining men of power and consequence on her husband's behalf – and she was in her element.

The previous occupant, from whom they had gained the manor and the estate, had perished at the battle of Hattin four years earlier. A brutish and unloved Scot, the third son of the Laird of Aberknockie had been unmarried and without kin. When he and his knights had failed to return from The Catastrophe, the reeve had simply assumed both his duties as ruler and his rights as landholder. There had been some grumbling at first, of course. With the growing realization that their lord and his retinue were not returning, the people of the valley wondered whether the decidedly unmartial reeve was the best man to protect them from the infidel. But once Father Rourke had given the reeve his blessing, any doubts the townsfolk and peasants might have had evaporated like the morning mists that were so typical of summers here in the Nouvelle Vallée de la Clarée. And so here they were, the Roquefeuils, hosting a banquet in honor of the brave Templars who had saved them from what they had feared most these past several years – the almost unthinkable depredations that might be inflicted upon them by the conquering Saracens.

And what a banquet it was. At the head of the great table sat the Roquefeuils, resplendent in their finest attire, and looking every inch as if the manor and all its appurtenances were theirs by right-of-birth. Seated along the table to their right were Father Rourke, several of the town's more noble burghers and their wives, the Roquefeuils' eldest daughter and her betrothed, and, near the foot of the table, Abbess Cecile. Fitz Alan sat alone at the foot of the table. To *his* right were arrayed Father de Ramla, Brother de Fonte, the Tawashi commander, William Turcault, the *turcopole* commander, and, nearer to the Roquefeuils, several more prominent townsfolk and their wives. The table was far from packed, a half-dozen more could have easily been seated, but there were enough guests for lively conversation. And it was the first occasion for such a celebration the townsfolk had had in many years. Madame Roquefeuil paused again to gaze around the room and marvel at her handiwork.

The discussion around the table ranged widely. Following a few pleasantries, the conversation began in earnest with the *poulains* regaling Fitz Alan and his men with accounts of life in the valley before The Catastrophe. They discussed the hardships of daily life, which Fitz Alan found to be not much different from those endured by people in Gascony or England, but seemed at pains to emphasize the simple pleasures and profound joys of life here in the East. They took turns telling tales of the pomposity and incompetence of the Laird, as he insisted on being called, who was both feared and reviled by all but a handful of the townsfolk and the lesser nobles in the valley. Fitz Alan and de Fonte spoke of the great siege of Acre, attributing the ultimate victory to neither the great Kings of Christendom nor the simple warriors who had finally broken the town's defenses, but to God himself. And the townsfolk drank toasts to the crusaders and their kings, and to the brave Templars who, they were sure, had delivered them from evil.

All the while, de Ramla was translating for the Tawashi commander.

It was a very agreeable evening, Fitz Alan thought, even if the *poulains'* gaiety seemed more than a bit strained. But, then, he thought, how could it not be? On the one hand, they had lived for years now in the shadow of almost certain despoliation at the hands of the infidel. On the other, they had little option but to carry on with life as they knew it; with the timeless rhythms of sowing and reaping, of birth and marriage and death, of keeping holy the Sabbath and observing the feast days. If their mirth and merrymaking seemed a bit strained, it was hardly surprising. How long could anyone live whipsawed between the hope that the angel of death, so undeniably afoot throughout *Outremer* in the aftermath of King Guy's terrible defeat, would pass over them and the near-certain knowledge that it would not?

Inevitably, the *poulains'* talk turned to the prospects for liberating Jerusalem. On the one side, there were those who saw it as inevitable, providing the pilgrims were bold and struck quickly for Jerusalem as their forebears had done nearly a century before. On the other, there were those who saw victory as inevitable providing the pilgrims proceeded with caution. Had not rashness and pride brought Saint Bernard's own expedition to grief within the lifetime of several of those at seated at the table?

"What's your view, Brother Michael?" asked Madame Roquefeuil.

"Don't have one, my lady."

"Come now, you are a knight of the Temple, an experienced warrior, well-versed in such matters. Surely you have some opinion."

"It is precisely because I am a knight of the Temple, my lady, that I have none. It is not for me, a humble knight-brother, to know such things. These matters are decided by my betters and, ultimately, I care little what course of action they settle on. For I am a Templar knight and as such I have but one concern: killing the enemies of Christ and His Church. It matters not to me whether I kill them in Acre or on the road to Jerusalem or outside the very gates of Hell. I go where I'm told and I kill who I'm told to kill. And for me, as for all Templars, that is enough."

Eloise Roquefeuil considered pressing her case, for surely this Templar knew more than he was telling. The tone of his voice, however, persuaded her that he was not likely to be any more forthcoming no matter what she said and she let the issue drop.

The convivial banter between the two opposing schools proceeded for some time and had almost played itself out when the conversation was interrupted abruptly by the unexpected interjection of the Tawashi commander. He banged his cup lightly on the table, causing all heads to turn in his direction. He then proceeded to speak in perfect *poulain* French. "It matters not whether your King Richard moves directly on al-Quds or approaches it via Damascus or decides to conquer Cairo instead – he will be defeated whatever he does. For his cause – your cause – is ignoble and unjust. Since arriving in these lands a century ago, you *Faranji* have done nothing but wage war on peaceful Muslims, unlawfully depriving its peaceful inhabitants of their homes, their lands and even their lives. In your barbarity and your lawlessness, you have slaughtered, raped and plundered across the length and breadth of Syria. You have brought your polytheistic cult to Dar al-Islam, you have despoiled our mosques and turned them into temples of blasphemy, and – worst of all – for a time, you deprived us of al-Quds, the holy place from which the Prophet, peace be upon him, ascended into heaven. Your cause is unjust, Christians, and Allah, who *is* justice, will soon purify the land of your iniquity. Saladin, whom you rightly fear, is not merely a great emir – he is Allah's terrible sword of righteousness. Allah has already used this terrifying sword to destroy the Christian horde at Hattin and to liberate Jerusalem from your unclean hands. All that remains now is for Him to strike with His sword of righteousness one last time and you and your kind will be swept from our lands forever. Whatever hopes you have invested in this Lionheart, infidels, abandon them. He is no match for the great Giver of Victory and his righteous and noble servant Saladin. Flee while you can, *Faranji*, or submit to the Exceedingly Merciful One. These are the only paths available to you."

There was stunned silence in the hall, as if the Devil himself had spoken. More than a few of those assembled crossed themselves to ward off the demon who was clearly present in the great hall this night.

Pausing to finish the measure of wine the Rule permitted at this hour, Fitz Alan, a measure of cold steel in his voice, replied simply but firmly, "Surely, my lord, you jest."

De Fonte and de Ramla exchanged nervous glances, for they had come to know Fitz Alan's convictions on this particular topic and feared where this might lead. Among the other guests around the table there was simply a stunned confusion, for none had expected either the Saracen's impassioned defense of the Muslim claim to the Holy Land or the white-mantled Templar's steely toned response to that claim. Of all the assembled guests, only Father Rourke smiled at Fitz Alan's response, for he suspected that this Englishman might just be a wee bit more than a brute dressed up in a monk's habit, and that there might no small measure of entertainment in all this, for him if for no one else.

"I do not, my lord," the Tawashi replied.

"Well, since you've been so kind as to share your views with us, my lord, let me return the favor. When did these lands become part of Dar al-Islam, as you call it?"

"My lord?"

"The question is a simple one, Saracen: when did the Holy Land pass into the hands of your race?"

"These lands have always been Muslim, *Faranji*. At least since the Prophet, peace be upon him, ascended into heaven from al-Quds, these lands been part of the House of Monotheism, the House of Islam."

"My lord, your ignorance of your own history, while not unexpected, is genuinely appalling."

"I have spoken the truth."

"No, you haven't, you lying bastard. Indeed, what you have said bears as much relationship to the truth as earth does to fire. Here is the truth, if you can bear to hear it: these lands from time immemorial were Roman and Christian. Christ was born here, was crucified here, was resurrected and ascended into heaven here. The first Christian communities were here. The Christian Roman Empire included all these lands. Antioch, Alexandria, Jerusalem, Damascus – these were Christian cities for centuries before your prophet was born."

The Tawashi shifted uneasily in his seat, unsure where this conversation was leading. "If you mean to say that before the Prophet brought enlightenment there was the *Jahiliyyah*, the time of ignorance, well, that is beyond dispute. However, once the Prophet, peace be upon him, revealed the Truth, the *Kuffar* chose to submit. The word of God conquered these lands, soul by soul."

Fitz Alan surveyed the hall; every eye was fixed on him. He chose his next words carefully. "Oh, there was a conquest alright, Saracen, but it was not the word of God that did the conquering. It was Saracen armies, driven on by lust for the riches of the Roman world, that conquered half of Christendom. And everywhere they conquered they despoiled Christian churches, plundered Christian cities, and forcibly converted the Christian faithful. No, Saracen, it was not the word of God that brought these lands under the yoke of Islam; it was fire and sword. And it is by fire and sword that we shall now take back what was taken from us, unlawfully, those many centuries ago. What was Christ's will be Christ's again. What was taken from him will never be taken again."

The Tawashi was spluttering now in indignation, his hand automatically reaching for a sword that no longer hung at his side. "This is infamy, *Faranji*! Blasphemy! The mischief of the Whisperer! These lands are part of the House of Islam – and they will ever remain thus, for once Islam is established in a land it cannot be disestablished. Saladin will erase the infamy of Christian polytheism from the land – he'll cleanse it with the righteous sword of Allah. Pray to your three gods, Christian, for your time has come."

Fitz Alan could no longer contain his contempt for the Tawashi and cause which he served. "The trouble with you people, Saracen, is that you want to have it both ways. You want to pretend that we are the invaders and usurpers; to portray us as conquerors and thieves who have unlawfully seized a land that belongs to another people. But you won't apply the same reasoning to yourselves. How convenient that you forget that *you* were the ones who four centuries ago conquered this land from its native Christian inhabitants, and with no greater warrant than you wanted its riches for yourselves. Bloody hypocrites. Sanctimonious bloody hypocrites. *You* are the thieves and conquerors, my lord. *You* are the ones guilty of unlawfully seizing these lands from their rightful lords. You may have deceived yourselves, Saracen, but you haven't deceived us – or God. He's looked into your hearts and he's judged you and found you guilty of grave violations of both natural and divine law. And that's the real reason he assembled and unleashed the Christian host nearly a century ago, and the reason he continues to war on you to this very day: to liberate the land where His Son once trod the earth and to avenge the injury you have inflicted on His Church and His people these past four hundred years. That's why we're here, Saracen, to do God's will. Not for plunder, nor land, nor glory, nor any of the other deceits you've circulated tonight, but to liberate the Holy Places and restore them to their rightful owner. The lies you tell yourself, Saracen, are your bloody business – they're no more to me than the braying of an ass. But I'll not sit idly by before God and have you peddle them here without challenge. Your people are thieves, apostates, homicides and rapists – nothing more. And while I and my brethren draw breath we will fight to drive you and your usurping band of brutes out of this holiest of lands once and for all." He turned to de Fonte, "Brother Arnaldus, bind this heretic and remove him from our presence that we might finish our meal in peace."

"*De par Dieu*, my lord!."

Emmanuele Volpiano finished relieving himself over the side of the Genoese galley and continued walking aft to where his lord and master, Alberto D'Asti, known to many simply as *Il Sinistro*, was dining with the ship's captain. He arrived to find that the two men had already finished their meal, and were now standing over a large table strewn with maps and charts.

"Thank you, captain, for a very satisfactory meal and an interesting conversation. But I have business now with my companion here – business that must be transacted in confidence. I'm certain you won't mind if we use your cabin for a short while."

The captain seemed not to know whether he should stay or leave.

"That's all for now, my good captain. You may tend to your affairs. If I have need of you I shall send for you."

The captain was angered by the man's arrogance. Ordering him about on his own ship – the insolence. He'd as soon have his men throw the bastard overboard as honor his request. But the man paid well – very well indeed – as did his master the Lord of Tyre. And given *Il Sinstro's* reputation, not to mention the menacing air about him, he wasn't sure that even the entire ship's company would be able to dispose of him. In the end, the captain simply acquiesced. "As you wish, my lord," he said.

"Come, Emmanuele, join me for a cup of wine while we make plans."

He gestured vaguely in the direction of a small table set against one of the bulkheads on which there was set a sealed half-barrel and several cups. Volpiano pried open the lid, scooped out a full draught of wine, and resealed the cask. He then sat himself down across the table from his lord.

"The captain, a good fellow, if a little thick, assures me that we will make landfall at Tyre in about two days time."

"Excellent news, my lord. The air on this vessel is as foul as any I've ever had to breathe. I shall be pleased to put ashore."

"It is good news, though in truth the air in Tyre is little better. In any case, it means that we should arrive at our destination a day or two ahead of our rivals. Now, what preparations have you made?"

Volpiano searched the table for the appropriate map. "Well," he began, "when we arrive in Tyre I'll assemble some of our men-at-arms. It's likely we'll have to pull them from the brothels and alehouses, and it might take a day to get them ready for the journey, but I reckon that we'll be able to muster something like three dozen men and maybe half-a-dozen knights. Add to that the seven of us and we should have sufficient strength to deal with whatever we encounter at the lazar-house. And if *fortuna* favors us, we will have recovered the relic and be halfway back to Tyre before the Templars realize what's happening. Ah, here it is," he said, having finally located a map that covered the territory in which they would be travelling.

"Here's the route I suggest, my lord," Volpiano said, pointing a mangled forefinger at Tyre. "We'll set out first along the coast road. It's in reasonable condition, or so I'm told."

"It is. I've travelled it many times myself before Hattin."

"Then we'll have to leave the coastal lowlands here," his mangled finger came to rest at a point where a spur in the coast road became a switchback zigzagging back and forth up the otherwise impassable wall of hills.

"Any possible danger along the way?"

"Doubtful, my lord. This remains part of the County of Tripoli; the Saracens have been busy elsewhere and have yet to press their advantage here. We might encounter small Saracen raiding parties, but even that is unlikely, or so I am told. More likely we'll encounter banditti, but they'd have to be very brave or very foolish to attack two score heavily armed men."

"Assuming we do not encounter any of these banditti, how long 'til we arrive at the monastery?"

"Still a day or so distant from Tripoli…. Two or three days to assemble our forces…. Another two days on the road…. Not more than a week, my lord. Providing there are no unwelcome surprises along the way."

"See to it there aren't, Volpiano. Montferrat wants that relic, and he wants it sooner rather than later. His prospects, I needn't remind you, and ours, turn on us recovering the Spear. He's promised me vast estates in his new kingdom if we succeed in our mission. And as I rise – or fall – so too do you, Volpiano, so do you. Get me that relic and you may ask for anything in my power to grant. Lands, women… anything."

Freedom, thought Volpiano – that would be nice.

"Let us drink to success, my old friend." D'Asti poured two cups of wine and offered one to his faithful vassal. "Glory, power, wealth," he said in his native Piedmontese.

"Glory, power and wealth," Volpiano similarly replied, raising his cup and then finishing its contents in a single draught. Needless chatter, though, was what he really thought of his lord's superfluous salute. Needless chatter. For what else, pray, would a man drink to? What else mattered in this world? Glory, power and wealth, indeed. If there were a holy trinity, surely these three things were its constituent elements. "Amen," was all he said aloud, though, "Amen."

26 July 1191

The day was oppressively hot, not a whisper of wind blowing to carry away their sweat and not a cloud in the sky to shield them from the scorching sun. The fires of Hell, thought Fitz Alan, not for the first time since reaching the Holy Land, could not be much hotter than this.

"How much farther to Heliopolis?" inquired Fitz Alan, referring to the town where they would leave this road for the one that would take them to Tripoli.

"Not more than half a day now, my lord."

"Right. De Fonte! Turcault!"

The two men appeared at his side almost instantly.

"Brother Arnaldus, take two men and scout ahead. Make sure there are no Saracen bastards on the road before us."

"*De par Dieu*, my lord."

"Master Turcault."

"My lord."

"How are the men?"

"Fine, my lord. Ready to fight."

"Good. My guess is they'll have plenty of opportunity to do so once we get a bit closer to Heliopolis. Make sure they're drinking enough water, William, it's a damned hot day."

"My lord." The *Turcopolier* smiled his lopsided smile as he turned his mount and rode back down the column.

"Alright Father de Ramla, tell me what to expect when we reach this town."

The Hospitaller adjusted himself in his saddle, wiping the sweat from his brow on the sleeve of his black surcoat. "The bad news," he began, "is that it's a large town, usually well garrisoned and full of fighting men. I accompanied a raid through the valley several years back, before Hattin. Struck fear into the hearts of the heathens all the way from Tiberias to here, so we did. And then we were turned back. The garrison at Heliopolis, Baalbek as the heretics call it, stopped us dead in our tracks. Nearly routed us, truth be told. Indeed, it was only by the grace of God that we made it out of this *valle lacrimarum* alive."

"Well, now I've had the bad news, what's the bloody good news?"

"The good news is that we don't actually have to pass through the town to get where we're going. There's a spur in the road about a mile this side of the town walls that will put us on the road to Tripoli and from there to Margat."

"Not having to take a well-fortified and garrisoned town – that's good news indeed."

"Not entirely. The spur itself is garrisoned. A small fortification, established not so much to deal with the likes of us, as to ensure that merchants using the roads in this valley pay what they owe to Saladin's tax collectors. A fortified toll house, really. But it really is fortified – and garrisoned. And I'm sure they'll try to collect the toll."

"Same bloody nonsense everywhere," Fitz Alan exclaimed. "Taxes and poxy taxmen."

De Ramla betrayed no emotion. One might as well complain about the weather as the taxman, for both were ordained of God.

"How should we proceed?" Fitz Alan inquired.

"We have no choice but to take the toll house. It dominates the mouth of the valley that runs toward Tripoli. There's no way round it. And if we don't do it quickly, the garrison from Heliopolis itself will be alerted. If that happens, they'll descend on us *en masse* and our goose'll be cooked, good and proper." The Hospitaller was thinking now of a different time, a time when his goose very nearly had been cooked in this valley. He did not relish the thought of such a narrow escape again. "No, we want this to be quick and quiet."

Fitz Alan could picture it. The banner trapped between the anvil of the fortified tollhouse and hammer of a Saracen horde striking out from Heliopolis.

"What're our options?"

"I am but a humble *poulain* priest, Brother Michael. You are the Templar warrior. You tell me."

Not for the first time, Fitz Alan felt a nearly overwhelming urge to smash this smug Hospitaller squarely in the face. "Look here," he said, "I don't know what foolish bloody game you think you're playing at, but I'm pretty sure you're not that simple. And I'm almost certain you're not a priest. And I'm bloody convinced you're up to no good. But no matter. I have my charge and I intend to carry it out. And you have knowledge that I both need and lack. So, tell me, Hospitaller, what's the best bloody way to tackle this tollhouse without calling the combined forces of Saladin and Satan down about our bloody heads? Tell me quickly, mind, for if you don't you'll know a side of me that most who do wish they didn't."

De Ramla smiled to himself. Fitz Alan's threats washed off him like so much water off a duck's back. He'd known harder men – men more capable of instilling terror in a man's soul – than this ever-so-earnest Templar. Killing rapists and slavers was one thing; doing harm to a Hospitaller priest was quite another altogether – especially for a man as devout as this Templar seemed to be. But he did need Fitz Alan's services. And he did know the situation better than the Templar did. "Very well," he said. "As I see it, we have two options. The first entails a direct attack on the tollhouse. We'd take it, of course, but our losses might be significant. And the garrison at Heliopolis almost certainly would be alerted. They'd be on our tail in an instant and would likely pursue us along the road to Tripoli, nipping at our heels all the way."

"Unappetizing. And the second?"

"The second entails a bit of a ruse."

"A bit of a ruse? You speak in riddles, man. What the devil d'ye mean, 'a bit of a ruse?'"

"I mean that we'll have to employ a subterfuge, a deception."

"I know what 'ruse' means, you Hospitaller bastard, but exactly what sort of ruse did you have in mind?"

"The Saracens at the tollhouse most certainly will not be expecting a Templar banner to appear at their front door. At worst, they're expecting merchants seeking to evade the tax man. So, as merchants we should appear. My thought is that four or five of us should approach the main gate, dressed as traders in some sort of dross or other. I'll speak with the guards. Put 'em at ease. Once they open the gate, you and the others will kill them. Then one of you will bolt the near gate open while the others will sprint to the far gate and open it. Once the two gates are open, the banner will charge through. If we move quickly and quietly we'll be through and half way to Tripoli before the Saracens have any idea what's happened."

"God save us," said de Fonte, crossing himself.

"We'll need God on our side to pull this off, right enough. But it sounds like it might just work. Arnaldus, you'll be with me and the good Father here. Have Brother Enyon and three other sergeant-brothers join us." He turned to the Hospitaller. "What about dress? We can't just walk up to their front door clad as Templars and Hospitallers now, can we?"

"Well, I've some local garb in my saddle bag. In my particular vocation, you never know just when you might have need of it."

"And we've some of the slavers' rags in ours'," said de Fonte. "Stripped 'em off the devils just before we sent them to meet their false God. As the good Father says, never know when you might need 'em."

"Right then. Let's get on with it. Get everyone dressed like Saracen merchants. Once we're ready, we'll approach the tollhouse and, God willing, seize the gate." He turned to the *Turcopolier*. "Master Turcault, once we've secured the near gate, you'll bring up the rest of the banner. We're not going to detain ourselves any more than we have to in that place; once we've captured the near gate, you'll assume we've captured the far one too, and you'll proceed straight through both and then head up the road as fast as you can. Understand?"

"Aye, my lord."

"Good." He turned to de Fonte. "Make ready, Brother Arnaldus. We are about to strike a blow for Christ."

"*De par Dieu,*" came his Gascon friend's reply.

Fitz Alan rose. Since issuing his order, he'd doffed his templar *cappa* and hauberk and changed into Saracen garb. In the brief period since, he'd bent his knee and prayed to God for the strength to check his baser impulses and fight as a true knight of Christ – not for his own wealth or honor, but for the glory of God and His Church. He prayed especially to be delivered from the sin of pride, for knew he was a proud man by both nature and upbringing and that he must constantly be on guard against his nature asserting itself. "*De profundis clamavi ad te, Domine; Domine, exaudi vocem meam.*" *From the depths, I have cried out to you, O Lord; Lord, hear my voice.* It was a prayer he'd been praying almost ceaselessly this past year; a prayer that was never far from his mind or lips. Having finished for the moment, he stood, called to his men to mount up, then hauled himself up into his saddle.

At his word, the five Templars and one Hospitaller dressed as Saracen merchants moved off in the direction of the tollhouse, leaving the rest of the mounted banner concealed in the blind where they had arrayed themselves out of sight of the enemy fortification.

Once they'd rounded the bend in the road, Fitz Alan saw the tollhouse. It was a short, squat fortification standing astride the road, a small tower on each side and a gatehouse set in the front wall. If de Ramla was to be believed, there was a similar structure on the far side, with a keep replacing once of the guard towers, and two ungated curtain walls linking the two. An ideal little fortification for extracting the wealth of merchants traveling up and down the valley. Impossible to bypass and difficult to storm. But then, Fitz Alan mused, they weren't merchants, and they certainly weren't interested in either bypassing the fortification or storming it.

As they approached the main gate, the sentry raised his hand lazily, signaling that Fitz Alan and his men should come to a halt. The man appeared to be wearing little more than a simple cotton tunic and leggings, rather than the mail hauberk typical of the more fearsome Saracen warriors. His turban was unwound across his chest, signifying that he really wasn't expecting any trouble. The man's sword hung on one hip and a small round shield hung awkwardly on the other. Fitz Alan observed the two guards on the wall above the guardhouse. They were similarly dressed and, he surmised, no more expecting trouble than their comrade below. The Templar scanned the fortification and guessed that there were two – perhaps three – men in each of the watchtowers to his left and right.

De Ramla commanded his little caravan to stop.

The sentinel spoke in a tongue that Fitz Alan neither understood nor cared to. De Ramla responded, and after some haggling, the Hospitaller produced a small sack of coins from his saddlebag. The guard counted out the coins and, declaring the requisite toll paid, waved them on. De Ramla passed through the guard house and into the courtyard, followed by de Fonte atop the slaver wagon they had appropriated a few days back and, behind him, the rest of the troop. Fitz Alan, at the rear of the column, approached the gatehouse. He was close now, close enough to see the sentinel's rotten teeth. Once he was close enough to smell the man's breath he took three quick steps toward him, simultaneously thrusting his dagger into the sentinel's belly and shoving the palm of his hand over the man's mouth. In rapid succession, the Saracen's eyes conveyed surprise and then fear and then death. In an instant, his spirit was gone and his lifeless body collapsed in a bloody heap at the Templar's feet. Fitz Alan wrenched his bloody dagger free of the still-twitching corpse, momentarily amazed at the agility he possessed unencumbered by his hauberk. He then looked back down the road, hoping to see Turcault and the banner, but they were nowhere in sight. Disappointed, the Templar quickly bolted the gate open, then turned and looked into the courtyard of the tollhouse. He saw Brother Enyon pull his bow out from its hiding place in the slaver wagon they had brought with them. Fitz Alan raced toward the wagon and retrieved his Saracen great sword, just as the Welsh Templar deftly notched the cord, nocked an arrow and loosed the missile in the direction of the stone staircase down which were descending a handful of Saracen warriors who had been manning the battlements. At this range the Welshman could hardly miss. The force of the impact knocked the first heretic violently backwards into his comrades, causing them to trip over him. One cascaded down the stairs; the other fell over the side, landing on his back with an audible grunt. De Fonte closed with the Saracens in a heartbeat and, as they struggled to regain their footing, first swung his sword and then thrust it, killing the two enemy fighters in rapid succession. There was shouting now from the guard towers and Fitz Alan saw the flash of crossbow quarrels as they began flying toward the Templars. One Saracen stepped through the gate of the keep, raising his crossbow to fire at the big Gascon, who was running back to the slaver wagon. Brother Enyon nocked another arrow, pulled the feather fletching to his right ear and then loosed the missile. The arrow struck the Saracen in the belly, the force of the impact causing him to double over and shoot his crossbow quarrel harmlessly into the dirt at his feet. The man staggered back a few steps and then fell dead against the half-open gate he had come through only heartbeats before.

It seemed to Fitz Alan that there were more Saracens manning the fortification than the half-dozen de Ramla had said would be there. Perhaps it was the changing of the guard. If so, there were likely to be twice the usual number of men then he's expected. Damn, he thought. De Ramla has got this totally wrong. Useless *poulain*. Damned bloody useless. He'd give the Hospitaller one last chance, he swore, and then God help him, priest or no.

"Arnaldus, we've got to get up and secure the far gate. If we don't, the banner'll be trapped in the courtyard and murdered one by one as they arrive."

"Easier said than done, my lord. By my count there are five or six of the bastards up there," de Fonte replied, gesturing in the direction of the keep in the northwest corner of the fortification, "and they don't seem to want us to take that far gate."

"Probably closer to twelve, less those three," he gestured in the direction of the stone staircase, "and the one at the gate. I think we caught 'em during the changing of the guard."

"God save us," came the Gascon's response.

"The good news is that other than those first three on the battlement and the one at the gate the rest seem to be holed up in the keep. Brother Enyon!"

"My lord."

"I want you to keep those Saracens' heads down while we cross the courtyard and enter the keep. Can you do it?"

"Just say when, m'lord. I'll bag one or two of those heretics and the rest'll keep their heads down, sure enough."

"Good man. Right, you men Make ready! When I give the command we're going to run like mad across the courtyard in the direction of that door over there," he pointed at the door to the keep, which was being held ajar by the body of the dead Saracen crossbowman, "and when we get in we're going to kill every bloody Saracen we see. No mercy; no prisoners. Kill 'em all. The rest of the banner will be here any moment now and we have to have 'em cleared out by then. Kill 'em all, brothers; God'll know his own."

Fitz Alan looked at the band of brutal and accomplished killers clustered around him. He knew every one of them would fight as if fighting Satan himself. "Right," he said, drawing his great Saracen sword, "Brother Enyon, bag me some game."

And with that the killing resumed.

King Richard and his chancellor, Bishop Walter, entered the courtyard of Acre's royal citadel and proceeded to seat themselves on one of the several benches arranged around its perimeter. The heat was blazing even at this early hour, and they were thankful for the shade offered by the fruit trees that ringed the marble-tiled space. Richard ordered one of the servants hovering nearby to bring them some water and some fruit.

"My liege," said the bishop, "there remains but one item on our agenda for today. We have spoken of it before, but I would raise it with you again. It is the matter of the crown of Jerusalem. A few days hence, the *Haute cour* will decide this matter once and for all – either Guy will be confirmed in his crown or Conrad will be named king. Your voice will carry much weight in the deliberations, my liege. You must be sure you choose wisely."

"This again, my lord bishop. Surely we have already decided this matter. Guy de Lusignan has the superior claim. What's more, he's my vassal and I owe him a duty of protection. Nor have I forgiven Conrad for the insolence he showed me upon my arrival in *Outremer*." Richard seethed again as he recalled how Conrad had refused him entry to Tyre, forcing him and his host to make camp outside the city's walls. The insolent bastard, he thought. He'd sworn vengeance on the Piedmontese cur for his unpardonable act of impudence, and now he was going to have it. "And do you forget that he fought beside us in Cyprus. Good God, man, he even renewed his fealty to me. No, my lord bishop, I am decided: my voice will be raised in support of Guy and against that dog Conrad."

The servant returned with a pitcher of water and two cups. He was accompanied by two other men, one carrying a large bowl of fruit, the other awkwardly hauling a small but heavy table across the marble-tiled floor. Once the food and drink was laid out on the table, the three servants withdrew, leaving Richard and his chancellor to resume their conversation.

"There can be no gainsaying the facts in this matter, my liege. Guy is your man by virtue of his holding in Poitou. He is also currently the king of Jerusalem – not a trivial consideration. And Conrad did wrong you at Tyre, my liege. These facts are not in dispute. But let me respectfully remind you, my liege, of some other facts that have a bearing on this cause. First, while Guy currently wears the crown, his legal claim to it is far from secure. He came to be king in the first place only by marrying Queen Sybilla – he has no claim to the crown in his own right and only a most dubious matrimonial claim to it now that she is dead. Second, the strict legality of his claim might not be such an issue if he could buttress his claim to the throne in some other manner – perhaps with a record of martial success. A history of victorious campaigns, glorious battlefield exploits, that sort of thing. These have sustained many a monarch in office when blood and marriage could not furnish the necessary warrant. But Guy de Lusignan has no such history. To be sure, his decision to depart Tyre and lay siege to Acre hints at such qualities. But this counts as nothing when set beside his monumental failure at Hattin. For many, perhaps most, his name has come to be synonymous with that terrible catastrophe. And this brings us to my third argument against his candidacy, my liege: few of the *poulains* have much confidence in Guy's ability to lead future expeditions against the Saracens. Even the Hospitallers have lost faith in him. None doubt that you are the one to lead the Christian host to victory over Saladin. But long after we've departed for home, sire, these men will have to fight to hold what you have won – on strictly martial grounds, on grounds of demonstrated military competence, would you rather have Guy, the hero of Hattin, leading that effort or Conrad, defender of Tyre?"

Richard stood and walked over to the ornate water fountain that dominated the center of the courtyard. He sat down on the lip of the massive bowl, dipping his hand into the cool water and splashing a little over his face. He knew he was a stubborn man, prideful even. And now that he had declared himself opposed to Conrad, it was difficult for him to reverse himself, even if only before his trusted confessor Bishop Walter. In truth, though, he knew that the chancellor was right. Conrad was an insolent dog, to be sure, and he would never forgive him his trespasses. For all that, though, the Count of Montferrat was indeed a respected warrior, and a proven leader as well. If anyone could hold on to what Richard would win back for Christendom, it was Conrad. And yet...

He rose from the fountain, splashed a little more water on his face, and returned to the bench. "What of the charges that his marriage to Isabella is irregular – that his marriage to Theodora is still valid and that he is thus a bigamist?"

"What of them, my liege?" the bishop responded. "The Bishop of Dreux saw no impediment when he performed the marriage, and the papal legate himself subsequently gave the union his blessing. The charge of bigamy – and indeed the charge of incest Conrad opened himself to when he serially married the two half-sisters Sybila and Isabella – carries no weight in the eyes of the Church."

Richard considered Walter's case, reviewing the pros and cons of shifting his support to Conrad. "You are most convincing, my lord bishop," he said at length. "For all your powers of persuasion, though, I simply can't bring myself to support Conrad over Guy. Not only will I never be able to forgive that Piedmontese dog for his impertinence at Tyre, but if I throw my support behind him now, Philip will appear to have triumphed over me – and his hand will be strengthened at my expense. If my cousin really does go through with his promise to quit *Outremer* and return to France, thus strengthened he'll be capable of even greater mischief."

Now, thought Walter, we are getting to the heart of the matter. This really was about Richard's interests in France and his ongoing struggle with Philip over the disputed Norman territory of Vexin. Liberating Jerusalem, while conferring honor and glory, would always take second place to Richard's regnal and dynastic interests. "My liege, we have long ago departed the realm of the optimal in this matter; it is simply not possible for you to satisfy all of your interests simultaneously. Difficult decisions must be made."

"Is there no way to square the circle? No way to advance our interests both here and in France? For if not, I will be forced to press Guy's case in the High Court – and if Philip continues to support Conrad with equal vigor we may find ourselves fighting each other rather than the Saracens.

"There may be a way, my liege. It's as likely to displease all parties as to satisfy any of them, but it might just work."

"Yes...."

"Make both men kings."

"What? Co-rulers of Jerusalem? I can't see that as a workable solution."

"No, my liege, not co-rulers. What I have in mind is this: have the Court declare Guy king and Conrad his heir. In effect, Guy would have only a life interest in the throne, which is fitting since he holds it now only by virtue of his dead wife's claim. Conrad and his progeny would succeed him, establishing a new dynasty. Both men get something, and the pot for both could certainly be sweetened in various ways if necessary. As Guy would be king for the foreseeable future, you would not appear to have defaulted on your duty to protect his interests. Philip's hand would not be strengthened in any way."

"What, then, is in it for my cousin?" asked Richard, his interest piqued.

"That which he desires above all else: to return home to France and tend to his affairs there."

"Including his scheming to recover the Vexin?"

"Presumably, my liege. But, as long as you are here on pilgrimage, the Church will protect your territories, including those Philip seeks to recover. From our vantage point, the beauty of this compromise is that it accelerates your campaign to recover Jerusalem. With Philip gone – and he needs to settle this matter before he can leave – you will be undisputed leader of the host; no need for further negotiations with your cousin. With Conrad placated and Guy satisfied, the crippling divisions within the Christian camp will be healed. United under one commander, the host can then move quickly to liberate Jerusalem. Once you have restored the holy sites to Christendom, you can then quit *Outremer* in a timely fashion and return to France to deal with Philip."

The bishop could see that his king was intrigued.

"And, my liege, once we have returned home to England, Conrad will have every incentive to protect what will eventually become his patrimony. If he fought like the devil to keep Tyre out of Saladin's grasping hands, imagine how hard he'll fight to keep Jerusalem in his own."

Richard pondered the scenario laid out by his chancellor. At length, a broad smile broke out on his comely face. "You have earned your keep this day, my lord bishop," he said. "You have earned it indeed. While your scheme has every chance of coming to naught, it might – might, I say – just pay off. How would you advise we proceed?"

"Well," said the bishop, "Philip can have not the slightest inkling the idea was yours, my liege. That will surely be fatal. Perhaps Toron can moot it."

"No, not Humphrey. He's a bit too obvious. Perhaps you might suggest it to Joscius," Richard said, referring to the Archbishop of Tyre. "He might see the advantage of such an arrangement."

"He might indeed, my liege. And if the plan were to be suggested by the archbishop, Philip will surely jump at it. I'll set things in motion at once."

At that moment, Richard's wife's hounds entered the courtyard, bounding toward their king and master. Richard stroked the two dogs lovingly.

"Make it so, Hubert. Make it so."

Fitz Alan and his men crossed the killing ground between the wagon and the keep without a scratch, thanks to the skillful shooting of the Welsh sergeant-brother they had left behind to cover their approach. In the space of just a few heartbeats, Brother Enyon had sent three shafts flying at the embrasures in the keep. Judging from the resulting screams, he surmised that he'd hit two of the Saracen defenders. The Welshman cursed himself for not making all three of his precious arrows count, but in the end it mattered little. None of the heathens dared show themselves again until the Templars had closed the distance to the keep and entered it by stepping over the corpse of the Saracen he had killed earlier. And by then it was too late. De Fonte and Fitz Alan were the first in. Fitz Alan caught sight of a Saracen to his right. The man was wielding a spear, attempting to thrust it into the Templar's side. The Templar parried the Saracen's weapon with ease, and then plunged his sword upward through the man's mail hauberk, under his ribs and into his heart. He was momentarily amazed at the ease with which his blade sliced through the Saracen's armor, but had little time to think about it as the keep's defenders were beginning to swarm about him and his little band of sanctified killers. He twisted his sword and withdrew it from the lifeless body before him just in time to contort himself violently and hack at another enemy warrior who appeared suddenly through a half-open door. A bolt of pain shot through his shoulder as it always did when he struck a blow for Christ. Blood, flesh and bone misted into the air as the Templar's sword struck home, separating the man's head from his shoulders.

The Templars moved on quickly, slashing and hacking at the half-dressed Saracen fighters swarming like wasps out of the rooms arrayed around the keep's main hall. After killing all those in the hall, they paused for a heartbeat to catch their breath and take stock. Fitz Alan, his blood up now, called to his comrades. "Templars," he yelled running toward the spiraling stone staircase that ran up the center of the hall, "follow me!" He took the steps two at a time, reached the next landing, and looked about him for enemy fighters. There were none. De Fonte, Brother Diarmait and Brother John were right behind him, covered in blood and gore and panting with the exertion of fighting and running up the stairs, but there and ready to fight.

"Looks like the Saracen bastards are done for, my lord," said de Fonte.

Then a shout sounded from the floor above them, a shout they instantly recognized as one of defiance and determination. The Templars did not understand its precise meaning, of course, but its tone, and the subsequent sound of swords and armor and men running purposefully about, left little doubt that it was a command and that the remaining defenders of the keep were rallying and preparing to attack the Templar troop. The clangor and din of the massing men also left little doubt in Fitz Alan's mind that he and his brothers were badly outnumbered and in real danger of being swamped by Saracens on the floor above. He looked to de Fonte for support and saw in his friend's eyes the mad lust for blood he had seen in the eyes of so many men in so many battles before. "Arnaldus?" he said.

"Slaughter the bastards," came the response, his friend's voice thick and menacing.

"Right, brothers." Fitz Alan's voice was hoarse and his mouth dry. He cleared his throat and bellowed, "*Non nobis!*" And with that, he raised his mottled and bloodied sword and charged up the narrow staircase.

Just as he and his men started up the stairs, however, a mass of Saracen warriors emerged through a large door on the next landing and surged down toward the Templars. The two masses of men collided in the narrow space, both sides doing their best to press forward and kill the other. The tightness of the space, coupled with the fact that the spiral of the staircase prevented the Saracens from swinging their swords freely while allowing the Templars to use theirs' unimpeded, denied the larger force the advantages it might have otherwise have enjoyed. Both sides fought like demons, slashing and jabbing and hacking at the enemy as if nothing else mattered in the world – as, indeed, at that moment, nothing did. The Templars exacted a heavy toll on the mostly unarmored Saracens, outmatching them in both skill and zealotry. Eventually, though, the sheer weight of numbers resulted in Fitz Alan's men being pushed back down the staircase and into the great hall.

Recognizing that if they tarried long in the open space of the hall he and his men would be massacred through sheer force of numbers, Fitz Alan shouted a command: "Templars! Back! Back! Through the gate!" They fell back through the gate, over the body of the Saracen whom Brother Enyon had earlier killed as he was taking aim at de Fonte. Once through, they turned and ran, hoping to get back through the guardhouse and perhaps to the safety of the banner that must by now finally be coming up the road. Two of their Saracen pursuers fell in quick succession, the first with one of Brother Enyon's arrows lodged in his throat, the second with one of the Welshman's missiles in his chest. Still they pursued, a murderous mass of heretics that Enyon quickly estimated to even now number more than two dozen. The Welsh Templar nocked his last arrow and sent it into the chest of a brightly festooned man who was bellowing commands and prodding the heretics forward. The man, one of the very few of the Saracen garrison wearing a mail hauberk, was thrown backward violently, dead before his aventail struck the ground. "Bagged 'im," Brother Enyon said, though no one was close enough to hear the words he always uttered when he had killed an enemy of Christ. The rest of the Saracen swarm, however, barely noticed their leader's death. Their blood was up and they continued their murderous charge across the courtyard in pursuit of Fitz Alan and his troop.

God save us, Fitz Alan thought, looking around for somewhere, anywhere, to mount a defense. He saw the far guardhouse and shoved his men in its direction, though the gate remained closed and there was no real hope of either escape or sanctuary there. "Make a line!" he yelled, though four men could hardly mount a serious defense against the horde that was scrambling across the courtyard. Nevertheless, four swords bristled and four men committed themselves to a last stand in the face of hopeless odds, motivated by love of Christ, lust for blood, and the forbidden pride of their warrior caste.

The first few Saracens crashed, woefully unsupported, into the little line of Templars. Fitz Alan stepped forward and raised his enormous Saracen blade. He flinched momentarily as a bolt of pain shot through his shoulder, then brought the blade down where the lead attacker's neck met his unarmored shoulder. The Templar had barely a heartbeat to reflect on the cutting power of the sword his friend the armorer had given him back at Acre before swinging it again. This time he chopped through the mail armor of the brute in front of him as if it were made of nothing more than leather. Lord, he thought, thou hast blessed me with the sword of righteousness. The remainder of the horde was crossing the courtyard now, only a dozen-and-a-half frothing brutes now, but all of them yelling and screaming the terrifying curses of men hell bent on inflicting death and slaughter. We're done for now, thought Fitz Alan, seeing no way out. By God, though, we'll take a full measure of these heathen bastards with us as we go. He turned to de Fonte, wiping the sweat from his eyes. "On the other side, Arnaldus."

"Indeed, my lord, though whether it be heaven or hell…." It was an old joke and the two men smiled grimly at each other.

The four Templars readied themselves for the Saracen assault.

"Thy will, Lord, not mine!" prayed Fitz Alan, his mottled and bloodied sword feeling heavy in his hand as he braced for the final onslaught.

They were close now, the enemy, and closing fast. As ever, he was ready to die, though now more than ever he was committed to taking with him as many of Christ's enemies as possible. "This is it," he thought, "Lord Jesus, receive my spirit. Forgive me my sins and prepare for me a place at thy table!"

Then the slaughter began in earnest.

The *Turcopolier* sized up the situation the instant he burst through the main gate and immediately led his men in a ferocious charge against the Saracens who had cornered Fitz Alan and his troop. The killing was awful, as it always was when half-organized and poorly disciplined fighters were caught in the open by mounted warriors. Templars and *turcopoles* crashed into the fleeing Saracens, hacking and slashing at the dismounted foe. Fitz Alan saw the *Turcopolier* smash in the skull of one of the Saracens, his forward motion combining with the vicious upward swing of his flanged mace to turn the man's head into a bloody porridge of bone, flesh and hair. "Come on, Templars!" he yelled, leaping at the nearest of the enemy warriors, his Saracen blade raised over his head. He slashed downward through the man's arms, which he had raised in a futile attempt either to surrender or to deflect the blade. Fitz Alan raised his sword again, the pain shooting through his shoulder, and finished the Saracen with a sharp thrust into his throat before moving on in the direction of the greater mass of enemy fighters. The other Templars followed, falling on the heretics nearest to them and slashing like men possessed. The blood pounding in his ears, Fitz Alan could hear nothing of the battle. He moved forward over ground that had been made slippery by the blood and gore spilled this day. He looked to his right and saw a sergeant-brother appear as if from nowhere, thrusting his arming dagger upward into the small of a Saracen's unarmored back. As the Templar sergeant withdrew his blade, the Saracen dropped to his knees, blood oozing from his wound. Fitz Alan watched as the sergeant-brother then kicked the man viciously in the back of the head, sending his face smashing into the dirt. The sergeant then bent over and slit the man's throat, wiping his blade on the dead man's tunic before disappearing once again into the thick of the mêlée. All around him, similar small battles were taking place, warriors focused on killing the man in front of them, oblivious to everything else in the world. Fitz Alan turned to his left, staying his blade at the last moment as a dismounted *turcopole* ran past him and launched himself against two half-clad Saracens who were standing back to back in the vain hope of keeping each other alive. The *poulain* slashed at the man closest to him, sending the Saracen's lance flying. He then closed quickly with the hapless man and swung his sword low, cleaving the Saracen's leg at mid-thigh and sending torrents of blood shooting across the courtyard. Hearing his companion scream, the second man turned around and, seeing the man collapse in a bloody and quivering heap, ran. Fitz Alan took three quick steps in his direction and, with a vicious hacking motion, severed the man's unarmored sword arm from his body. The Saracen dropped to his knees, staring at his severed limb in disbelief. Fitz Alan finished him off with a sharp downward slash that crashed into the top of the Saracen's unturbaned head, exposing hair and bone and brain alike. As the Templar withdrew his sword, the man fell forward face-first, blood oozing from his severed limb and mangled head.

One by one the Saracens fell, until the courtyard across which they had charged so certain of victory only heartbeats before was nothing more than a mass of still and still-twitching bodies lying in flooding pools of warm blood and gore.

"Hold!" Fitz Alan bellowed, "Hold!" He could barely contain himself, his heart pounding in his chest and his thirst for blood not fully slaked, but knew he must if they were to get out of this place alive. "Brother John, Brother Matthew," he called thickly, "dismount and secure that gate!" He pointed in the direction of the large wooden doors they had just come through. "The rest of you secure the courtyard and make certain these Saracens bastards are dead. Thump their eyes. If they move, gut 'em! No prisoners!"

He turned to the Turcopolier who had dismounted beside him. "What took you so bloody long, William?" said Fitz Alan, wiping the sweat, blood and grime from his face with the sleeve of his bloodied disguise.

"Bit of bother, my lord. Enemy horse came up the road behind us. Stumbled into us, they did. There were lots of them, my lord, so even though they were only Bedouin auxiliaries it took us a while to send them packing. But we're here now, my lord, as you commanded." He smiled lopsidedly at the Templar.

Fitz Alan took a long draft of water from his squire, who had appeared out of nowhere as he always did after a battle. It was warm, but slaked his thirst nonetheless. "Thank you, Thomas," he said. The Templar then turned back to the *turcopole* commander. "And not a moment too soon, William. We'd have been done for had you been delayed much longer. Wounded?"

"Mostly just scrapes, bumps and bruises, my lord. Nothing serious. Except...."

"Yes?"

"Except for one man, my lord. One of mine."

"He was one of mine, too, William. Who was it?"

"Jean Moreau."

"Good man, was he?"

"One of the best. I've known him since he was but ten years of age. A good Christian and a good fighter. Survived Hattin, he did." The *Turcopolier* crossed himself, "God rest his soul."

"Take some time to get him buried properly, William. And don't worry, I'll see that de Ramla does right by him. But let's be quick about it, eh? We need to be out of here before your Saracen horse return or those heretics over yonder in Heliopolis wake up."

"Thank you, my lord!" The *Turcopolier* turned and barked a command at the native horsemen who had so tenderly carried the body of their dead comrade into the courtyard. The men set about digging a hole in which to bury their friend.

"My lord?"

"Brother James."

"Quick count of the enemy dead, my lord. Thirty-eight altogether."

Thirty-eight, thought Fitz Alan. A far cry from the dozen or so de Ramla had predicted. It was fortunate indeed that these men had not been anticipating trouble; for had they been they'd've slaughtered both the advance party and the remainder of the banner. Fitz Alan was furious at the Hospitaller and intended to express his displeasure.

The Templar rode over to where de Fonte and de Ramla were pulling on their white and black *cappae* respectively. "De Ramla! Be thankful I have need of you, you incompetent Hospitaller bastard, or I'd have your bloody guts for garters. Thirty-eight Saracen devils were garrisoning this fort. Not the dozen or so you claimed would greet us."

"I have no explanation, Brother Michael. When I was last here, there were fewer than twelve. I can only imagine that the Turks have been having trouble with the local Arabs and have been forced to increase the garrison…"

Fitz Alan cut him off. "Spare me your excuses, Hospitaller. I trusted you to provide insight into the Saracen disposition and you let me down. I've never had much faith in your abilities, either temporal or spiritual. Now I've none. But I need you at the moment, in your capacity as priest. Get yourself ready and say a prayer over that brave *turcopole* who gave his life today for Christ and His holy Church, d'ye hear me? He fell in the service of God and deserves no less. And do it right, mind, or you and I shall quarrel!"

"I have no need of instruction from you when it comes to the performance of my office, Templar," the Hospitaller replied, indifferent to the scorn dripping from Fitz Alan's tongue. "I'll do my best to rest his soul, irrespective of your *commands*." He uttered the last word with barely concealed derision.

Fitz Alan turned away from the Hospitaller, irritated and disgusted. The pain in his shoulder, which had been bad enough during the battle, was nearly intolerable now. "Get the men ready, Brother Arnaldus," he grunted. "We're moving out once the *turcopoles* have buried their dead comrade."

"Aye, my lord. *De par Dieu!*" The giant Gascon then slung his shield over his neck and shoulder, wheeled his mount around and began organizing the sergeant-brothers for the remainder of their long journey toward Tripoli and the Priory of Valsainte.

VI

Brother Enyon did what he always did in the aftermath of a victorious battle: he recovered as many of his precious arrows as he possibly could. The supply of arrows, good arrows at any rate, was always meager here in *Outremer*, where the crossbow was the most common missile weapon and the manufacture of quarrels the highest priority. "If I were back home in Wales," he muttered to himself, "there'd be arrows aplenty and I wouldn't have to scrounge around on the battlefield like some dog picking through a rubbish heap." Of course, he thought ruefully, if I were back home in Wales I'd be wallowing in some stinking gaol now – or worse. He continued recovering the arrows – prying a few out of doors and shutters, but digging the major part out of dead enemy bodies – renewed in his conviction that serving Christ here in the Holy Land was infinitely preferable to any life, or death, he might have had back in Monmouthshire. *Non mea voluntas sed Tua fiat*, he prayed, not for the first time that day; Not my will, Lord, but Thine be done.

"Arnaldus!" Fitz Alan was looking in the direction of the keep where they had nearly been overrun. "Take a few men and search the keep. Look for quarrels, food, water... anything we might be able to use."

"*De par Dieu!*"

Fitz Alan was striding across the courtyard now, trying to keep his men focused on the tasks that needed to be done before their spirits inevitably sank and they collapsed of exhaustion. They were bone tired, he knew, drained by both the emotional and physical exertion of the day's fighting. But there'd be time enough for rest later. Now, they had to prepare themselves as best they could lest the enemy were to suddenly appear and they find themselves unprepared either to fight or flee.

As he walked, he noticed Turcault and a handful of *turcopoles* laying their dead comrade to rest. De Ramla was presiding, for once, thought Fitz

Alan, doing something useful. "You men!" he called to a small group of Templars drinking water from a small cistern near the far gate. "Drink your fill and then prepare that cart," he motioned in the direction of the slavers' cart that had been part of their subterfuge to gain entry to the toll house, "for the journey. I want everything that we can carry loaded up and ready to go before the hour of None. And find some horses. Those two," he pointed to the dray horses that had been slaughtered in the opening moments of the battle, "will be of little use to us on the march."

"*De par Dieu!*" replied the senior sergeant-brother, wiping his mouth dry with the tight-fitting sleeve of his brown *cappa*.

Fitz Alan then climbed the stone stairs leading to the top of the eastern curtain wall. Once on the battlement he looked toward Heliopolis and, reassured that nothing menacing was taking place in that direction, walked to the south wall and looked back along the road they had travelled earlier that day. He could see several dead Bedouin and a few dead and dying horses where Turcault's men had fought off their attack, but that was all. No sign of danger in that direction either, though the lay of the land meant that he could not see much farther down the road than where it opened into the valley. Fitz Alan then turned around and began surveying the interior of the toll house. More charnel house than toll house now, he thought to himself. Dead Saracens lay all over the courtyard, dark pools of thickening blood forming oversized halos about their lifeless heads and torsos. Hell is a little fuller today, he thought; the devil will be well pleased. Then again, he reflected mournfully as he glanced in the direction of the *turcopole* burial party, heaven is a little fuller too. I hope you are pleased to receive your faithful servant, Lord; for I am saddened by his death. He crossed himself and recited a short prayer: *Requiem æternam dona eis, Domine; et lux perpetua luceat eis.* Eternal rest give to them, O Lord; and let perpetual light shine upon them.

Satisfied that the banner was in no immediate danger, Fitz Alan then began to make his way back toward the stairs leading down into the courtyard, for there was yet much to do and little time to do it. Before he could descend the steps, however, de Fonte appeared on the battlement and walked purposefully toward him.

"What news, Arnaldus? Please let it be favourable."

"It is, my lord. The keep is packed to bursting with bows, quarrels, lances, maces, food, even wine – and gold, a king's ransom in gold. Seems tax collectors do well enough in these parts."

"As doubtless they did when our Savior walked these roads. And I'm certain they are as reviled now as they were then. No matter. Make sure the men have all the food and weapons they need. Pack up whatever we can on the slavers' cart. And put some people to work making that gate impassable – spike the gate shut, pile up debris, the usual things. Turcault and the banner seem to have given those Bedouin demons a drubbing, and I doubt we'll see them again, but there's no telling who else might come down that trail to our disadvantage. No use making it easy for them."

"And the gold – there's enough there to make us both very wealthy?" de Fonte jested, his battle-scarred face contorted into what for him passed for a smile.

"There was a time, my friend; there was a time...."

"Indeed there was, Michael – and it wasn't that long ago."

"Seems like a lifetime, Arnaldus," replied Fitz Alan. "Pass a few coins to each of the *turcopoles* and bury the rest. If we pass this way again, we'll see if we can carry it back to King Richard. Bastard's always short of money and if he really is going to liberate Jerusalem he'll need all he can get."

"*De par Dieu!*"

"And, Arnaldus."

"Yes, my lord."

"See that William takes some for the family of that fallen *turcopole*."

"My lord."

The two Templars then descended the stairs and set about organizing the banner for what they both knew would be a long and hazardous march to Tripoli.

Had circumstances been slightly different, there would have been euphoria in the banner after the hard won victory at the toll house. But the inevitable – and intended – effect of the Order's strict spiritual discipline was to dampen any celebration of personal achievement, any tendency toward the kind of pride that would transform the selfless acts of martial virtue recently performed into sinful acts of murderous vice. They had fought well, better than well, and among lesser men there would have been jubilation and self-congratulation. Among the Templars, though, there was none of the euphoric banter that always punctuated the victories of more temporal warriors. The warrior-monks and their local auxiliaries rode on in silent prayer or contemplation, speaking only when the practical demands of the march demanded it. If there was a common sentiment among these battle-hardened veterans it was one of thanksgiving and humility – a sentiment best captured and expressed in the Templar battle hymn: *Non nobis, non nobis, Domine, sed nomini tuo da gloriam*. Not to us, not to us, O Lord, but to thy name give glory!

On and on they rode, along dusty roads or, where necessary to skirt a village or avoid other travelers, through rough tracks in the rolling foothills to the east or west of the valley. They stopped once, briefly, to water the horses at a small stream that bisected the road. Other than that, they pressed on as quickly as was prudent, intent on covering as much ground as possible before nightfall.

As dusk began to descend, Fitz Alan raised his hand to signal that the day's march was at an end. "Gonfanier, give the order."

The standard-bearer broke formation and turned to face the column. "Make camp, brothers, on God's behalf!" he bellowed.

Once the order given, the column instantly transformed itself into a hive of frenetic, though ordered, activity. Fitz Alan directed the men to a spot a few hundred feet from the road where they would be partly concealed from any passersby. He doubted they'd encounter any at this hour, but years of experience dictated that this was the prudent thing to do. Once off the road, the men began to unencumber their horses. Some then led the mounts off to be watered and fed; others pitched tents and prepared cooking fires; everyone had a task to complete before they could rest and all applied themselves with an energy that belied the bone-deep weariness that Fitz Alan knew afflicted all of them without exception.

"Brother Matthew, Brother Luke!" the *turcopolier* bellowed. "You have the first watch. You," he stabbed an unmailed finger at the smaller of the two *poulains*, "set your picquet a half-mile or so up the road. You," he pointed now at the other, "set your's a half-mile in the other direction. Any sign of danger, get your backsides back here as quick as you can. I'll have someone bring you some food once it's ready, so don't worry about missing the evening meal. No sleeping now, boys. We're deep in Saracen territory and the enemy is everywhere. Be watchful. And prayerful."

"Yes, my lord," they responded in unison.

"Alright, boys, off you go. And God be with you."

As the two *turcopoles* headed off in opposite directions, Turcault turned back to the encampment. The smell of burning wood and roasting meat was in the air now, and he realized how hungry he was after the days fighting and marching. I'd better find Father de Ramla, he thought. He'll need to say vespers before the men can eat and he'll want a couple of men to help him with the preparations. First things first, though, he thought. The *turcopolier* looked about and, seeing a large cedar tree on the edge of the encampment walked quickly toward it. For at that moment what he needed, above all else in the world, more than food, more even than rest, was to empty his near-to-bursting bladder as quickly as he possibly could.

Arnaldus de Fonte handed a cup of wine to his old friend Michael Fitz Alan. The office of compline was completed, and like most of the other Templars they were gathered around one of the numerous fires dotting the encampment, enjoying the evening drink permitted by the Rule. The night was warm, but both men sat close to the fire anyway, drawn to its comforting flames.

"We'll need to be moving again by the hour of Prime, Arnaldus."

"I'll let the men know before they bed down for the night."

"Good man."

De Fonte pushed the embers of the fire around with a long stick, exposing the glowing orange-red coals and sending embers crackling into the air. The dancing flames reminded both men of other fires in other lands – some, like this one, small and benign; others, infernos, as malign as the fires of hell. The two men sat in silence, each partly caught up in their own thoughts and partly entranced by the flickering flames. At length, de Fonte broke the spell.

"What troubles you, friend? You seem not yourself tonight."

"My shoulder pains me, that's all," replied Fitz Alan rotating his arm slowly in the vain hope that doing so would provide some relief.

Both men drained their cups of the last few drops of wine, and Fitz Alan motioned for his squire Thomas to refill them.

"Been a hard day, Arnaldus. I don't think the Lord will mind much if we take two evening drinks rather than the prescribed one."

"The wedding feast at Cana would seem to support that point of view," replied de Fonte, "though I'm not sure the Grand Master would see it that way."

No, he probably wouldn't, thought Fitz Alan. But then the Grand Master wasn't here to register his disapproval, was he? He took a healthy draught of the warm, dark liquid, feeling its restorative effects flow outward from his belly to his extremities. Combined with the soothing effects of the fire, the wine made him feel more relaxed than he had felt since they had departed the Christian host and crossed into heathendom.

"Again, Michael, you seem troubled."

"You know me too well, old friend. The truth of it is, I *am* troubled. Have been since we set out on this fool's errand."

"Been a bit nip and tuck at moments, truth be told, but so far I'd say things have gone quite well. No reason that you should be troubled by our progress thus far."

"No, it's not that," Fitz Alan replied. "It's something else, something Fr. Arkwright – God rest his soul – said to me on his deathbed." Thomas emerged again out of the darkness, silently filling their cups before disappearing again into the night. Both men drank deeply.

"He warned me that this mission, undertaken on behalf of that Godless bastard Richard and his false bishop, was a test, a trial. By the time it was over, he said, my true colors would be revealed: the world would know me to be either a true knight of Christ or merely a worldly one playing at piety."

"A test?" de Fonte responded. "Of what? Your fidelity to the ideals of the Order? If such it is, then you need not concern yourself overmuch: you have proven yourself worthy many times over. You fight for Christ with all the skill and strength and resourcefulness of your namesake, whom Our Heavenly Father esteemed so much that He entrusted him with the heavenly host."

"My fighting skills are not really the issue, though, are they? At least not my temporal ones. I think the good Father's point was that ultimately it was not the exterior battle that mattered, but the interior one; not the worldly fight against Christ's enemies, but the spiritual one against our own fallen nature. It means battling against anger and wrath, and above all, pride. It means battling and killing the worldly knight within. This is the war that Fr. Arkwright spoke of; ultimately the only war that really matters. And though he had faith in me, Arkwright was fearful that in this place, this land both holy and unholy, the Evil One would prevail and reclaim my soul. The farther we travel up this valley, Arnaldus, the more I fear the good father's concerns may have been justified."

De Fonte poked at the fire again, but it was dying now and nothing he could do could bring it back. "It's a difficult balance," he said at length. "To be a knight, but meek and lowly; to be a monk, but a ruthless killer. Perhaps it is not really our struggle at all; perhaps it is only through God's grace that we can walk this narrow path. In any case, I really do not see where you have departed the path of righteousness, Michael. I cannot see the Fitz Alan of old, except when it comes to your temporal fighting skills. These are undiminished."

"How many men have we killed – have I killed – since Acre?"

"Dozens. Scores, perhaps." Came de Fonte's reply.

"And why is this killing not counted as murder? Why does it not violate every precept our Lord taught when he spoke at the Mount of Beatitudes? Why does it not contravene the fifth commandment?"

"You know the answer, Michael. It is because of our inward disposition. We fight and kill, neither for love of self nor for the riches of this world, but for God and the riches of the next. It is the object of our love that sets us apart from – above – the earthly knight. For us, God; for him, Man."

"And if the proper inward disposition is lacking? If anger and wrath and pride – those fatal symptoms of temporal knighthood – are present in a man's soul? What then, Arnaldus?"

"Such a state of affairs would make the killing murder. But you long ago put such vices aside, Michael. Do you forget that I knew the old Michael Fitz Alan. You are not that man."

Fitz Alan looked deeply into the dying fire. "Anger, wrath and pride, Arnaldus – this is the unholy trinity that first brought me to Temple Ewell in search of salvation. And it was at Temple Ewell that I thought I had crucified the earthly knight who had so delighted in living according to these so-called 'virtues'. Grace bent my will toward God, and the disciplines of the Rule produced both virtuous habit and, I thought, virtuous disposition. But since coming here, since confronting the evils of this land, I have felt once again the stirrings of anger and wrath; I have tasted again the bitter gall of pride. When I ordered those slavers killed...."

"That was justice," exclaimed de Fonte, "God's will."

"Was it? Or was it merely undisciplined rage and hatred masquerading as justice? Was it God's will, or *my* will arrogantly supplanting His? Was it *caritas* that moved me, or hatred?"

De Fonte reflected for a moment, taking time to finish his wine. At length he replied. "Only you can answer those questions, Michael, though for my part I think Fr. Arkwright would have approved of your actions. I will say only this: it seems to me that if a man can ask such questions of himself, he need not concern himself excessively with the state of his soul."

"Perhaps," said Fitz Alan as he drained his cup, "perhaps."

De Fonte rose. "The hour is late, my friend, and we've a long and trying journey before us tomorrow. We should part now and get some sleep."

"Of course. *Congé,*" he said, dismissing his friend with the prescribed formal command.

De Fonte nodded and set off toward the palliase his squire had laid out for him near the center of the encampment.

Yes, thought Fitz Alan, a long and trying journey indeed. The English Templar then rose, turned his back on the dying fire and headed off into the darkness.

28 July 1191

The *Haute cour* of *Outremer*, never the most serene of bodies, was in utter and complete turmoil. Guy and Conrad had just been recalled to the chamber to hear Joscius, the Archbishop of Tyre, announce the terms of the grand bargain agreed by the assembled magnates. Guy, he said, was to retain a life interest in the crown of Jerusalem and to be granted hereditary title to Acre and any lands liberated in the south; Conrad was to be awarded hereditary title to Tyre, Sidon and Beirut, and named heir to the throne of

Jerusalem. Not surprisingly, neither Guy nor Conrad was pleased with the decision – both raised strenuous objections to its terms, arguing alternately with the archbishop and each other. The two men were soon joined by their respective partisans, who, having exhausted their more reasoned arguments during the earlier deliberations, were left with nothing to exchange now but insults and threats. Matters quickly spiraled out of control and it seemed as if the shouting and cursing might at any moment give way to physical violence.

Eventually, though, Richard, through sheer force of personality, was able to restore order in the hall. The threat of violence averted, he spoke briefly to the assembled magnates. "My lords," he began, "I am no more pleased with this compromise than any of you. How could I be, given my own well-known preferences. But what choice have we? As you all clearly recognized during our deliberations, there is no practical alternative to this arrangement. Please do not let heated spirits or bruised sensibilities stand in the way of victory. We are here to fight Saladin; to restore Jerusalem to Christendom. What chance have we against Saladin and his band of heretics if we continue to fight amongst ourselves? This compromise is not perfect; I know that you are all to some degree disappointed and frustrated by its terms. Indeed, I share those sentiments. But I am willing to put my own preferences, my own interests, even my own duties to one side if it means that we will have peace within our camp. For absent peace and concord among ourselves how can we prevail over the ancient enemy. As the Gospel says, 'a house divided against itself cannot stand.' So I say to you today, accept this grand bargain; put an end to the division within our house. For if you do, great victories lie in our future. If you do, future generations will praise you, not only for your valor and martial prowess, but for your prudence and self-command as well. If you do, you will go down in history, not as the men who bickered while the Holy Land was despoiled, but as the men who redeemed Jerusalem and returned it to its rightful owners."

God, Philip thought, but the man was insufferable; the sound of an ass braying directly in his ear would be easier to suffer than his self-serving cant. Having decided that he had heard enough, he turned his back on his cousin and left the chamber, his entourage in tow.

"A moment, cousin," called the Marquis of Montferrat, "I would have a moment of your time."

Philip barely turned to face him, "In the corridor, for I can suffer no more of this."

They left the great hall and proceeded together some way down the corridor before seating themselves in a small alcove. "What do you want of me, cousin?" he said coldly. The two men had once been close, but since Philip had decided to return home to France, they had parted ways.

"I have a proposal for you, my lord king."

"A proposal? What have *you* to offer *me*, cousin?"

"What you want most, sire: to harm that bastard Richard."

Philip leaned forward, intrigued now by what the marquis had to say. "You have my ear, cousin. Speak your peace."

"As you might well imagine, I am unsatisfied with the decision of the *Haute cour* – I am king of Jerusalem by right and the only just pronouncement would have been one that confirmed that fact…"

"If you are here to try to convince me to change my mind, save your breath. I cannot be moved on this matter."

"No, my lord, that is not my intention," Conrad replied quickly. "I understand why you agreed to go along with this ill-starred *compromise*, and I accept your decision. I mention it merely to underscore that, despite appearances, despite the recent unpleasantness between us, we have a common cause against Richard. In your case, that cause flows naturally from the fact that he is your great rival in France; in mine, from the fact that he has denied me what is mine by right – Jerusalem. I'm sure you'd agree, my lord, that at heart we share an interest in bringing harm to Richard, for any harm that comes to him here only strengthens your hand in France and mine here in *Outremer*."

"I have no desire to see the pilgrimage fail, if that's what you're suggesting." Philip's voice was still cold, though no longer icy.

"Nor do I, my lord king, for who now has more to gain from a successful campaign against the Saracens than I. Sidon, Beirut and ultimately Jerusalem will only be mine if we are successful," the marquis continued. "But it doesn't mean that Richard should receive all the honor and glory."

"No it does not. The man already has a grossly inflated sense of self – God help us should it be inflated further still."

"Then we are agreed?"

"We are agreed," Philip replied, "that neither you nor I have any reason to love Richard. Beyond that…. What is it, then, that you would ask of me? Perhaps then we'll see if we are in agreement."

"As you wish, my lord. Here is what I propose: that upon quitting the Holy Land, you turn over your portion of Acre and the Acre hostages to me."

"What?" Philip was stunned by the request. "Is that what this is all about? Money and land?" he sputtered, furious that he had been put upon in this way. He began to rise.

"Please, my lord, hear me out. Think of how this will hurt our common foe. If you leave the hostages here in Acre, Richard will be able to exchange them for the True Cross, captured by Saladin at Hattin." Conrad knew that Saladin was no longer in possession of the relic. He didn't know who *did* possess it, but he knew it was neither Saladin nor Richard. Conrad, though, wanted those hostages for himself, and could think of no better way of motivating Philip to turn them over to him than to invoke the specter of Richard in possession of the True Cross. "Think of what that will do for his reputation, my lord. The great Richard, King of England, Duke of Normandy, Duke of Aquitaine, Duke of Gascony, Lionheart, liberator of the True Cross. Think of how that will strengthen his hand here in the Holy Land. Think of how it will strengthen his hand in France."

He saw a look of horror flicker momentarily across Philip's face.

"If on the other hand," he continued quickly, "Richard cannot offer Saladin what he wants, then it is unlikely that the Saracen will turn over the most holy relic. Richard may still prevail over Saladin, but he won't be sainted. And he won't be able to parade the Cross through the French lands he seeks to add to his empire."

"And Acre? Why should I give you half of Acre?" Philip asked somewhat hoarsely, his mouth made uncomfortably dry at the thought of Richard armed with the True Cross rallying lord after lord to the now-holy Angevin cause.

"Because, my lord king, it will serve as a sword pointed at Richard's back. With my forces quartered in Acre and Tyre, he'll never have complete freedom of action in the south. Again, my lord, a distraction, a complication

– an additional consideration that will keep his ravenous attentions away from France."

Almost in spite of himself, Philip found himself giving serious consideration to Conrad's proposal. He had dedicated himself to smashing the Angevin empire, to restoring the ancient kingdom of Francia. And a distracted Richard could only help advance that cause. And what did he care of Jaffa, or Acre or Beirut or Sidon. Or Jerusalem, for that matter. After all, he was only here because that devious priest the Archbishop of Tyre had tricked him into taking the cross. Almost as soon as he had arrived in this Godforsaken place, though, he had realized it was a mistake. France, not *Outremer*, was Philip's Holy Land and it was there he needed to apply his talents. It galled him to enrich Conrad thus, but ruling, he had learned, was all too often about making such unpleasant decisions. No, considered in the balance, Acre and a few hundred hostages were ultimately nothing to him. A distracted Richard, on the other hand, was invaluable.

"Very well, cousin. I will grant your request. I will give you my half of Acre and my portion of the hostages. I do so, however, on condition that you do everything in your power to keep Richard's gaze on Jerusalem – and to keep the True Cross out of his hands."

"My lord king, I swear to you this most solemn oath: I vow to do all in my power, as long as I draw breath, to frustrate Richard's schemes here and in France. If it is in my power, I will keep his attentions focused on *Outremer* and will keep the relic of the True Cross out of his grasping hands. So help me God."

With that, both men rose and clasped each other's forearms. If the friendship they had once shared had not been fully restored, they were at least allies once again. Both men smiled as they imagined Richard's reaction to the news that Conrad was now in possession of half of Acre and, more deliciously, half the Acre hostages.

1 August 1191

Emanuele Volpiano was the first to spy it. He had been scouting the road ahead of the Lord of Montegrosso d'Asti's main force when he and two of his most trusted knights had decided to follow a spur in the road leading east through a narrow pass in hills. Expecting danger, they were surprised when opportunity presented itself instead.

"Benicio," bellowed the Astigiani knight, "carry word back to Lord d'Asti. *Fortuna* favors us this day. Nothing to do with the Templars or the Holy Lance, but good fortune nevertheless. Tell him we have found some fat Cistercian fruit ripe for the plucking. Go!"

"My lord." The man-at-arms turned his mount around and bolted back down the road they had just traveled.

Volpiano turned to his remaining companion. "A day's ride out from Tripoli on what is likely to be nothing more than a fruitless fool's errand. Then this. You just never know your luck, Albericus. You never know your luck."

"No, my lord." Albericus had learned long ago both to agree with his master and to say as little as possible while doing so.

Volpiano looked back down the hill at the monastery in the distance. He marveled at the richness of the lands, tended by white-robed Cistercian monks, apparently unmolested as yet by the Saracens. Olives, lemons, grapes – even a fishpond. They'll have treasure house, he thought. Stuffed with gold, or at least silver, and who knows what else, a rich house like this. He felt his mouth water and his heart beat a little faster. After what he had suffered during the defense of Tyre and then the siege of Acre, he felt he was due some compensation. And not just the blessings of his lord, but real wealth or glory or power. Justice, he thought, would be done this day. If nothing else he would enjoy seeing these Cistericans jump and dance at his command. God, but he hated Cistercians. In truth, he hated all churchmen. But as a result of the childhood years he'd spent being raised by these bastards he harbored a special loathing for these white-clad monks. God's teeth, but they had made him suffer – how they'd abused him, ridiculed him, tormented him. Above all, how they'd humiliated him. And all because he didn't take to their lessons as quickly as the other children; all because he was the smallest and weakest and most vulnerable of the poor souls in their care. Well, he'd avenged himself on them since then; whenever possible, whenever the opportunity presented itself, Volpiano had repaid the debt he believed he owed them. And he'd sworn he'd continue to do so as long as he drew breath. Now, when he'd least expected it, *fortuna* had presented him with another opportunity to avenge himself on the odious white-robed bastards that had destroyed his youth. The mere thought of his tormentors suffering at his hand was enough to make his mouth water.

The Astigiani adjusted himself in his saddle then spat into the dry soil in the shadow of his mount. Looking down at the monastery, his eye went directly to one particularly portly monk carrying two large baskets on his back and shuffling about like a woman. That one, he thought to himself, will suffer first. And what he will suffer will truly be terrible. He'll tell me what I want to know. And if not, no matter; for I'll have placed another weight on the scales of justice. He spat again. Besides, he thought, if the fat one dies a gruesome death, the tongues of the other white-clad sodomites will surely be loosened. And if the next one doesn't talk, I'll kill the next one and the next one and the next one until there are no more. By the bowels of Christ, I'll kill every last one of them all if I have to. The thought of sending a score or so Cistercians to hell brought a smile to his face. Yes, he thought, let them all resist to the bitter end, for I will find their deaths delightful. Delightful indeed.

The Lord d'Asti was pleased by the news he'd just received from Volpiano's man. He'd never had many scruples about plundering fat little churches. Indeed, he'd made something of a career of it in Piedmont. And the prospect of plundering this inconsequential, but likely quite wealthy, little monastery in this godforsaken corner of heathendom troubled him not in the least. For though he was already a fabulously wealthy man, he had a war to finance. A very expensive war. And every little bit of treasure he could extract from his tenants, his vassals or the Church helped keep his host in the field. No, he had no scruples about plundering this fat little monastery; none whatsoever.

As the column approached the place where Volpiano and his man were maintaining their vigil, d'Asti raised his hand to signal a halt. He then rode with Volpiano's messenger the last half-mile or so to the spot where his trusted lieutenant had concealed himself. "Volpiano! What news of our white-robed friends down below."

"My lord," came the reply. "They suspect nothing. They go about their business as if Hattin had never happened and they were not now on the frontier of heathendom. Stupid bastards!" he spat in the direction of the monastery.

"Good, good. How do you think we should proceed?"

Volpiano had been thinking of little else since dispatching his man with news of the monastery to his lord. "Little subtlety is required here, my lord. Let me take the column down the road to the main gate. The sight of it will likely induce them to give us all we want. But if not, we'll storm the place and start putting the fat little swine to death. After a few have been sent to the heavenly banquet, the rest will start to sing like the heavenly choir."

D'Asti considered Volpiano's suggestion for only a heartbeat. "Very well. Take the column and bring me their treasure. Do what you deem necessary – and do not fail me. Whatever they have, I want. No excuses."

"No excuses, my lord," Volpiano replied. And with that he spurred his horse back in the direction of the column, excited at the prospect of both serving his lord making these Cisterican bastards pay once again for all the pain and humiliation that they had inflicted on him.

Emanuele Volpiano led a dozen knights and twice as many mounted men-at-arms down the winding road leading to the monastery's main gate. As they approached the entrance, a solitary white-robed monk emerged from the monastery and walked purposefully toward them. "Hold," he said to his fighters, motioning that they should stay where they were. He then rode slowly in the direction of the man walking toward them. The man wore the white robe of the Cistericans, and was quite probably the abbot of the house, but he had a decidedly martial air about him. Nothing at all like the effeminate swine he'd spied earlier carrying the two baskets on his back. He was tall and broad shouldered. He had thick black hair about his tonsure and a hard face disfigured by what seemed to be a fighting scar that stretched from his right nostril all the way to where his jaw line gave way to his neck. Volpiano stiffened, sensing that this man might be a spiritual warrior now, but he had been a more temporal one at some point in his past. His left hand moved instinctively to the hilt of his sword as he used his right to bring his mount to a halt.

"I am Emanuele Volpiano, a pilgrim in the service of Conrad, Marquis of Montferrat and King of Jerusalem. Who are you?"

"I am Abbé Pierre and this is my house, Belmont. You are welcome here. I can offer you hospitality – water, wine, olives, even a little cheese – and in return ask only that you tell us of developments beyond this holy place. We have so few visitors and hear so little of the outside world. Yet what we do hear is deeply troubling."

"The world beyond your little plot is troubled indeed, Abbé. The Saracens have taken most of *Outremer* and have despoiled dozens of houses like this. But we are here to take back the Holy Land, for King Conrad."

"Surely, if you are a pilgrim facing the Saracen horde, you are here to take back the Holy Land for Christ rather than Conrad."

"I am here to fight for Conrad, Abbé, my king, the sole and rightful King of Jerusalem. Which brings me to my purpose. In order that the fight may be carried to the Saracen, our king and his vassals have needs."

"Needs, *mon fils?*"

"Yes, Abbé, needs. In particular, we need treasure that we can use to sustain the pilgrimage. As I'm sure you understand, such an endeavor can be sustained only at great cost. In times of necessity, all are expected to contribute to the common good."

"What are you asking, monsieur? We have little, and what we have I have already offered to you. And we have asked for precious little in return."

Volpiano was ready to gut the white-clad man standing before him, but managed to restrain himself, at least for the moment. "Let us not play games, Abbé. We care not for food or water, though we may accept your offer of wine. We are here to requisition whatever treasure we can carry with us." He looked toward the monastery. "You have what appears to be a thriving house here. You have property, you have tenants and you probably trade in various commodities. Therefore you must have treasure. In the name of the king, I must insist that you turn it over to us at once."

"And, assuming we have any such treasure, what will happen if we refuse?"

"What treasure you have will be requisitioned by whatever means necessary. This is war, Abbé, and in times of war, necessity trumps all other considerations."

"I am afraid that you misjudge us, my lord. We have no treasure, save the redeeming body and blood of our Lord, and the ciborium, paten and chalice through which it is administered to the faithful. And I'm afraid that we cannot let you have those."

"I do not believe you, *priest*," he hissed the word, his voice dripping with contempt and all pretense of civility fallen away. "I have dealt with old women like you before. A little corporal persuasion and, miraculously, temporal treasures always seem to appear."

The Abbé was a hard man. He had been a warrior before committing his life to Christ and the Cistercians, and had seen carnage and suffering almost unimaginable to most of his brothers, even here where suffering and death were commonplace. As a result, he knew when he was in the presence of a killer. And he knew he was in the presence of one now. "The strong do what they will," he said to Volpiano, "and the weak suffer what they must."

"Scripture won't help you, priest. Tell me where you conceal your treasure and we will leave you in peace," he lied.

"It's not scripture. And I doubt very much you will. In any case, I will not permit you to desecrate our holiest treasures."

"Look, priest, would you really sacrifice all of your brothers for a few pieces of dross? Are you so committed to earthly wealth that you cannot see your way to sacrificing a few pieces of silver to support your king's pilgrimage to Jerusalem? Is your pride such that you will not accede to my request, even though it be lawful and just? You profess to be a man of God, yet will not support God's warriors fighting to liberate the holy places. What sort of man are you? What sort of *Christian* are you?" Volpiano spat. "A bloody hypocrite, that's what I say. And a traitor too," he concluded menacingly.

The Abbé stiffened, the old warrior in him asserting himself after so many years of being scourged and willed and prayed into submission. For a heartbeat, he wished that he had his old sword. Were it in my hand now, he thought, I'd teach this dog a thing or two about humility. But an instant later the monk he had become was back in control, pushing aside such dark thoughts and silently begging the Lord's forgiveness for his momentary flash of knightly arrogance. The Abbé looked Volpiano directly in the eye. For a moment, the Piedmontese knight thought the priest might actually draw a sword out from under his cassock and try to kill him. But the Abbé had no sword and no such intention. "Get thee behind me," he said loudly. Then he turned his back on this demon sent to test his faith and began to make his way back toward the monastery.

The monastery fell without resistance, and its inhabitants were quickly rounded up by Volpianos's men and gathered in the courtyard. The Piedmontese knight rode his black *destrier* up to the assembled monks, looking them over with utter disdain. His horse whinnied, its breath misting in the early morning air.

"Cistercians!" he bellowed. "Your abbot has betrayed his king, the most noble Conrad. He has refused His Grace aid and counsel in time of war and has thereby committed an act of treason. I have therefore arrested the false priest, Pierre. I have also confiscated the monastery in his charge and put its resources at the service of its lawful king. You are now direct subjects and vassals of King Conrad of Jerusalem – warriors in his just war to liberate the Holy Places from that most heinous demon Saladin. As the king's deputy, I now lawfully claim authority over you. And, in the name of His Grace, I order you to submit!"

Abbé Pierre, bruised and battered as a result of his treatment at the hands of Volpiano's henchmen, looked up at his tormentor through bloodied and half-shut eyes. "In this house," he declared defiantly, "we recognize the authority of Christ and the Holy Father alone. You have no jurisdiction here, knight. We are subjects of no earthly king, least of all that near-heretic Conrad. Depart these holy precincts, I say! Leave now or you and your men will face the wrath of Christ and His Holy Church!" He turned to address the assembled knights. "You men! Sinners! Repent now and accept my lawful authority. If you do, I shall absolve you of all your trespasses and remit whatever penance you have been condemned to perform. Refuse," he coughed, then spat a mouthful of bloody phlegm into the dirt beneath Volpiano's horse, "follow this servant of the Evil One, and I will damn your souls to eternal torment in the fires of hell. In Christ's name, I command you, here and now: choose!" He raised the battered and bloodied crucifix still hanging from his neck, shoving it in Volpiano's face. "Choose!"

Volpiano dismounted his horse and walked calmly toward Abbé Pierre. He looked into the abbot's eyes and, seeing nothing but defiance, smashed the cross into his face and, while his victim was trying to regain his footing, deftly drew his dagger and thrust it upward into the man's unprotected belly. Blood oozed instantly from the abbot's wound, spreading slowly down the length of the killer's blade and onto Volpiano's mailed fist. Abbé Pierre's eyes momentarily registered surprise, for he did not expect to die this day, and then… they registered nothing. The abbot was dead. Volpiano twisted the blade free of his victim's bowels and pushed the carcass away. The abbot's lifeless body fell backward slightly, then dropped in a crumpled heap to the ground, its empty eyes facing heavenward in silent supplication.

The monks began to pray, joining their supplications to their fallen abbot's.

"Shut up, you bastards, or I'll have every last one of you skinned alive!"

Silence returned to the courtyard.

"Bring me that one over there," he pointed toward the man he had earlier spied carrying the two baskets. "Strip him down and tie him to that tree so that his backside is pointing toward the good brothers here. I'm sure more than one of these sodomites is already intimately familiar with it," he paused, fumbling in his saddlebag, "but now they are all going to come to appreciate it in its full glory." He pulled a small, pear-shaped object from the bag and held it up for all to see. It was about six inches long, consisting of a metal body divided into spoon-like segments and a screw where the stalk of an actual pear would ordinarily be. "This," he declared, "is called the Pear of Anguish. It looks like a simple metal pear – until I do this." He twisted the screw until the spoon-like segments began to spread outward. "Innocent enough, you might think. And so it is. Until it is inserted into a part of the body, the mouth or the anus, and expanded to its full extent. Then it inflicts the most awful pain. Excruciating really. I've seen the fiercest of knights reduced to quivering women by these four simple leaves. I have discovered, however, that words cannot really do the device justice; its true potential can only be conveyed through demonstration. Benicio," he called. One of the bigger brutes attached to his entourage stepped forward.

"My lord."

"Apply this device to the treasonous monk before us."

"Yes, my lord." He took the Pear and approached the quivering monk lashed to the massive cedar in the monastery's courtyard. He tried to insert the device, but the monk squirmed and writhed, making it impossible. Benicio punched the man hard in the side of the head, then grabbed his tonsure and shoved the monk's skull into the tree trunk. The trussed man collapsed into unconsciousness. Volpiano's man then forcefully inserted the device into the monk's anus.

"Ready, my lord."

"Proceed."

Benicio began to turn the screw. After several heartbeats, the Cistercian was revived, not quite sure what was happening to him but very sure he didn't like it. A few more heartbeats and the monk was screaming, alternately begging for mercy from God and his tormentor. The latter looked to Volpiano, silently seeking further instructions.

Volpiano raised his hand to stay the torture. "Brother monk. I am going to ask you some questions. Every time you answer me honestly, I will have my man here turn the screw to the left. When he does so your pain will decrease. Every time your answer is less than satisfactory, I will have him turn it to the right. When he does your pain will increase. Enough bad answers and the pain will become unbearable. Shortly thereafter, you will die a horrible, and ultimately pointless, death as your insides spill out into the dirt between your legs. Do you understand me, monk?"

"Father, if it be possible, let this cup pass from me: nevertheless, O Lord, not my will, but thine."

"No. My will reigns here." Volpiano then nodded to his man. Benicio turned the screw one full rotation to the right. The screaming intensified.

"Your king has need of your resources if we are to defeat the heretics and liberate Jerusalem. Where is your treasure hidden, monk?"

"My treasure is stored up in heaven," he gasped defiantly through gritted teeth.

Volpiano looked to the other monks, who were variously sobbing and seething. "Will you good and holy men allow your brother to continue to suffer like this? Any one of you can redeem him. Any one of you can spare him the passion he is about to endure. All it will take is for you, any one of you, to tell me where your treasure is concealed. Once I have that, I will release you all and my men and I will be about our lawful and holy business. You have my solemn oath."

No one responded.

"Very well. Benicio, you must be more persuasive." Another turn of the screw. Blood and feces now began to drip down the monk's legs, pooling in the dirt beneath him. The waves of pain convulsing his body were nearly unbearable, and he screamed like a demon, praying for death.

"You'll all go through this ordeal, you bastards!" Volpiano roared. "Each one of you in turn will be lashed to that tree, until I have what I want. And why should you resist me? I am no Saracen. I do not demand that you abandon the true faith and worship that false prophet Mohammed. I am a man of God, a Christian like you, seeking your help to liberate Jerusalem. Help me do God's will and all this unpleasantness will come to an end."

The suffering monk sputtered something.

"What's that, monk? Have you come to your senses?"

"Yes," came the barely audible reply.

Volpiano had the device removed. Even in his crushed and broken state, the monk was under no illusions. He knew they were all dead men, destined to be with their Lord and Savior before this day was done. The only question was how much pain and suffering he and his brothers would have to endure before they were released from this *valle lacrimarum*, this vale of tears. The monk himself was of course willing to undergo this terrible passion – even to be martyred for Christ. He was not, however, willing to see his brothers martyred on his account. So he began to talk. Through tears and vomit and blood, he began to talk, divulging everything Volpiano wanted to know.

"There, there," Volpiano said to the suffering man, stroking his head, "now your suffering ends."

The monk whimpered in gratitude.

"Davide, get this poor wretch a blanket. You two," he pointed to two men of his command whose names he knew not, "find out if he is telling the truth. Quickly now. We've tarried here long enough." The two men ran off in the direction of the stables, where the broken monk had confessed the monastery's treasures to be concealed.

After a while, the two men returned with several liturgical vessels and a few small bags of money. "This is all that we could find, my lord," said the smaller of the two.

Volpiano took the moneybags, weighing them expertly in his hands. "Not as much as I'd hoped for, but enough to justify this little detour. Very good, we can supplement it with other goods. Benicio! Assemble the good monks here in the stables. Not our friend the talkative one," he gestured toward the monk quivering in the blanket in a pool of his own blood and feces, "but all the rest of these holy men. Move them quickly, now, we haven't all day." He turned to the remainder of his band. "The rest of you: take what you can carry and make ready to resume the march!" There was a flurry of activity as some of the Piedmontese knights marched the Cistercians off in the direction of the stables while others fanned out through the monastery gathering every bit of moveable treasure they could find.

D'Asti, Volpiano and the rest of their band of killers left the monastery early the next morning, the packhorses they had seized from the monks' stables weighed down with all manner of valuables. The horses alone would bring a small fortune once D'Asti and his men returned to Tyre and brought them to market. Then there were the books, statues and carvings, all of which would fetch a handsome price in Tyre or Genoa. Finally, there was the Abbé's ring and crosier, countless silver crucifixes, the monastery's liturgical vessels and a couple of small bags of silver and gold coins. Not as much plunder as the Lord Montegrosso d'Asti had hoped for, but as Volpiano had said, more than enough to justify a day's delay in their expedition to Valsainte.

D'Asti looked back over his shoulder to see several columns of smoke rising from the now lifeless Cistercian house. He felt satisfied that things had gone as well as they had. Volpiano had had the broken monk nailed to the crossbeams of the monastery's main gate in a gruesome parody of the Crucifixion. Not absolutely necessary, d'Asti thought, but Volpiano disagreed and he and his men seemed to take some satisfaction in the act. But then there was the very efficient way his vassal had handled the killing of the monks. That *was* necessary, he believed, for witnesses could be very messy things. And Volpiano had made it happen in such a painless way – painless, at least, for d'Asti. The Cistercians, still stunned by the treatment of their brother at Volpiano's hands, had been effortlessly herded into the monastery's one wooden building, the stables. These had then been barred shut and set alight. All three-score or so of the self-righteous hypocrites had perished therein, leaving no one to report d'Asti's misdeeds to Conrad or Richard or anyone else who might cause trouble. No, the plunder may have been less than he might have hoped for. But, he thought, the death screams of the monks still echoing almost melodically in his head were well worth the price. Well worth the price, indeed.

142

VII

4 August 1191

This day, like every other since they had departed Acre, dawned with the cloudless blue sky and the blistering heat of high summer in *Outremer*. Despite the fact that they had only just completed their early morning worship, the men were already sweating profusely. But if the heat and exertions associated with breaking camp and preparing for the days march wore on the men, they gave little indication of it. Absent was the testiness and complaining typical of worldly warriors dealing with the quotidian rigors of campaigning. For the Templars, such mortifications were simply another way of atoning for their sins; another way of paying the price for their trespasses in this life so that they wouldn't have to pay quite so much in the next.

Fitz Alan, seemingly immune to the Syrian sun, mounted his destrier. "Brother de Fonte," he called out, pitching his voice so that all could hear. "Have the banner mount up and prepare to depart."

"*De par Dieu*, my lord," came the reply. Turning to the sergeant-brother serving as gonfanonier that day, he continued, "Brother Joseph, call the men to their mounts."

The Templars and their auxiliaries mounted their horses in silence and formed a column two abreast. Fitz Alan and de Ramla assumed their positions in the van of the column; de Fonte assumed his in the rear. Turcault moved up and down the column, ensuring that everything was in order. When he was satisfied that the banner was ready to move out, he approached Fitz Alan. "The banner is prepared my lord. We can set out at your command."

"Very good, master Turcault. Have the *gonfanonier* signal the advance."

Turcault did so and the banner set off on the day's march. The *turcopolier* then dropped back to take up his position alongside de Fonte in the rear of the column. As he did so, he looked up at the brilliant blue sky, lamenting the absence of even a wisp of sheltering cloud. Resigning himself to another day of blazing heat, he wiped his brow with his sleeve and prayed silently: Father, if thou be willing, remove this cup from me: nevertheless not my will, but thine, be done. He waited for a strengthening angel to appear to him, but as he looked along the long road stretching before him all he could see was a score or so of the most formidable killers ever known to man. After a moment of reflection, he concluded that that was enough; for while an angel might be helpful, all the strength he really needed this day could be drawn from the sight of this body of holy, disciplined and deadly killers.

The Templars had rested over the midday hour, tending to their horses and equipment, consuming a little food and drink and taking advantage of whatever shade they could find. They were on the road again now, scouts patrolling a half-mile ahead of the main body now that banner had entered the foothills skirting the Beqaa and was encountering blind turns more and more frequently. De Ramla and Fitz Alan had dropped back to the rear of the column, replacing de Fonte and Turcault who had taken up position in the van. Not a word had passed between the Templar and Hospitaller since they had set out that morning.

"De Ramla," said Fitz Alan, "I would speak with you... in private." Both men slowed their mounts until they had drifted out of earshot of the rest of the column.

"Speak your mind, Templar, but if it's about the trouble back at the toll house you're wasting your breath. I have no idea why there were so many Saracens garrisoned there – I gave you my understanding of the situation as I knew it based on my experience. That I was wrong is beyond dispute; that I somehow misled you is an infamy. In either case, I am finished explaining myself. If you've any more recriminations, I suggest you waste neither your time nor mine expressing them."

"What's done is done, Hospitaller, and what's said is said. It is true that you were wrong about the garrison. But in suggesting that your motives were impure or that you lack courage or competence... Well, let us simply say I may have been a little..." he searched for the right word, "intemperate. It is a vice I continue to struggle with. I would ask you to pray for me that I might exercise greater self-command in the future." Fitz Alan didn't like this *poulain* priest, and he certainly didn't trust him – at least not fully. He was, after all, a man in the service of King Richard and Bishop Hubert, and only God himself knew what those two bastards were really up to. But Fitz Alan knew he needed the Hospitaller. And he also instinctively valued the man's combination of toughness and piety. In that respect, if no other, the Hospitaller reminded Fitz Alan of his recently deceased confessor and friend Father Arkwright. And for that reason, if no other, he was willing to give this *poulain* priest another chance to prove his worth.

"Fair enough," replied de Ramla, "I shall pray to our Lord and Savior that you come to enjoy ever more fully all the fruits of the Holy Spirit, but most especially that of 'self-mastery'."

"Given all that has passed between us, that is good of you indeed."

The two rode on in silence.

"Tell me, Father de Ramla, why do you serve the Angevin king and his bishop? I have known them a very long time – their interests can hardly be the same as yours'."

"You might assume as much, but here in the East, things are seldom as they appear," was all the Hospitaller said.

"That's true everywhere, is it not. It is certainly true where those two are concerned, whether here or in France?"

"Perhaps. But I think it especially true in *Outremer*. Those with little experience of the Holy Land always expect life here to be simple and uncomplicated; for things to be as they appear to be. Christian versus Muslim; God versus the Evil One. They expect, even crave, a moral clarity here that is typically lacking back home, wherever home is. When in due course they are confronted with the harsh complexities of life in the East, the deceits and deceptions that are part of the normal pattern of politics here as elsewhere, the result is almost always a kind of shock. So if life here is in reality no more complex than it is elsewhere, it often feels that way to the uninitiated. The distance between appearance and reality always seems greater here than it seems elsewhere."

The Hospitaller's words rang true to Fitz Alan.

"Take, for example," de Ramla continued, "our enemies the Saracens. To those who know not better, they are simply an undifferentiated mass of heretics, a single race of brigands who have unlawfully seized the Holy Land

and who hold it against the will of God."

"Is that not the truth of the matter?"

"Yes and no. They are heretics and blasphemers, to be sure. And nothing can justify their infamous aggressions against Christ and His people. But they are as riven with factional infighting as any kingdom in Christendom. Sunnis and Shia, Nizari and Sufi; Fatamid and Ayubbid; Arab and Turk and Kurd and Bedouin; and the list goes on, each with their own interests and beliefs and aspirations. The distinctive dress of the various warriors you have encountered on the battlefield only begins to hint at the range of cleavages within the Saracen world. They may all be Muslims, but they are otherwise as diverse as the peoples of the Christian world, perhaps even more so."

"I am well acquainted with the variety of warriors in the Saracen horde – though until now I attached little significance to the distinctions between them save that some are better archers, while others better horsemen. I am indeed thankful to have a more complete picture of the cleavages underpinning their more superficial differences."

"*De rien*," de Ramla replied, smiling a smile that Fitz Alan was sure had seduced many a maiden.

"There is one faction I do not really understand, however. And I wouldn't care about them overmuch, save I am told their lands are not far from our final destination. The Assassins – or Nizaris as I believe they call themselves – what can you tell me about them?"

"Now, there's a very interesting race," de Ramla replied, "a very interesting race indeed."

"How so?" inquired Fitz Alan, adjusting himself in his saddle and resisting the urge, not for the first time since midday, to reach for his now only half-full skin of water.

"Well, for one thing, they are considered heretics by Saladin – indeed, he has more than once tried to stamp them out."

"And how did that end up?"

"No love lost between them, to be sure. They loathe and distrust Saladin, and he loathes and distrusts them. But they both also fear each other. The Assassins worry that if Saladin finally extinguishes the Christian presence here, he will turn his attention back to them. For his part, Saladin fears that the greater his success against us the more likely it will be that the Assassins might make yet another attempt on his life. For the last twenty years or so the two sides have maintained an uneasy peace. Few believe, however, that it is a peace based on anything other than expedience. Should either side see the advantage to it, or come to believe that the other side was about to strike first, they'd be at each other's throats again in a heartbeat."

"Surely that provides us with an opening. Has no one attempted to bring the Assassins in on our side."

"There was a time when such an alliance seemed within our grasp. Two decades ago, the Assassin leader approached King Amalric of Jerusalem and offered to provide intelligence and fighters in return for support against Saladin's predecessor Nur ad-Din. There was even talk that the Nizari leader would be baptized. It came to naught, however; for your Order was extorting an annual tribute of two thousand gold pieces from the Nizari and feared it would lose that tribute if an alliance were agreed. A Templar knight put paid to any possible rapprochement between our two peoples when he murdered the Nizari ambassador to Jerusalem. Since then, however, we Hospitallers have worked quietly to re-open negotiations and draw the Nizari into an alliance. But their leader has a long memory and seems to have decided that the Assassins' long-term survival is best served by playing Saracens and Christians against each other – to maintain a kind of balance in which neither we nor Saladin have the strength or inclination to threaten them. Since Hattin, though they have not abrogated their treaty with Saladin, they have tended to favor us with various kinds of support – surreptitiously, of course. Mark me, though, should it ever appear that we are gaining the upper hand over Saladin, that could change in the blink of an eye."

The two rode on, each contemplating how a single man could change the course of history.

"None of this, though, really answers your question, does it?" It was de Ramla who broke the silence.

"Not really, but it does hint at an answer. Something's going on here that I am not privy to; something related to factionalism among the Saracens – or maybe merely the pursuit of glory or power or wealth on the part of the Angevin. But then I've suspected that all along. Richard and his false bishop going to all this effort to recover a holy relic – never rang quite true to me."

"Oh, they're interested in the success of our little expedition to Valsainte alright; King Richard seems to believe that if he can't recover the True Cross, the Holy Spear is the next best thing. On that score, you may rest assured. You may also rest assured that the success of this expedition is *my* highest priority. You are correct in your assumption that my interests and those of the king and his bishop are not always precisely aligned. But in this instance, there is simply no daylight between what they seek and what I seek – or, I presume, what you seek. We must get to Valsainte." The Hospitaller paused to drink deeply from his waterskin. "I know you have questions about me, Brother Michael. Doubts even. And I'm afraid that it is in the very nature of my…," he searched for just the right word, "… *vocation* that I remain something of a mystery to you. But, even if at times it appears otherwise, you can count on me to do as I'd said I'd do."

Fitz Alan said nothing in reply. He was warming to this Hospitaller priest. Despite all the differences in background and experience, he sensed that ultimately they were both cut from the same bolt of cloth. But there remained something about the priest that troubled the Templar. Perhaps it was the mysteriousness he himself had mentioned; perhaps it was his association with Richard and the bishop; perhaps it was nothing more than the fact that he was a *poulain* and a Hospitaller. Whatever it was, Fitz Alan was wary of him. *You can count on me to do as I've said I'd do*, that's what the Hospitaller had said. Well, we'll just have to see about that, won't we, Fitz Alan thought. We'll just have to bloody wait and see.

6 August 1191

The *turcopolier* received the report from one of his men who had been scouting the road ahead. After questioning the man, he reined his horse about and rode back to the rear of the column in order to apprise Fitz Alan of the situation. "Afraid our luck's run out, my lord. There's a Saracen village straddling the road ahead and there's no way 'round it. Unless we want to backtrack and enter the valley proper we're going to have to go through it."

They had indeed been fortunate thus far, Fitz Alan thought. They had managed to avoid both traffic and settlements by travelling along the eastern edge of the valley, screened from the main road and major towns and villages by a range of low hills. Now, however, the little-used road had brought them to an enemy village that they could not simply bypass. The dangers were obvious to all. "Is it garrisoned?" he asked.

"My scout says it didn't appear to be, but he couldn't be entirely certain."

De Fonte, who had halted the column, joined them in the rear. Tucault repeated his report to the Gascon.

"Suggestions?" Fitz Alan asked.

Turcault scratched his beard. "Yesterday we passed a spur in the road that led over the foothills and onto the main Beqaa road. We could turn around, follow that spur and take our chances in the open in the valley."

"We'd avoid this particular village, but such a course would cost us several days. It would also expose us to other dangers as well, other villages, Saracen patrols."

De Fonte nodded at Fitz Alan's words. "Alternatively we could force our way through the village," he said. "There's no doubt we could fight our way through, even if it is defended by some sort of militia or a...."

Fitz Alan cut him off mid-sentence. "But we might suffer casualties in the process – and, more ominously, they might be able to send someone to call for help. If that happens, who knows what dangers we'll encounter farther along the road."

"Not sounding promising so far," said Turcault.

"There is a third way," de Ramla interjected. "We could send an emissary and negotiate free passage through the town. Such an approach would involve reciprocal promises: we'd promise to pass through peacefully; they'd promise to let us do so. Neither side would molest the other."

Fitz Alan turned over the possibilities in his head. "Might just work. If we give them some of that gold we picked up back at the toll house in return for a promise of silence, it might just work. We wouldn't want them sending word of our presence to the local garrison, would we?" He thought about it a bit more, carefully gauging the risks and balancing them against the alternatives. "It's perilous, to be sure: the bastards might take the gold and still send word of us. But de Ramla's plan seems the best of several bad possibilities."

"Shall I prepare to treat with them?" asked the Hospitaller.

"Yes. And Master Turcault?" he said turning to the *turcopolier*.

"My lord."

"You will accompany Father de Ramla."

"You do not trust me, Michael?"

"I have found it helpful when treating with the enemy to have two sets of ears at the table: one for listening to the primary interlocutor, the other to listen to what's going on in the background. As the *turcopolier* is the only one of us who speaks the Saracen tongue, it makes sense for him to be your second set. As to the question of trust, that is earned. I trust Master Turcault with my life." Left unspoken was the distance the Hospitaller priest had yet to travel before he too enjoyed such unqualified trust.

"Indeed," came the frosty reply. "Master Turcault, if you would make ready. 'I must work the works of him that sent me, while it is day: the night cometh, when no man can work.'"

The two men then mounted their horses and rode up the road leading to the Saracen town.

He saw them enter the town. The first two riders bore red crosses pridefully displayed on almost-white mantles. They were followed by more riders with crosses on brown robes, and even more with the hated image painted on their black and white helms. *Faranji*, he thought, spitting a partial measure of his hatred of the infidels into the dust-caked rooftop. *Faranji*. And if his uncle knew half as much as he claimed he did, not just ordinary *Faranji*, but *Templars* – the worst of all the murdering infidel devils. Allah be praised, he thought, for sending these *kuffar* his way. Allah be praised for braiding his fate with theirs' this day.

Abdul Rahman ibn Omar al-Aziz was not a killer – at least not yet. He had been orphaned at the age of seven, his father martyred– or so he had always been told – by men dressed like these, men dressed in the colours of blood and blasphemy. Since that terrible day, the day his uncle had broken the news of his father's death to him, he had dreamt of nothing but vengeance, of killing those who had taken his father from him. And every day since then he had prepared himself for the moment when he could make his dream become reality – the moment when he would finally exact his revenge on the Christian dogs who had killed his noble father and widowed his saintly mother. He had devoted years to learning the arts of war, to mastering the bow and the sword and otherwise steeling himself to the hardships of war. Now, on the eve of manhood, he was not yet a killer; for the opportunity to take from the infidels what they had taken from his father had not yet presented itself. But he had prepared himself well; he was as proficient with the bow he was now stringing as any archer in Saladin's host. And the opportunity to avenge himself on these murderous devils had finally presented itself. No matter what the imam had said, no matter what arrangement had been struck with these infidels, he would seize the opportunity Allah had given him. He would avenge his father.

His first arrow struck one of the brown-clad *Faranji* in the throat, killing the man instantly. Even before the corpse had slumped lifeless in the saddle, his second arrow clattered off the helm of the third man in the column. He had loosed it too quickly and had missed his mark by half an arms' length. He could hear the blood pounding in his ears now, feel it coursing more quickly through his veins. He took a deep breath to calm himself, wiped the sweat from his brow, then knocked another arrow. He intended to aim carefully this time, but the fear and exhilaration of his first battle had its usual effect on the unblooded and he loosed the missile too quickly. The arrow clattered harmlessly along the cobbles in the road. He took another deep breath in a futile effort to calm himself, then knocked another arrow and stepped back into the open. He aimed and loosed again. He thought he saw his arrow strike the chest of the white-clad *Faranji* at the head of the column, but stepped back behind the cistern before he could be sure. He clumsily knocked yet another arrow, fired blindly in the direction of the enemy column, then quickly stepped back behind the cistern. His hands were trembling now and he was sweating the cold, clammy sweat of a man in fear for his life. He cursed himself silently for his weakness and prayed that he might find the strength to complete his task, to make these *kuffar* pay for what they had done to his father, to his mother. Strengthen my hand, O Giver of Victory, he prayed, strengthen my hand that justice may be done this day.

Abdul Rahman ibn Omar al-Aziz knocked an arrow and stepped out of his hiding place.

He spotted one of the *Faranji* dogs trying to conceal himself in the doorway of one of the buildings in the street below, drew his bow and took careful aim at a brown-clad infidel.

Fitz Alan rode at the head of the banner as it snaked silently through the town. The parley with the Saracens had gone well, he thought, very well indeed. Terms had been agreed – in return for the Templars promising not to despoil the town, the villagers had agreed to neither molest them nor report their presence to the local garrison – and had been agreed quickly and with a minimum of bother. The Saracens had even agreed to last-minute request that they furnish a dozen hostages to ensure the Templars safe passage. Truth be told, he had been more than a little surprised that things had gone as smoothly as they had. And he had half-expected some sort of deceit or treachery – which was why his men were in full mail and prepared for a fight as they picked their way through the winding streets. But true to their word, the Saracens had cleared a route through the town and left them unmolested. The Templars had just passed the town square, about half-way to the town's far gate, and had seen neither hide nor hair of its inhabitants. At least along the main road, the town was utterly deserted, forsaken. All was proceeding as they had hoped, Fitz Alan thought. God willing, they'd soon be through the town, rid of their hostages and back on their way up the valley.

The Templar column moved quietly along the main road, its silent passage punctuated only by the sound of hooves clacking on cobblestones and the occasional whinny of a horse. They were approaching the town square now and the road had narrowed considerably, framed by tall buildings on either side. Ideal ambush territory, Fitz Alan thought. Like every other man in the banner he was scanning the windows for any signs of danger. The sooner we're through this town and in open country again, he thought, the happier I'll be.

"Arnaldus."

"My lord."

"Take one of the sergeant-brothers and scout the square ahead. We'll be following the north road," he gestured toward the road directly opposite the one they were on. "Make sure it's as quiet as this one has been."

"*De par Dieu*, my lord," de Fonte replied reigning his horse back to collect Brother John.

Fitz Alan looked down the road, searching the square they were about to enter. All clear, he thought. Perhaps the Saracens have kept their word and we might actually be permitted to pass through this godforsaken town without incident. Just then, de Fonte and Brother John rode past him to scout the way forward. As they did, they drew his eyes to the large building on the far side of the square. He scanned the windows thoroughly, but saw nothing suspicious. Then, just as he was about to turn his attention elsewhere, he thought he saw something move, not in the windows but on the roof. It was a furtive movement, the kind of motion he had learned to look for while campaigning in Normandy and Gascony. Instinctively, he raised his crossbow from its resting place on his horse's withers.

Then the missile struck.

It was an arrow. A short, black, ugly arrow of the kind used by the Saracen horse archers. It made a thrumming sound as it flew past Fitz Alan, who instinctively spurred his mount and shouted to the banner to seek cover. His men reacted as they had been trained, dismounting and availing themselves of whatever protection they could find. All save Brother Matthew, the day's first victim, who was hanging lifeless in his saddle, the shaft of the deadly missile protruding from his slashed and gory throat.

A second arrow caromed off the piebald kettle hat of Brother Luke, who had taken a moment too long to dismount, and skittered along the street cobbles. The man was dazed, but signaled to Fitz Alan that he was unharmed.

Fitz Alan stood tall in his saddle, preparing to rally the banner. He knew from long experience that if they stayed too long in this canyon of a road they'd likely be cut to pieces, especially if additional attackers appeared along their flanks or to their rear. Better to rush forward now, he thought, even if it meant exposing themselves for a short time.

He began calling to the men to move forward, pointing them in the direction of the building where he had earlier seen movement.

Then it happened. He felt a hammer blow to his left shoulder, the force of which nearly threw him from his saddle. He gasped in pain, then struggled to right himself and regain control of his mount. He looked down at his shoulder and there saw a short, black, ugly arrow shaft protruding from his woolen *cappa*.

De Fonte was at his side in a heartbeat. "Are you alright, Michael?" he asked, fearing the worst.

"Not sure," replied Fitz Alan. "Can't see any blood, but it hurts like the devil." Without warning, he grasped the shaft of the arrow and pulled it out of his *cappa*. The broad arrowhead was unbloodied though badly bent. "Mail stopped it. Fortunate for me that that demon prefers broadheads to bodkins." Broadheads were wide and barbed, made for slashing the flesh of unprotected men and horses. Bodkins, on the other hand, were needle-nosed and unbarbed, ideal for penetrating mail.

A visibly relieved de Fonte smiled and nodded in agreement. The two men retreated into a nearby doorway, just as Turcault arrived.

"Either of you two see anything? Is it just the one attacker or are there more?" Fitz Allan queried.

"I saw nothing, my lord. Seems to be just the one," said Turcault.

"I didn't see anyone else, Michael," replied de Fonte. "Just the one in the building across the square."

"In that case, there's a change of plan. Initially, I thought we'd best ride through the ambush, but now...." He looked back toward the rooftop whence the Saracen arrow had come, but saw nothing.

"Brother Enyon," Fitz Alan called to the Welsh archer, who was huddled a few doorways down stringing his bow.

"My lord," came the reply.

"Bastard's on the roof of that big building on the other side of the square. Can't see him now, probably in hiding behind that cistern, but he's up there alright," he said pointing to the large rooftop reservoir. "My guess is that he'll step out to loose a few arrows in our direction and then conceal himself again. I want you to bag him. Think you can manage it?"

Brother Enyon pondered Fitz Alan's request for a moment. There was a lot to consider in essaying a shot like this: distance, windage and elevation at a minimum. Then there was the timing of the shot – he'd have to get the rhythm of the Saracen's attacks and loose his arrow a heartbeat before the man actually revealed himself. He performed the various calculations instinctively and almost instantly. "Bit tricky, my lord, bit tricky. But I can do it, alright."

Just then, the Saracen appeared, loosed two half-aimed arrows and disappeared again. The first bounced harmlessly off a wall; the second, though, sank deep into the hindquarter of the dead sergeant-brother's horse. The animal bolted down a side street, its lifeless rider still hanging from its saddle and a blood-red stain spreading across its white caparison to create a grim parody of the Templar mantle.

"Anyone hit?" called Fitz Alan.

"Just Brother Matthew's mount," came de Fonte's reply.

"Right! Enyon, make ready. Turcault!"

"My lord."

"Get your men ready to move out. Once Enyon's bagged his prey, we'll want to move quickly through the square."

"My lord," he replied, rising to a crouch and running quickly back toward where his men had half-assembled out of the enemy archer's range.

"Arnaldus."

"My lord."

"Retrieve Brother Matthew's body, if you can. We'll want to bury him once we've cleared this cesspit of a town."

"*De par Dieu!*" he said, dashing across the narrow road and racing down the sidestreet that had swallowed up the dead Templar's horse only a few moments earlier.

Fitz Alan then turned to the Welsh archer beside him. "Now, Brother Enyon," he said, drawing his sword, "let us be about our Father's business."

Brother Enyon stood erect in the doorway, only half-concealed from his Saracen opponent, both prey and predator. Tricky little shot, he thought. He had worked out the range and elevation easily enough, years of experience suggesting the angle he would have to raise his bow if his arrow was to strike home. Windage was more of a problem, though the air was still down near the ground and, if the plume on the Saracen's headgear was any indication, only slightly left-to-right on the rooftop. The real challenge was going to be the timing. The distance to his target, coupled with the short time the man was exposed, meant that he would have to loose the shot before his prey actually appeared from behind the cistern. A tricky shot, indeed, he thought. Even trickier than that one he'd made back in Wales before he had joined the Order. God forgive me, he reminisced, but that was some shot. Damned forester never knew what hit him.

Enyon counted the heartbeats between the Saracen's appearance, twenty-five, thirty, thirty-five, forty. The Saracen appeared again and loosed two arrows in the direction of one of the only half-concealed sergeant-brothers. The arrows narrowly missed their target, prompting the Templar to retreat even farther around the corner of the building where he was seeking to conceal himself. The Welshman knocked an arrow and raised his massive yew warbow, adjusting and readjusting it according to feel and intuition rather than conscious thought. He had entered a kind of trance, a state of mind in which distance, windage, elevation, and timing were all being worked out almost without him being aware of it; a state of mind in which he did not think about where to aim his bow, but simply let his eyes and muscles and instinct do the work. Fifteen, twenty, twenty-five. He inhaled. Thirty. Thirty-five. Then exhaled slowly. Forty. The Welshman loosed his goose-fledged arrow and watched it arc toward the rooftop cistern. It's in your hands now, Lord, he thought. It's in your hands now.

Fitz Alan marveled at the archer's concentration, at the focus and intensity the Welshman brought to the murderous task he had been assigned. He knew what Welsh and English archers were capable of, having seen them ply their deadly trade in Gascony and Normandy; the best were capable of near-miraculous feats. But he knew, too, the limits of their collective abilities – and he was certain that what he had asked the Welsh Templar to do was at or near those limits. He knew that there were few in the East, indeed in all of Christendom, who could make this shot. He was almost certain, though, that Enyon was one of them…. Almost.

Then Fitz Alan heard the harp note of Brother Enyon's bowstring being released and the whir of the ash missile departing his bow. A heartbeat later, the Saracen archer appeared from behind the cistern raising his short bow and aiming in the direction of some unseen victim. He watched the sergeant-brother's arrow arc toward the target, and in that instant knew beyond doubt that the Saracen on the rooftop was a dead man.

The steel-tipped ash arrow was descending slightly when it struck the Saracen. It hit him just above his left eye, punching easily through his skull and plunging deep into his brain. The force of its impact snapped the man's head down and sideways, almost knocking him off his feet. He staggered backwards a couple of steps and, for a heartbeat, seemed to regain his balance. Then the Saracen collapsed suddenly into a lifeless heap, as if, Fitz Alan thought, some diabolical alchemist had transmuted every bone in his body into blancmange.

"Bagged 'im, thanks be to God" said Brother Enyon. He then dropped to one knee, crossed himself, and began praying, "*Non nobis domine…*"

"*Non nobis domine*, indeed," said Fitz Alan, smiling. "*Non nobis domine*, indeed."

"Brother de Fonte!" barked Fitz Alan.

"My lord."

"Assemble the hostages."

"Yes, my lord," the Gascon replied, turning and heading in the direction of the slaver's cart in which the Saracen captives were being transported.

Fitz Alan poked at the meager fire in front of him, contemplating the day's happenings. The half-day journey since they had dispatched the Saracen archer had proceeded without incident and they had subsequently made good progress up the valley. He poked at the fire again, watching the smoke waft lazily upwards toward the darkening sky. He had been comforted, as always, by the compline prayers, even though they had been led by de Ramla and even though they had been offered in the hurried way necessary when they were in the field. But the brute fact was that Brother Matthew was dead. His lifeless body had been recovered by de Fonte and secured to his warhorse. The sergeant-brother had then accompanied the banner for one last ride, escorted en route by two of his comrades. He had been laid to rest in a simple ceremony not two hundred paces from where the *beauseant* was now planted near the center of their encampment, his soul departed and his body awaiting the resurrection promised when Christ came again in glory to judge the living and dead.

Fitz Alan spat into the glowing embers of the fire. He was furious, with himself to be sure, and with de Ramla, but mostly with the Saracen dogs who had promised him and his men safe passage and delivered instead nothing but deceit and death. He poked at the fire again, glimpsing in its burning depths the eternal fires of hell – fires to which, he swore to himself, he would from this day forward send as many of the heretic bastards as he possibly could. He would kill them to avenge all their heinous felonies: their lawless usurpation of the Holy Land, their despoliation of Christendom's most holy places, their slaughter of innocent pilgrims, their murder of his fellow Templars at Hattin – the roll of their crimes was endless, he thought, and he would kill them to avenge all their contemptible offenses. Most of all though, he would kill to avenge young Brother Matthew – a good man, a man entrusted to his care – a loyal servant of Christ and His holy Church who was travelling under a flag of truce and who had been maleficently murdered by these oath-breaking bastards. Queen of Heaven, pray for me, he plead silently; for, though your blessed Son commanded us to love our enemies, in truth I hate this race of vile demons. I have seen too much of their evil ways, too much of their cruelty and wickedness, too much of their blasphemy and corruption. Spitting a third time into the fire, he vowed to himself that as long as he drew breath, he would fight and kill these evil bastards – fight and kill them until all of *Outremer*, nay all of God's creation, has been cleansed of their defiling and debasing presence.

"Why are you assembling the hostages?" de Ramla asked, striding up to Fitz Alan and puncturing his reverie.

"To implement the terms of the truce, of course," came the Templar's ominous reply.

The Hospitaller was stunned, his face uncharacteristically betraying his inward disposition.

It took him a few heartbeats to recover his composure. "You can't do that," he finally replied, flatly yet firmly.

"I can and I will," said Fitz Alan, turning his back on de Ramla and walking resolutely toward Arnaldus and the hostages.

De Ramla followed, quickly catching up to Fitz Alan and grabbing the Templar by the sleeve of his *cappa*. "I cannot permit such a crime, Brother Michael. The hostages are under my protection and I say they shall not be harmed."

In less than a heartbeat, Fitz Alan had rounded on de Ramla, his Saracen sword flashing through the air, coming to rest not a hand's-breadth from the priest's throat. "Do that again, Hospitaller, and I'll fillet you like a herring, Rule or no. As to the hostages, they die – here and now. Justice demands nothing less."

De Fonte and Turcault appeared as if out of nowhere. "Michael," said de Fonte, gesturing toward the sword hanging menacingly in the air, "put up your sword, old friend. We don't want any needless bloodshed, do we?"

"Who's to say it would be needless?" Fitz Alan replied, his eyes not leaving de Ramla's. A few heartbeats later, however, he honored his friend's appeal and slowly lowered his sword.

"What's all this about, my lord?" queried Turcault.

"Brother Fitz Alan wants to kill the hostages in retribution for the death of Brother Matthew," de Ramla responded. "And I have forbidden it. They are innocents and under my protection. I will not see them butchered without justification or cause."

"Without justification or cause?" sputtered Fitz Alan, barely able to contain his disdain for the Hospitaller. "Brother Matthew's death was all the justification or cause necessary. The Saracens attacked us under color of truce – honor and justice demand that we punish them for their perfidy. As to your right to forbid anything in this matter," he addressed de Ramla directly, "I simply don't recognize it. The banner is in my charge and I decide who lives and who dies, not you. Arnaldus."

"My lord."

"Proceed as I have commanded."

"*De par dieu.*"

"Brother Michael, have you thought through the consequences of this action?"

"I consider this to *be* a consequence – of their actions, not mine."

"And it is. But have you thought through what killing the hostages will cost? What it will cost our cause here in the East? What it will cost you? Think this through, Brother Michael. Before you commit this act, I pray you, think it through."

"Perhaps we should hear him out, Michael," said de Fonte.

"Indeed, my lord," said Turcault. "Perhaps we should hear what our Hospitaller friend has to say."

Fitz Alan seethed. He wanted someone to pay for the death of Matthew, to pay for all the crimes the heretics had committed here in the Holy Land. He didn't want to hear what the Hospitaller priest had to say, didn't want to hear why he should not kill these depraved creatures. From somewhere deep within, though, he heard a voice urging him to hear de Ramla out. He sheathed his sword.

"Speak your peace, Hospitaller. But quickly, mind. We have work to be about."

"As to your claim that justice demands what you propose," de Ramla began hurriedly, "I have only this to say: since the Saracens in my custody are in no way guilty of perfidy, you have no just cause to punish them for perfidy. Was Brother Matthew's death not the work of a single man – nay, a single *boy* – acting *motu proprio*? There is no evidence that the Saracens who agreed to the truce were culpable for the acts of this lone wolf acting on his own initiative. Killing the hostages would be a grave injustice."

Fitz Alan glowered at de Ramla, barely able to contain the rage against the Saracens that had been building since his arrival in the Holy Land. "Look here, Hospitaller," he said, "The bargain we struck – *you* struck – with these bastards was simple enough: they promised to arrange safe passage for us; in turn, we promised that we would do no harm to them. We kept our end of the bargain, they failed to keep theirs'. And as a result, a good man is dead. It is only just that they forfeit the bond pledged to ensure their compliance with the bargain; that they pay the price all agreed should they renege on their promise. Indeed, I know of no other definition of justice."

"Brother Michael," de Ramla responded. "Surely you can see that the fault lies neither with those who treated with us in good faith nor the hostages themselves. Killing these innocent souls in these circumstances would not be an act of justice, but of justice perverted to vengeance and malice. But even if this line of argument is not persuasive, surely you would concede that we must consider our own interests in this affair. If word gets out that we are murdering hostages without cause, who will parlay with us in the future? And what if we need to return this way? Shall we be met with sullen silence or active resistance? We must keep our word, Brother Michael, not because it is the just thing to do, but because it is the wise thing to do."

"If word gets out?" Fitz Alan spat derisively. "We travel swiftly, de Ramla, so I doubt very much that word of this incident will overtake us. And if it does, surely that would be a welcome development. Perhaps the fame of our killing hostages in payment for treachery will disincline others to so lightly betray us. As to the return journey, perhaps next time these good townsfolk promise safe passage they will be more diligent in ensuring that it is delivered."

Seeing that things were not going well, the Hospitaller priest drew the last arrow from his quiver. "If nothing else will persuade you, Brother Michael, perhaps you will consider the effect that murdering these innocents will have on your pilgrimage here in the East. I speak here not of your temporal journey to Jerusalem, hallowed though that may be, but to your interior pilgrimage from worldly knight to knight of the Temple of Solomon. What would Saint Bernard, who grasped so clearly what it meant to be a true knight of Christ, think of such an act as you propose to commit? Would he laud it as a deed of great virtue, signifying a man's realization of the ideal of the New Knighthood? Or would he condemn it as the vicious act of a base and sinful knave, the crime of a worldly knight mired in monstrous error and condemned to eternal death? Once you answer that, Brother Michael, you'll know what you must do. You'll know whether you are truly one of Saint Bernard's new knights or merely another of Satan's knaves."

Fitz Alan had been fully prepared to let de Ramla have his say, fully prepared to let the Hospitaller break himself futilely against the shoals of his fixed purpose; for he had resolved that, once the priest had completed his peroration, the lives of the hostages would be forfeited in payment for the Saracens' perfidy. He had anticipated and rejected the Hospitaller's arguments from military necessity and natural justice, and, his mind made up, he felt he was proof against anything that de Ramla might have to say. But he was wrong. The priest's final argument passed though Fitz Alan's armor with ease, penetrating deep into the Templar's soul. He was almost physically staggered by the force of its impact. *Would he laud it as a deed of great virtue...? Or would he condemn it as the vicious act of a base and sinful knave?* Although his face and body betrayed nothing, the Templar was reeling inside. It was, he thought, as if de Ramla knew his innermost doubts and fears; as if the Hospitaller were aware of his vexing suspicion that he was incapable of realizing the Templar ideal, of decisively breaking the chains binding him to the Earthly City and its warrior caste. But how could de Ramla know such things? How could he know to pluck the one chord that might have Fitz Alan singing a different tune?

"Well, my lord, what's it to be?" asked de Ramla, shattering Fitz Alan's reverie. "Much hangs in the balance. I would have your answer, Brother

Michael… and I would have it now!"

"The braying of an ass – you open your mouth, de Ramla, and all I hear is the braying of an ass. Your words are like the blows of a child's wooden sword, ineffectual and harmless," Fitz Alan heard himself saying, though in truth the Hospitaller's words had hit him with all the force of the Saracen's arrow the previous day. His mind was racing now with the weight and implications of what de Ramla had just said. He still believed killing the hostages was warranted, and he loathed the thought of being bested in any way by the Hospitaller, but what if the priest was right? What if his motives, and thus the act of killing the hostages, were the fruits of hatred and vice rather than justice and virtue. What if it were pride and vainglory rather than love of justice spurring him along this road? Had he really drifted so far from the path of righteousness he had committed to upon entering the Order? Was it really possible that vengeance and hatred and pride had blinded him to the will of God? If that were the case, then he had departed the narrow Templar path to salvation and entered instead upon the broad highway to damnation. He had travelled the latter road all his adult life; it was not a road he cared to travel any longer.

"Arnaldus."

"My lord."

"Stay your hand for the moment. I am still inclined to make the Saracens pay for their treachery, but justice demands that I give careful consideration to Father de Ramla's words. Have the banner ready to move at Prime; I'll render my final judgment before we depart."

"*De par Dieu*, my lord."

And with that, Fitz Alan pushed past de Ramla and set off in the direction of Brother Matthew's still-fresh grave, hoping to find there a dark and quiet place where he might think, where he might pray, and where he might find the wisdom needed were justice to be done.

8 August 1191

The tent pitched outside al-Kharruba was smaller and less well-appointed than the massive pavilion Saladin had occupied outside of Acre, but more than spacious enough for a man who had spent most of his adult life campaigning in the field. He was sitting cross-legged on a large cushion, poring over various reports regarding the disposition of the host when the tent flap parted and his brother Saphadin the entered the tent.

"Greetings, brother. Please, join me. We have much to discuss," said Saladin, putting down his papers and motioning that Saphadin should seat himself on one of the sumptuous cushions strewn along the right hand wall of the tent. "I shall have some food and drink brought for us."

The Sultan motioned to a servant who had been concealed in the shadows and the man departed the tent to do his master's bidding.

"Thank you, my lord. I have been out surveying the Christian positions most of the day and am in need of sustenance."

They passed the time speaking of inconsequential matters until the servant returned and finished laying out three serving platters: one of pickled vegetables, yoghurts, spicy pastes and *murrī*, a brine sauce made from fermented barley and wheat flour; one of thin slices of roast kid seasoned simply with cumin, dry coriander and little pieces of cinnamon bark; and, of course, one containing *sanbusāj*, the little triangular pies filled with meat or cheese that the sultan loved so much. The servant then placed a final platter of breads and a large pitcher of water before them and, anticipating his master's wishes, disappeared, leaving the two brothers alone to speak of weightier matters.

"What news of the *Faranji*, al-Adil?" Saladin asked, casually dipping one of the deep-fried pies in the spicy-paste condiment and consuming it in one bite.

"For the moment, they seem content to be rebuilding Acre's walls and otherwise availing themselves of the city's earthly pleasures. I have seen no sign that they are preparing to move against us."

"Good. As you have said on many occasions, the longer they tarry in Acre the stronger our position becomes."

So the old fool does occasionally take what I say to heart. Maybe there's hope for him yet, thought Saphadin, ever contemptuous of his older sibling's lack of strategic sense. "My spies tell me, though, that there have been some interesting developments *within* the Christian host – developments that might also bode well for us, my lord."

"Indeed," said Saladin, leaning forward slightly either in anticipation of his brother's report or to better avail himself of the platter of breads lying just beyond his easy reach.

"It seems that both the Duke of Austria, Leopold, and the French king, Philip, have quit Syria for home. Most of their vassals, it seems, have opted to remain and fight under Richard, but their departure has weakened the infidels nonetheless."

Saladin's eyes widened as the implications of the news dawned on him. "Your knowledge of the infidels is remarkable, brother. Your spies must be well-placed indeed."

"They are, my lord – the *Faranji* are despicable creatures, bereft of honor; they would sell their own mothers for a few pieces of silver. But they are useful nonetheless. Beyond what I have already shared with you, consider this piece of information: my spies tell me that that dog Conrad of Montferrat has inherited Philip's share of the Acre hostages and that they are with him in Tyre." The Sultan looked at him quizzically, not grasping the significance of this bit of information. "This means, my lord, that they are not currently in Richard's possession. And given what we know of the hostility between these two men, it may not be within the English king's power to deliver them to us as agreed – at least not according to our agreement, and perhaps not ever."

"Allah smiles upon us, brother," said Saladin, sensing that this created possibilities that had not existed earlier that day. If Richard were not able to keep his end of the bargain, then perhaps he would be amenable to pushing back the date on which they would consummate their bargain.

"Perhaps, my lord, perhaps. We must not forget that we, too, are unable to meet the terms of the agreement. We are no longer in possession of the Cross; we can't raise the remainder of the agreed two hundred thousand-*dinar* ransom; and our own emirs are being less than forthcoming when it comes to turning over the sixteen hundred Christian prisoners in their possession – they were expecting these men to *yield* hefty ransoms, not be part of one."

"What of it?" asked Saladin. "If Richard can't deliver, he can hardly insist that we do."

"My lord, the news from the infidel camp is welcome, but ultimately it changes very little. Someday soon, Richard will force Conrad to return the hostages to his possession. Every day we tie the infidels down in Acre is a day that we grow stronger and they weaker; every day we delay them is a day that we can strengthen our fortifications and reinforce our host. But be not mistaken, my lord, the day of reckoning is near. On that day, Richard will press us to honor the terms of the surrender agreement and we will be unable to do so. And on that day he will slaughter the hostages."

Saladin's jaw dropped. "What about your earlier assurances that he would not do so?"

"If you recall, my lord, I did not guaranty such an outcome; I merely said it was likely. And I also suggested that we be prepared to meet the terms if pressed to do so. Now that we cannot do so, I fear that the hostages are lost."

"Why? Why would Richard do such a thing? What possible advantage is there in such slaughter?"

"My lord," Saphadin began to explain, "Richard has a simple choice to make: if his first love is God and the things of the next world he will find a way to spare the innocents; if, on the other hand, his first love is himself and the things of this world he will kill the hostages. My experience with the *Faranji* teaches me that, with precious few exceptions, they love themselves and the riches of this world more than they love – or fear – God. And from what I've seen, the *Faranji* king is no different. If I judge correctly, and I fear I do, Richard is typical of these brutes, worshipping nothing more than power, glory, wealth and pleasure. And if that is true, the hostages are as good as dead."

"That the infidels neither love nor fear God is obvious – were it otherwise they would embrace the one true faith. And that Richard serves none but Richard is beyond obvious. Even so, why should he kill the hostages? Where is the glory or riches in that?"

The man's lack of strategic sense is staggering indeed, thought Saphadin. He picked up a slice of spiced kid meat, dipped it into the *murrī* and popped it into his mouth. Once he had swallowed it, he proceeded to explain the situation to his brother. "Consider, my lord, the *Faranji* king's options. If he wishes to prevail over us, and to do so quickly so that he can return home and defend his patrimony against Philip's machinations, he cannot leave the hostages at Acre. He would have to detach a sizable detail to mount guard on them and would also have to divert scarce resources to feed them. And there would always be the danger that they might rise up and overthrow the garrison – which would be the end of Richard's campaign in the East. Nor can he take them with him on campaign. The problem of guarding and feeding them while in Acre would be nothing compared to the challenge of doing so while on the march. Nor can he simply free them without securing the promised ransom in return. His fighting men would resent the forfeiture of promised monies; his priests, the failure to procure the relic that they worship so blasphemously; and the families of the men we hold hostage, the failure to secure the return of their loved ones. Nor do I imagine Richard has much interest in returning several hundred capable warriors to us without receiving at least a comparable number of those we hold back into his own host. No, if he wishes to advance his worldly interests, and to take Jerusalem before the rains come, Richard has no choice: he must dispose of the hostages – even if the lives of those Christian prisoners in our custody are forfeit in exchange.

A knowing look spread across the sultan's face. He now saw the inexorable logic of the situation and conceded to himself that his adversary had little choice in the matter. Were the tables turned, he thought, I would doubtless do the same. "Very well," he said, taking a draft of cold water from the cup before him, "the hostages are lost to us. Given that, how should we proceed?"

"We must squeeze every drop of advantage from this situation. And that means delay, delay, delay. We must offer him partial payment, additional hostages, the Holy Spear if we have it in our possession by then…. Anything that will keep him negotiating and thus anchored here in Acre."

Saladin nodded pensively.

"And while Richard and his host are wasting away here, we must redouble our efforts to strengthen our positions at Jaffa. The *Faranji* are totally dependent on the sea for food, water and all the necessities of war – they will not march on Jerusalem until they have secured a suitable port to sustain them as they move inland. Jaffa is their best option – and they will surely attempt to seize it before they move into the hills around Jerusalem. We must improve its defenses so that we can keep it out of their hands."

"I will see that the command is given."

"Beyond that, my lord, we must also make preparations to attack them as they march south along the coast. We must scorch the earth before them; we must harass them at every turn. Then, once they are worn down we must find a suitable spot and mount a major attack on the infidel horde. If we can open gaps in the *Faranji* column, or if we can draw them into one of their typical ill-disciplined charges, perhaps we may bloody them so badly they will abandon the march. We might even, insha'Allah, inflict on them another Hattin," he smiled at such a pleasing prospect, though he doubted the infidel had so soon forgotten the schooling they had received in that terrible battle. "In any case, we cannot permit them to rove about at will – morale in our host is already low; standing idly by while the *Faranji* parade up and down the land as if it were theirs' cannot but lower it further – perhaps fatally."

"I will assign two of my more competent emirs to scout out a suitable location. And I'll have the master of the baggage train prepare to move our main encampment to Caymont. I'm told that if we are to follow the inland route and outflank the Christian horde we will almost certainly have to move through the pass there. It thus seems wise to move our stores from here to there. Will there be anything else, brother?"

"Nothing, my lord, except this: Once, many years ago, I advised you to avoid a pitched battle with the Christians, at least until their battle formations had dissolved into formless masses of individual knights. That advice still stands. If they catch our host in the open before we have broken their formations their heavy horse will destroy us. We must be patient, grinding them down, pricking them and pricking them until they begin to fall apart. Patience and timing are everything, my lord. Victory or defeat – all that separates the one from the other is patience and timing."

"As always, you speak wisely, al-Adil," Saladin responded.

"If Allah has not yet smiled upon us, my lord, at least he is no longer frowning. If He wishes it, and if we act wisely, we may yet defeat Richard and his infidel horde and drive the *Faranji* from our lands once and for all. As I say, all depends on patience and timing. Once they begin their march down the coast we must harass them, awaiting the moment of greatest promise. Then we must strike them at their weakest point with everything we have."

"As always, my brother, your words shine light where I see only darkness. I shall do as you suggest and, insha'Allah, together we will make that infidel

Richard rue the day he set foot in *Dar al-Islam*."

I, too, pray that Allah favors us in this endeavor, thought Saphadin; for these *Faranji* are formidable fighters, and Richard is more formidable than most. Without the help of the All Powerful, I fear that all may be lost – the battle, the campaign, even the empire. Still, where once there was only cause for despair, now there was hope. It is, he thought, as the Prophet, peace be upon him, has written: *And be not weak-hearted in pursuit of the enemy. If you suffer, they suffer too; and you hope from Allah what they hope not.*

"Indeed, my lord," was all he said. "I thank you for your hospitality and bid you good night."

With that he drained his cup of water, rose to his feet and pushed through the flap of the tent and into the darkness gathering beyond.

He awoke with a start, heart pounding, clammy, straining to breathe, a cry of terror stillborn in his throat. Desperate to escape the hell-fire all around him, he pushed aside the sweat-soaked linen and rolled off his palliasse, starting to pray the paternoster even before he had scrambled to his knees. *Pater noster, qui es in caelis, sanctificetur Nomen tuum....* He chanted the ancient prayer slowly, as he had been trained, struggling with each word to calm himself, to focus on the reality of the waking world, to push from his mind's eye the fiery vision that had roused him so violently from his sleep. *Adveniat regnum tuum. Fiat voluntas tua, sicut in caelo et in terra...* Thirteen times he chanted the prayer, its rhythms gradually drawing him fully out of the horrors of his nightmare and into the relative peace of the waking world. *Panem nostrum quotidianum da nobis hodie, et dimitte nobis debita nostra sicut et nos dimittimus debitoribus nostris.* Just as the first wave of terror began to subside, however, he found himself nearly overcome by a second. For with the clarity of wakefulness came the awful realization that the dream – the terrible, awful dream – was back.

He lay on his palliasse for what seemed like an eternity, exhausted yet not daring to close his eyes, shocked that the nightmare had returned. When he first entered the order a little over two years ago, he had viewed the dream as a curse, a nightly foretaste of the eternal punishment that he had earned in this life. But as his friend Father Gabriel had taught him, the dream was less a curse than a scourging; less a foretaste of his fate, than a clarion call to abandon the path of perdition and seek the path of righteousness. As he had immersed himself more fully in the disciplines and rhythms of the life of the order he had come to see the truth and wisdom of the old priest's words. Seeking relief from his dream, and forgiveness for the many sins it recalled, he had entered the Order. Through its Rule, he had found the path of righteousness: selfless devotion to God and His Church; adherence to the simple disciplines of prayer, fasting, and good works; a life of poverty, chastity and obedience. And as he travelled this path, he found the purpose, the fulfillment and, finally, the peace that he had come to believe God had intended for him all along. Mercifully, over time, he had also found relief from the terrible nightmare. Sleep was no longer a foretaste of death, but a blessed relief from the exertions of the day.

Now, however, the night-terror had returned.

And he knew why.

And he knew what he must do to banish it once more.

The sun was not yet fully above the hills to the east, and the banner was shrouded in morning shadow. But the Templars were packed, mounted and eager to begin the day's march. Fitz Alan surveyed the men and horses under his command and thanked God yet again the He had seen fit to put such an instrument in his unworthy hands. With men like these, he thought, all things were possible.

He rode to where de Ramla, Turcault and de Fonte were assembled, just out of earshot of the main body of the banner. "I have made my decision," he said flatly, concealing from his companions the ordeal he had endured to reach it.

De Ramla adjusted himself in his saddle, preparing to renew his objections to the killing of the hostages. Turcault and de Fonte remained perfectly still, ready to accept without question whatever Fitz Alan decided.

"The hostages may live. Master Turcault, release them. Two per mount, with as little water as necessary to get them where they're going."

"*De par Dieu*, my lord," he said, spurring his horse in the direction of the hostages.

De Ramla began to say something, but Fitz Alan silenced him with an icy glance. "Open your mouth, Hospitaller, and I may reverse myself yet again." He then reined his mount around and rode off toward to assume his position at the van of the column. "Gonfanonier!" he barked.

"My lord".

"Make ready to begin the days march."

"*De par Dieu*, my lord."

Fitz Alan looked back only once, catching a glimpse of the now-redeemed hostages galloping off in the direction of home. He then turned back to the task at hand. "Brother John," he said to the gonfanonier, "sound the advance."

Brother John bellowed the call in the prescribed manner.

And with that the banner lurched forward, pushing ever further up the valley – ever deeper, Fitz Alan thought, into the valley of the shadow of death.

VIII

12 August 1191

Fitz Alan stared at the monastery from the edge of the trees. So that's it, he thought. That's what we've come all this way for, killed all these bastards for – that's the Priory of Valsainte. Impressive enough, he judged, though he had seen houses in France, and even England, that made this look like little more than a country church. He turned to de Fonte, who had spent the hours since dawn scouting the priory and its approaches. "What d'ye think, Arnaldus?"

The two Templars were about a mile distant from Valsainte, on the crest of a wooded ridge that concealed them from view should anyone be looking in their direction. From their vantage point to the rear and slightly above the priory they were afforded a relatively good view of the buildings and surrounding lands.

"Looks promising, Michael," came his friend's response. "Basically, we're looking at the back of the priory, which as you can see is set on that little promontory. The valley side falls away into a heavily wooded slope, except there where an earthen embankment forms the wall facing the valley."

Fitz Alan saw the strange feature, which looked less like a wall or embankment and more like a rock-littered ramp leading up into the priory.

"Clearly not designed by a Templar," de Fonte said. "Not even a Hospitaller would build a fortification with a ramp leading over the wall."

"Not a fortification, though, is it. Maybe something to do with its function as a hospital."

De Fonte shrugged and continued with his assessment of the situation. "You can also see that its front gate is facing away from the valley onto the plateau and that it is connected to the Tripoli road by a spur that crests the slope there," he pointed to a spot about a mile from the priory were a modest but well-maintained road emerged from the valley, "then winds past that small collection of buildings, through that the little copse there," he pointed

171

to a small stand of trees, "and straight to the front gate."

Fitz Alan surveyed the priory, looking for anything that might cause them trouble. The location of the church created a blind, concealing most of the cloisters and all of the central garden.

"I'd like to have a better look at that space beyond the church, but I can see nothing amiss. Any reason not to simply ride up and knock on the front door?"

"Just one," de Fonte replied. "See that copse down there, just down the road from the front gate?"

"Yes."

"Look carefully."

Fitz Alan strained to see what bad news lurked in that little thicket of trees. At first he saw nothing; then, just as he was about to press de Fonte for more details, something moved. He focused his gaze ever more intently on the small grove of trees, but could make out nothing clearly. "I saw something move down there," he said to de Fonte. "Monks?"

"Afraid not. Didn't see them at first either, Michael, but once the sun was full up in the valley they came down from the priory to relieve two other men in the copse. They're picquets – bloody Saracen picquets."

Fitz Alan was surprised. He'd half-expected to encounter some sort of Saracen patrol or raiding party once they'd turned onto the main Baalbek-Tripoli road, but he wasn't really expecting them to be in the priory. The only real question now was whether they had been sent here purposefully or were simply raiders who had happened upon the lazar house by chance. Either way, he thought, the bastards now stood between the Templars and the holy relic they were pledged to recover. And as far as Fitz Alan was concerned, that meant that they were as good as dead.

"How many?" he said to de Fonte.

"Can't say. I've only seen the four, but I'd wager that there's many more within the priory's walls. What I *can* tell you is that they're Turcoman horse-archers," De Fonte spat out the words with palpable disgust, "*maudits laches!*"

Thanks be to God for that, Fitz Alan thought. Ill-disciplined light horse they could deal with, depending on the numbers; Mamluk or Kurdish heavy horse, well, that would have been another matter all together.

"How do you want to proceed, Michael?"

Fitz Alan surveyed the battlefield with a practiced eye. This was not the first monastery he'd attacked, though he'd thought when he'd joined the Order he'd be finished with such things.

"We'll move dismounted through those woods down there," he said, pointing toward the heavily treed slope below the priory's walls, "and work our way up to the embankment. The hillside looks steep, but manageable. Once we're on the slope we can enter through the monks' dorters. If the Saracens have rounded everyone up, they'll be holding them in the refectory or the gardens – maybe even in the church itself. There'll no doubt be some too ill to leave the infirmary, but not many I should think. In any case, the dormitory is likely to be empty, so we should be able to enter there undetected."

"And once we're in?"

"Unless I miss my mark, this is just a small band of horsemen. Perhaps they were sent here to acquire the relic; perhaps they've just found their way here while in search of a few easily slit throats and some easy plunder. Either way, we're probably looking at no more than two-dozen of the bastards. And piss-poor light horse at that. If we can get up that ramp without being detected, if we can catch them unawares, if Brother Enyon can get himself situated in that bell tower so that he can rain death down on the heretics, and if we can kill the picquets before they flee to bring help, I think we can carry the day."

"That's a lot of 'ifs', Michael."

"What was it Father Arkright used to say? 'The gods favor the bold?' Fitz Alan laughed aloud at the thought of the old priest's favorite bit of pagan wisdom. "Of course, if you have a better plan...."

The Gascon thought about it for more than a few heartbeats, but had to concede that Fitz Alan's plan not only had merit, but was without serious rival. "No," he said, solemnly. "Let's just pray, though, that God can distinguish between bold and reckless – and that He does not have in store for us another bloody cock-up the likes of which we suffered back there at the toll house."

Fitz Alan nodded in agreement.

And began praying for exactly that.

Fitz Alan led the advance. It seemed to him, as he pressed beyond the first few yards, that the wood would thicken to an impenetrable thicket. He walked slowly up the steep incline, trying to maintain his footing while pushing through the ever-more-dense undergrowth. He feared that the sound of the banner moving so clumsily up the densely treed slope would carry all the way to the priory and beyond. After he'd thought about it for a moment, however, he came to the conclusion the trees themselves probably muffled any noise he and his men might make. In any case, they'd know soon enough.

As he pressed deeper into the wood and further up the hillside, he began to wonder if they were still moving in the right direction, toward the place where the wood thinned out and eventually gave way to the earthen embankment that would take them into the priory. A bird clattered off from its perch, startling the banner into a hedgehog-like posture, bristling with swords and lances and bows. Fitz Alan, heart pounding and blood still hammering in his ears, signaled a halt and motioned de Fonte to join him in the van of the column.

"Reckon we're still moving in the right direction, Arnaldus?" he asked.

"Can't see a thing but trees, trees and more bloody trees," the Gascon replied. "If I were still a wagering man, I'd stake a few small coins that we're still on course, but….". He shrugged.

"Alright, then. That'll have to do. We'll keeping moving as we have been."

De Fonte half-rose from where he had been crouched alongside Fitz Alan and was about to return to his position at the rear of the column when the air was rent by the unmistakable sound of a human scream. It came from some distance away, beyond the woods, and was muffled by the trees. But there was little doubt that is was human, and that it's cause was pain.

"Questioning the poor bastards. God and all his holy saints deliver them," said de Fonte as he crossed himself.

"We may not be saints, Arnaldus, but it's likely to fall to us to deliver them."

Fitz Alan rose and motioned the banner to follow suit. They pushed on ever deeper into the trees, ever further up the steep hillside. The undergrowth was even thicker here than it had been, with shrubs and young ferns vying for what little light there was in the perpetual semi-darkness under the dense foliage above. Another scream, longer this time, and even more blood-curdling. Fitz Alan stiffened and the hair on the back of his neck bristled, but he pressed on and the banner followed him.

It took him another hour before he could see the clearing – an hour punctuated by the scream of the lazars suffering at the hands of the Saracen horsemen. As he approached the tree line, he halted the banner and motioned for de Fonte to join him. The two then moved forward cautiously so that they could see what lay beyond the wood.

"We've undershot a bit, but not enough to make a difference," Fitz Alan said. Another scream pierced the air, louder and clearer now that they were closer to the priory and free of the wood's embrace. "We'll have to cross that open ground to the base of the rock face there," he motioned with his mailed hand at the rocky outcropping that formed the east wall of the priory. "We'll be visible once we leave the wood, but it's only about a hundred paces to the wall, then perhaps a hundred more to the embankment. Unless they've put picquets out on the wall it's unlikely they'll see us."

"Pity we can't see the embankment from here. It looked so smooth and inviting from back on that hilltop, but I doubt it'll be so when we actually have to…." He was interrupted mid-sentiment by another blood-chilling scream, this one ending with a suddenness that left neither Templar in doubt as the fate of its author.

"I fear we haven't the time for a closer look, Arnaldus. If we are to deliver any of those poor souls, we must act quickly. Go back and bid the men prepare for battle. We'll move in a single column. And tell them to move quietly. I want to conceal our presence as long as possible."

"*De par Dieu*," de Fonte replied.

Fitz Alan had been down on one knee while he and de Fonte were surveying the battlefield. Without rising, he drew his sword and held it in front of himself, grounding the point so that the weapon formed a crucifix. He bowed his head and prayed. *Non nobis domine, sed nomini tuo da gloriam.*

And then he rose up from the earth.

And prepared to kill the enemies of Christ and His Church.

Fitz Alan covered the distance from the tree line to the rock wall in a few heartbeats, then moved along the rocky outcropping to where it began to disappear into the earth. Once the remainder of the men had crossed over, he stole a quick glance over the wall and up the embankment. All clear, he thought. No picquets and no one shouting the alarm – a good sign; a very good sign indeed. Perhaps God had heard his prayers and decided to show them some favor. He motioned the banner to follow him, then stepped around the corner and ran up the sloping embankment. It was steep, steeper than he'd thought it would be, nearly impossibly so – but only nearly. He was breathing hard now and his heart was thumping and the blood was pounding deafeningly in his ears. He had to scramble the last few dozen paces on his hands and knees, such was the steepness of the embankment, but he made it to the top and then crossed the forty or fifty yards of level ground between the crest of the embankment and the wall of the nearest building. Then the others began arriving and he moved along the wall, partly to make room for them but also to locate the large window they had earlier spied from their vantage point on the hilltop up the valley. By the time all the Templars had made their way up the embankment he had located the opening in the wall. He motioned to two of the sergeant-brothers standing nearby to prise open the window's wooden shutters, which they did with remarkable ease. He then peered briefly into the room, withdrawing his head before any possible defender in the room might be able to slash at it. The room was darkened, though, and he could see little. Still, the fact that he neither the removal of the shutters nor the appearance of his head had elicited a challenge or cry of alarm suggested that they could enter it in relative safety.

"De Fonte and I will enter first, followed by Brother John and Brother Simon. Once we've secured the room, you," he nodded toward Turcault, "will follow with the rest of the banner. The trick now will be to move quickly and quietly. Once we know where the Saracen bastards are, we'll rush 'em and hack 'em to bits. Until then, we need to conceal our presence. And pass the word: once fighting commences, no quarter is to be given. Understood? I had my fill of Saracen prisoners back in *Espérance* and want no more. If we're going to kill the bastards, let's just do it honorably... in battle."

Both men nodded.

"Right then, let's be about the Lord's work." And with that Fitz Alan heaved himself up to the sill of the arched and now-shutterless window and launched himself into the priory. He landed hard and, half-expecting to be attacked by some disease-crazed lazar or cunning Saracen, dropped immediately into a defensive crouch. Once it was clear that no attack was forthcoming, he relaxed his stance and took a moment to look about. As his eyes slowly adjusted to the darkness, he realized that he had not entered the monks' dormitory as expected, but rather some sort of storeroom or larder. Barrels of wine, sacks of flour and grain, and large wheels of cheese were carefully arranged around the room; from the rafters hung salted meats and smoked fish. Stairs dropped down through a vaulted door on the far side of the chamber and Fitz Alan took them carefully and quietly. He could hear voices now, some in French, others in what he took to be the barbarous tongue of the Saracen horsemen. A movement to his left as he cleared the stairs made him twist around, again half-expecting to be attacked, but it was just a rat scurrying out of the Templars' way. Fitz Alan looked back to see that his three companions were with him, though he knew it was not really necessary to do so. A few more steps and he came to a landing supporting two sets of steps. One set – obviously the night stairs – led up to the church; the other down to a walkway that topped the cloisters. He motioned to de Fonte to follow him, and they both quietly made their way down the short flight of stairs.

The two Templars emerged in a shadowed doorway that opened onto the walkway atop the priory's cloister. Below them was the source of screaming that had punctuated the Templars' approach through the wood. The scene was nightmarish. Scattered around the square lay perhaps fifty dead and mutilated bodies, most of which were dressed in the habit of the Order of Saint Lazarus, though more than a few wore the garish dress of the Turcoman horse-archers. It was obvious that the brothers had offered the Saracens stiff resistance, though it was equally obvious that their attackers had ultimately bested them. The garden was also crammed with dismounted horse-archers, perhaps a score of them, all watching the goings on at the far side of the square. Fitz Alan followed their gaze and discovered the source of the screams that had raised the hairs on his neck during their approach. There the Saracens had constructed a half-dozen makeshift crosses and had nailed to them a number of pitiable-looking men whom he supposed were the survivors of the garrison. Four of the brothers were quite obviously dead. Three of them were still nailed up, copious volumes of dark blood congealing beneath their crucified and tortured bodies. The forth was on the ground beneath his now-empty cross, the nails having evidently torn through his diseased flesh and released him from the beams of wood. A fifth was being interrogated by a small, bowlegged Saracen who was bawling at his victim in palpable frustration. A good sign, Fitz Alan thought, for it meant he has not yet learned what he wanted to know. The final brother seemed only half-conscious, barely able to raise his head from his chest.

The two Templars slipped back though the door and up the steps to the larder. De Fonte stuck his head out the window and motioned the rest of the banner to join them inside. Once they were all in, Fitz Alan sat down with Turcault and de Fonte.

"Suggestions?"

"A quick rush, Michael," said de Fonte. "If we can get our men quietly to the ground floor we can take them all in one quick rush."

"Perhaps leave Brother Enyon up on the walkway so he can skewer their leader – sounds like the bastard deserves a slow death, but I don't suppose we've time for that," Turcault contributed.

Fitz Alan thought it over for all of two heartbeats. "A sound plan, my lords. Master Turcault, get the men sorted. We'll have at 'em as soon as we're in position. Tell Enyon to wait until he hears us charge, then he's to shoot anyone he deems worthy of his ministrations."

"My lord," said Turcault, turning away to organize the attack.

The battle, if a battle it was, was over almost as soon as it started. Brother Enyon's arrow had found its mark, not only killing the Saracen warlord, but pinning him to the empty cross upon which he had so recently crucified the Lazarite brother. The charge had surprised the enemy fighters, who were in any case unaccustomed to dismounted combat, and none survived the initial onslaught. Only one even managed to get off an arrow before dying, but the short, squat bolt had caromed harmlessly off Brother John's mailed sleeve. De Fonte's sword finished the man before he could reload or draw his own blade.

Fitz Alan was still breathing heavily from the exertion of the rush. He stooped to wipe his bloodied mace on the shirt of one of the fallen Saracens, then rose and pointed to two of the *turcopoles* standing nearby. "You men," he said, "cut that poor soul down."

The two men dutifully complied, gently cutting the cords that bound his upper arms to the crossbeam and laying him out carefully on an unbloodied patch of grass.

"Now fetch him some water. Quickly, mind." One of the men dashed off in the direction of the well. Fitz Alan then turned his attention to the man on the ground. "I'm Brother Michael, Knight of the Temple," he said, gently shaking the man. "Who are you?"

The man slowly roused himself to consciousness, and, not realizing that he had been delivered from the fate suffered by his companions, he recoiled in fear.

"You are with friends now, brother. Fear not."

The man tried to speak, but Fitz Alan could not make out what he said.

"Here you are, brother, drink this. It'll help you speak," he said, passing the man a large cup of water. Once the Lazarite had taken a deep draught of the cool water, he tried speaking again. "It's *father*," the man replied, "Father Jean Duval. Of the Order of Saint Lazarus. Chaplain of this house. And who are you?"

Fitz Alan introduced himself again, then proceeded directly to the heart of the matter. "I have need of your assistance, Father. We have been sent here by Richard, king of England and leader of the pilgrimage, to recover an object that was deposited here some decades ago. Do you know of what I speak?"

"Indeed, I do. That bastard," he gestured in the direction of the piniomed carcass of the dead Turcoman warlord, "sought the same thing. And I'll tell you what I told him: I have been told that the Lance lies secreted somewhere in the church – beyond that, I have no knowledge of its whereabouts."

"What do you mean, you have no knowledge of its whereabouts?"

"Just what I said. None of us knew anything about it, other than the tales we were told of it being brought here by the Templars many years ago. Personally, I thought it all just a bit of a fanciful story intended to give our charges a sense of purpose – you know, guardians of the Holy Lance and all that. Today's events would seem to have proven me wrong."

"But you think it lies hidden in the church?"

"That is what we were all told," the priest replied. "And that's certainly what those Saracen devils believed. They tore up the church looking for the relic. In the end, though, they found nothing. As to the truth of the matter...." he shrugged, "I doubt there's anyone alive knows where it is truly concealed."

"Thank you, father," Fitz Alan said, struggling to conceal his disappointment. "I'll see that someone helps you pack your belongings – we can't be certain that others won't come here looking for the relic and you won't want to be here unprotected if they do." He motioned to Brother Simon to look after the Lazarite priest, then turned to the *turcopolier*.

"Master Turcault!"

"My lord," came the reply.

"Set the men about searching the church for the relic. And have someone check to see that our two horsemen cleared those two Saracens out of the copse outside the front gate." He had forgotten about the two men detailed with killing the picquet until that very moment.

"Already done, my lord. Two more Saracens dispatched to the devil's cellar. And we've started searching for the relic. The heathens made a good start of it before we got here, though. They've been through all the more obvious possibilities. I can see why that bastard crucified by Brother Enyon was so frustrated – no obvious place left to look."

"Search the less obvious places, too, William. Much depends on recovering that relic."

"We'll give the place a thorough going over, my lord. If it's here, we'll find it."

"It's here alright. The man who brought it here told me so. The question is, where?"

"Indeed, my lord. I've also sent a man back to bring up the horses and squires and Father de Ramla, my lord. They should be here before nightfall."

"Good. Once they arrive, make certain the horses are fed – and then see that the squires prepare something hot for the men. Seems to me there was meat and cheese aplenty in the larder. See that the men each receive a small cup of wine, too, eh? They fought well today and deserve what the

Rule permits."

"My lord," said Turcault, turning away to organize a small knot of *turcopoles* who were lying, spent, under a large shade tree on one side of the garden.

Fitz Alan covered the short distance across the central garden quickly and entered the church via a door that led into the south transept. He surveyed the building, astonished at the amount of damage the Saracens had managed to inflict in so short a time. It seemed that every statue had been toppled; every window smashed. Benches were upended. The high altar had somehow been overturned and the tabernacle wrenched from the wall and smashed open. Chalices and candles and crucifixes; patens, and pyxes and ciboriums – liturgical objects of every kind were strewn about the sanctuary floor. Even the life-size crucifix that had been suspended from the top of the chancel arch had been hauled down, the cross and image of Jesus crucified both smashed to splinters by infidel horsemen driven nearly mad by their lust for the relic and their loathing of the Christian faith.

At length, he came upon the Marian chapel – or what had once been the Marian chapel. The statue of the Lamentation had been toppled from its plinth and smashed, the image of the crucified Jesus ripped from His grieving mother's plaster embrace. But the twelve-starred halo' of the Queen of Heaven was still plainly visible on the azure wall of the alcove that had housed the statue, as was the ornately sculpted crucifixion scene that adorned the plinth block upon which the statue had rested. The plinth itself rested on a massive stone block that had been sculpted to resemble the cloisters surrounding the garden outside. At the center the cloister was an arched vault, bearing a close resemblance to the main entry to the church, into which was built the chapel's small tabernacle. It was empty now, of course, its precious contents strewn about the floor of the chapel, and its door hanging awkwardly off its hinges. Great beauty, Fitz Alan thought, created out of love of God and marred by the lusts of man. Moved by both the soaring magnificence of the chapel and the terrible ugliness of its desecration, the Templar went down on one knee and prayed the Salve Regina. *Hail, holy Queen, Mother of Mercy, our life, our sweetness and our hope. To thee do we cry, poor banished children of Eve; to thee do we send up our sighs, mourning and weeping in this valley of tears. Turn then, most gracious advocate, thine eyes of mercy toward us; and after this our exile, show unto us the blessed fruit of thy womb, Jesus. O clement, O loving, O sweet Virgin Mary. Pray for us O holy Mother of God, that we may be made worthy of the promises of Christ.*

When he was finished, he crossed himself, stood up and approached the alcove to inspect it more closely. As he got closer, details that had been invisible from the far side of the altar suddenly came into sharp relief. He noticed for instance that some script had been carved into the crucifixion scene on the plinth block. Along the left of the colorfully painted carving were the words *I am Alpha and Omega, the beginning and the end*; along the right, *I am the way and the truth and the life*; along the bottom, *No one comes to the Father except through me*; and all along the top alternating symbols of alpha and omega.

Something tugged at his memory. The words were familiar, of course, for he had heard them at mass and recited them at prayers many times. But this was different. There was something important about these words, felt, something he needed to recall but couldn't. *I am the Alpha and the Omega; No one comes to the Father except through me.* What was it about these phrases that darted in and out of the range of his memory like a Saracen horse archer pricking the Christian host?

And then Turcault was in the chapel. "Pardon me, my lord."

"Yes, William. Have you found anything?"

"No my lord, but the squires and horses have arrived."

"And? Haven't we already spoken of this? Get the horses fed first, then the men."

"I beg to report, my lord, that the priest is not with them."

"He's not…." Fitz Alan's mind was racing now, suspicions flowing as freely as the wine at the wedding feast of Cana. That bastard, he thought. That treasonous bloody, Hospitaller bastard. He's betrayed us. To whom, God only knows. But he's betrayed us, sure as night gives way to day, he's betrayed us."

"It would appear so, my lord."

"What do the squires say?" Fitz Alan asked.

"They say he simply mounted his horse and rode off to the north. He said nothing of where he was going or what he was doing. Simply mounted up and rode off."

"And what do you make of it, William?"

"Same as you, I should think, my lord: he's a lying, stinking traitor. What else could it be?"

I'll kill him, Fitz Alan thought. Next I see his treacherous face, I'll gut him like a trout and watch him flop and writhe in agony until his spirit finally departs for the underworld.

"Nothing we can do about it now, though, is there William?"

"Reckon not, my lord. Not now, at any rate. Maybe later, though, God willing."

"God willing. But for the moment, we've our duty to do. This church has been ransacked twice now, and no one's turned up a bloody thing. Do you have any notion, any whatsoever, where this relic might be concealed?"

"In truth, my lord it could be anywhere. Buried under the floors, in the ceilings, mortared into the walls.... Anywhere. Might even be at the bottom of the midden. If I really wanted to hide it in a place like this, my lord, I assure you none would ever find it."

"Suggestions?"

"None that are practical, my lord. If we could talk to the man who hid the thing, we'd surely know. Barring that, however...."

And then it struck him. Like Saint Paul on the road to Damascus, the truth had struck him. Fitz Alan *had* talked to the man who had hidden the relic, his friend Father Arkwright. What was it he said on his deathbed? *If you do decide to accept this commission.... I am the Alpha and the Omega.... No one comes to the Father except through me.* Jesus wept, he thought, regretting the blasphemy immediately. Is that it? Could it really be that simple?

"Master Turcault," he barked, impatient now to test his theory.

"My lord."

"Bring me two strong men."

"My lord?"

"Two strong men to pick out that sculpture there," he said, pointing to the crucifixion scene on the plinth block. "I've a strong notion, William, that what we seek is there, concealed behind that carving of our Lord on His holy cross."

Turcault barked a command at the sergeant-brothers Simon and John who were searching through the detritus of another chapel in the transept

183

opposite. Within a few heartbeats they presented themselves to Fitz Alan.

"Pluck that sculpture out of that block," he said. "Quickly, mind. We can't be sure there aren't more of those damned heathens heading this way."

Brothers Simon and John had been using short swords pilfered from dead Saracens to pick and probe their way through the church in search of the relic. At Fitz Alan's command they immediately set about using these weapons to try to work the carving out of its setting. The two Templars scraped and chiselled at the mortar holding the scene in place, trying to separate the carving from its setting as quickly as possible. But it was laborious work and progress was painfully slow. Fitz Alan quickly grew impatient with their slow progress and pressed them to move more quickly. The two men redoubled their exertions, but to little appreciable effect. The mortar yielded at its own pace and it seemed there was nothing that could be done to accelerate the work.

A few moments later, de Fonte appeared. Fitz Alan apprised him of the situation, expressing his concern that if they kept on at this rate they'd be here until morning.

"Mind if I try?" the massive Gascon asked. Fitz Alan nodded and the two sergeant-brothers stopped their chiselling and stepped aside so that de Fonte could approach the plinth block. They had anticipated that he would use his sword like they had, but that given his size and strength he would be able to chisel more rapidly. Instead of his sword, though, he drew his Turkish mace, a yard-long wooden club tipped with an immense flanged metal head. He stepped forward and applied the weapon to the scene of the crucifixion with the same force that had smashed so many heathen skulls. One of the metal protrusions struck the crucified Christ in the side, causing the scene to shatter and sending bits of Golgotha flying in all directions. He had to hit it twice more in the same spot before the entire block shattered into a thousand shards, revealing the small vault it had concealed since Father Arkwright had sealed it up over two decades before. Fitz Alan joined de Fonte and both Templars peered through the cloud of stone dust, straining to see what was in the hollow of the plinth.

The cavity was dark and dusty and emitted a faint odour of musty leather. Fitz Alan reached in and withdrew a small buckskin bag and carefully placed it on the altar behind him. Turcault and the two sergeant-brothers crossed themselves and offered silent prayers of thanksgiving as Fitz Alan used his arming dagger to cut the desiccated leather bonds that secured the opening of the bag. The Templar knight then carefully opened the bag and peered inside.

And there it was, the Spear of Longinus, the Spear of Destiny. It was bigger than Fitz Alan had imagined – perhaps a full hand's-breadth in length. It was fashioned in the shape of an ash leaf, just like every spear tip he had ever seen, and looked to be made of iron. It was rusted and pitted, except for the leading third, the killing part, which was obviously old but in remarkably good condition. The neck, where the spearhead would once have been fitted to a long wooden shaft, was shrouded in a band of gold leaf that secured to it a single iron nail, about three inches in length. Fitz Alan turned the relic over and saw that the gold leaf bore an inscription: *Lancea et Clavus Domini*, the Lance and Nail of the Lord.

He looked around and saw that his companions were all on their knees, overawed by the majesty and holiness of the object before them. He had been mesmerized by the Lance, and had treated it like an oddity, but now realized that he was standing before two of the holiest relics in all Christendom, two relics that had actually pierced the sacred flesh of Christ and been bathed in His holy blood. The realization prompted him to drop to his knees, too, and to pray that his impiety be forgiven.

After a while, he rose and bade his companions do the same. "We must be about the Lord's work," he said, "and we can't do that if we remain on our knees all day, can we?" He then reverently replaced the relic in its bag.

"Your commands, my lord?" inquired Turcault.

"The horses and men need to be fed. Set the watch, and let's have some picquets set to watch the road. De Fonte," he said, turning to his friend, "ask Father Duval if he'd do us the honour of leading us in Night Prayers after supper. After that, we'll bed down for the night – I think we could all do with a good night's sleep. We'll leave for Acre at dawn. Questions?"

There were none.

"Alright then, let's get moving."

"My lord," Turcault and de Fonte replied in unison.

When the two had left, he dismissed the two sergeants.

And then he was alone with the relic.

And he sensed its awesome power.
And his heart trembled in the presence of God.

13 August 1191

As soon as the stars began to fade and a smear of light appeared in the east the column had set out. Alberto Forno Canovese, Lord of Montegrosso d'Asti, rode at its head. He wore an unadorned red surcoat over his hauberk and a spangelhelm with broad nasal on his head. His kite shield was slung on his back, the simple device of Montferrat, a red band atop a white field, visible only to those riding behind him. Unlike those of the rest of the three-score men in his *eschielle*, d'Asti's helmet cover reproduced that device, as did his quilted, mail-lined *chausses*, which were striped in red and white. He was riding a black stallion, which alone of the squadrons' sixty plus mounts was wearing a mail-lined caparison of red and white.

Il Sinistro was determined to get his hands on the Holy Spear; for his master, Conrad of Montferrat, wished to have it, and if his master wish something, he would move heaven and earth to furnish it. It was a race, and he knew it. But he had pushed his men hard, tarrying only briefly to plunder the abbey at Belmont. And now, as he crested the rise and entered onto the plain of Valsainte, the prize was in sight. He had only to reach out and grasp it and his master would be well pleased.

As the last man in the squadron left the valley, Canovese motioned the column to halt.

"Albericus," he said.

"My lord."

"Take two men and scout the road ahead. Nothing looks amiss, but I don't want any surprises."

"Yes, my lord," he said, calling out two men-at-arms and riding off toward the priory.

"Volpiano," *Il Sinistro* barked.

"My lord."

"Arrange the men for battle. Three *conrois*. I'll lead the first, Albericus the second, you take the third."

"Si, my lord," came Volpiano's reply. He then reined his warhorse around and began bawling orders at the men to form up into three *conrois* or waves. These men had never trained together, so it proved difficult, but Volpiano showed himself up for the challenge.

Fortuna, Canovese thought, not for the first time, was a fickle bitch. Just because she smiled on him at the last monastery didn't mean he could assume she would at this one. So he had his men arrayed for a fight, just in case the Templars or Saracens or anyone else had beaten him to the prize. He had not clawed his way this far in life, he thought, not proven so useful to the Marquis, by trusting in the inconstant goddess of fate. He preferred instead the stern discipline of *virtú*. He believed in mastering *fortuna*.

And then he heard it. A sound he'd heard once before, long ago. What was it, he thought? Where have I heard that before?

And then, as suddenly as it began, it was over.

And he remembered.

And his heart skipped a beat – for the sound he had heard was the Templar battle hymn. The monkish bastards had beaten him to the prize. They had cheated his master of the object of his desire.

The light was growing, though the dawn proper had not yet arrived. A few *turcopoles* in piebald kettle-hats still moved about the outer courtyard, making a few final preparations for the day's ride, but otherwise the banner was ready to depart Valsainte.

"Master Turcault," Fitz Alan said.

"My lord."

"Have the *gonfanier* signal the advance."

"Yes, my lord."

The plan was simple. The banner would retrace its route back to the Beqaa and from there south to Galilee and then west to Acre. Fitz Alan had considered other options. The Armourer's map suggested at least two alternate routes, one back along the coast road; the other to the sea fortress at Gibelet and thence via ship to Acre. Ultimately, though, he had settled on the inland route; for, although there were myriad dangers along that route, at least they were familiar dangers. Who knew what new perils waited for them along the coast road or on the high seas?

At the *gonfanier's* command, the column lurched forward. The lead horses had moved only a few paces toward the priory's main gate, though, when it was halted by the sudden appearance of the two picquets who had been posted to watch the road. They were galloping as if the devil himself were in pursuit, their horses' hooves throwing up great clods of earthen road behind them. They were through the gate in a few heartbeats and curbed their mounts beside the *turopolier* who had ridden forward to meet them. The three men exchanged words and gestures, then Turcault rode over to Fitz Alan.

"Trouble, my lord."

"Go on."

"These two report that there is a large body of armed men approaching the priory, a few score – maybe as many as sixty. They are coming up the road from the valley. They couldn't be certain, but they didn't think they were Saracens."

Fitz Alan's mind was racing. If they weren't Saracens they could only be Christians – and in this part of the world, that nearly certainly meant Montferrat's men. And if they were already emerging from the valley, they would be at the priory's ruined gate in no time. That left the Templar with a choice: he could have his banner charge the enemy horsemen or he could have them dismount and try to defend the priory. If he had had more knights or even more sergeant-brothers, his decision would have been simple. But the *turcopoles* were not trained in the ways of the Templar charge; they were light horse who fought in the manner of the Saracen horse-archers. Nor, however, was the priory easily defended against so many men. As he knew only too well, it had not been designed as a fortress and he was now down to only about a score of fighters. To charge or to stand and fight: these were his choices. And neither was good.

Then he remembered that he had the relic of the Holy Lance in his saddlebag – remembered the stories of how the spear had put fire in the bellies of the outnumbered and besieged defenders of Antioch; how it had miraculously summoned the spirits of Saint George, Saint Demetrius and Saint Maurice to fight alongside the garrison as its sallied forth in one last desperate attempt to break the siege and carry on with their pilgrimage to Jerusalem. How those saints had delivered the pilgrim host from certain destruction and had spurred it on to liberate the Holy City from the Saracens.

In that instant, Fitz Alan knew what he had to do – and that he had precious little time to do it. He turned to Turcault de Fonte. "My lords, we can't hold the priory against a force that size. So we are going to charge them." He fumbled for a moment with his saddlebag, then withdrew the relic. "And like Bohemund at the siege of Antioch, we're going to charge them under this." He held the relic aloft. "Affix it the *Beauseant*," he commanded. When it had been done, he reined his mount around so that he could address the banner.

"Templars," he began. "The enemy will be upon us in mere moments. Not heathens, but fellow Christians – men who would seize from us the holy relic we have fought so hard, bled so much, to recover for Christ and His Church. They'll be on us soon to kill us and take from us this Holy Lance. But as long as one of us draws breath, they shall not have it! On our sacred honor, the thieves shall not get their grasping hands on it; they shall not seize it from us and put it in the service of their own sinful lusts and evil schemes. No, we're going to hold it – whatever the cost – and return it to the pilgrimage so that it can be used in the service of God, so that it can be used in the sacred cause of liberating Jerusalem. Much depends on what we few bretheren do here today. I know that you will not disappoint, for you are the finest warriors in all of Christendom, nay the world! And I know, too, that this holy relic," he pointed to the lance, lashed now to the *Beauseant's* own spearhead, "touched by our Lord and Savior Himself, is endowed with great powers – powers that will protect us and fortify us as we strive to do what God has called us to do. The past teaches us that the relic can deliver victory where defeat seemed certain. And that was in the hands of mere pilgrims. Imagine what victories are possible when it is wielded by those who fight under the *Beausant*! Templars!" he bellowed, surveying the column with evident pride. "Prepare for battle! Prepare for victory!"

For a few heartbeats, the assembled Templars were utterly silent, stunned by what they had just heard. Until a few moments before, they had expected nothing more than a hard day's march and now, suddenly, they were faced with the prospect of imminent combat and death. Fitz Alan could see the play of emotions on their faces. Fear, dread, uncertainty – the usual panoply of human sentiment on the verge of battle. But he also saw serenity and determination on those faces, happiness even; for he was calling these men to fight and kill and die for Christ and His Church – and that was a tiding of great joy. Indeed, Fitz Alan felt a similar serenity, a similar joy; for he, too, realized that he had been given yet another chance to do what had been born and raised to do, to do what God had called him to do, to do penance for the monstrous sins of his past.

Other men on the verge of battle might have raised their voices in raucous shouts of enthusiasm or bravado. But that was not the Templar way. As the enemy approached the outnumbered Templars, Fitz Alan nodded to de Fonte and the colossal Gascon began to sing. "*Non Nobis Domine, Domine!*" his mellifluous voice holding the first "*Domine*", before finishing abruptly with the second. *Not unto us, O Lord.* The song pierced the banner's silence, calling the men to readiness for battle. Swords and maces were drawn; lances couched. A horse whinnied. A heartbeat later, a score of throaty voices sounded the refrain: "*SED NOMINE, SED NOMINE. TUO DA GLORIAM!*" *But unto* thy *name, unto* thy *name, give glory!*

And with that, the *gonfanier* tilted the *Beauseant* slightly forward and twenty Templar warriors thundered through the gates of hell and into battle.

Il Sinistro saw them first, a swarm of horsemen emerging from the gates. He could just make out the white robes and crosses of the two leading horsemen. Templars, he thought. Damned whore-son Templars. And they've beaten me to it; they have the Lance. The thought of these thieves cheating his master of the relic caused an enormous anger to well up inside him – an anger that quickly became rage and that erupted a heartbeat later in an ear-splitting roar of pure fury. I'll kill the bastards, he thought, his ire stoked by the impudence of these vile monks. I'll kill every last one of the filthy bastards and then I'll take the damned relic from them. Christ on His Cross, he thought, they may have won the race for the Lance, but I'll be damned if they simply walk away with it. I'll kill every last one of the swine before I let that happen. By the bowels of Christ, I'll crucify every last one of the accursed sodomites before I let that happen. Canovese then savagely roweled back his spurs, sending his *destrier* charging toward the approaching Templars. His sword was out of its scabbard before the horse had taken two strides; by the time it had taken three, he was screaming at his men to follow him.

And they did, the first two *conrois* at least, lowering their lances and roaring out their battle cries and viciously spurring their warhorses to the attack.

And a few heartbeats later forty of the Marquis of Montferrat's best men-at-arms collided with twenty of the Temple's best mounted warriors on a plain deep in the heart of Saracen-held Syria.

And then the killing for the Lance of Longinus began in earnest.

The Templars covered the first fifty yards or so at the canter. Tightly packed, almost knee-to-knee, eight across and two deep, they formed a small but fearsome wedge of flesh, spirit and steel. As they closed to within a hundred yards or so, Fitz Alan could see the enemy horsemen desperately trying to hold their formation. But the ground was uneven and, while many were excellent riders and fighters, they were unpracticed and ill-disciplined. Gaps began to open up in the line. That was all Fitz Alan needed. *"Beauseant!"* he cried and the banner roweled their horses to a unstoppable gallop. Thundering now toward the enemy, Fitz Alan gripped his Saracen sword tightly. Directly to his front, he picked out his target. A bearded man, wearing a helmet and mail, he was carrying a lance in one hand and had kite shield looped over the other in such a way that he could hold both it and the horse's leather-covered mail reins. Fifty yards now. The blood pulsed in his ears and he felt as if his heart was about to burst. Twenty yards. He stood in his stirrups and leaned forward in his saddle. The enemy horseman raised his lance and pointed it directly at Fitz Alan's chest. The Templar was so close now that he could almost tell the color of his eyes. The man leaned forward at the last moment, thrusting his lance toward his Templar opponent. In a motion that he had practiced countless times, Fitz Alan used his sword to deftly flick the man's lance back across his body, thus exposing the man's neck. The Templar drove past the now defenseless rider, delivering a vicious downward stroke that sliced though the man's coif and bit hard into his neck. Fitz Alan felt a sharp stab of pain in his right shoulder, but held onto the sword and let his forward motion wrench it from the man's spine. He marveled once again at the killing power of the Saracen sword the armorer had given him. Vaguely aware of the screams and cries all around him, he allowed the force of the charge to carry him into the second *conroi* of the enemy force. Fitz Alan began hacking and chopping at the mass of horsemen, first to his left and then his right, all the time keeping his *destrier* moving forward. He could sense it now: the enemy force was broken. The brawl would continue for a short while, but he sensed that it was now only a matter of time. *Resist the Devil and he shall flee*, he thought. Providing the Templars continued to fight as if they were fighting the devil himself.

To his left Fitz Alan saw de Fonte use his massive mace to smash the head of an unarmored horse. The beast died instantly, its forelegs buckling first and pitching its rider forward over the horse's shattered head. De Fonte then swung his mace around and caught another man full in the face, just below where the broad nasal of his helmet ended. The force of the blow sent a thick gobbet of tooth and blood and bone spraying into the air. The man shot backward, lifted by the Gascon's immense strength over the rear cantle of his wooden saddle and onto his back, writhing and frothing as he lay dying on the ground.

Fitz Alan was through the two enemy *conrois* now. "*Beauseant!*" he called and the standard bearer quickly rallied to his side. "*Beauseant!*" he called again. Within heartbeats, the Templar banner was forming up around him as they had so many times in practice and on the battlefield. The enemy horses were running everywhere now, their riders desperate to escape the Templar warriors. A dozen or so had been rallied by one of the enemy leaders, who was desperately trying to form them into some sort of battle formation. That was all Fitz Alan needed to see. "Templars!" he yelled, pointing to the half-formed mass. "*Beauseant!*" This time, he spurred his horse to the gallop right away, a dozen of his men packed tightly behind him. His blood was up now and he could barely think straight. Kill the bastards, he thought, kill them, kill them all. And then he was moving through them, hacking with all his might against anything wearing a red surcoat, a merciless, ruthless killer at work in the fields of the Lord, all the while pressing forward, slashing as many of the red-coated demons as he could before emerging from their annihilated formation. The enemy was in general retreat now, fleeing back toward the third conroi that stood motionless a few hundred paces from where the battle had raged. Those poor few souls who found themselves wounded or unhorsed were quickly dispatched by the Templars, who showed exactly the degree of mercy they knew they would be shown if the circumstances were to be reversed. Fitz Alan began to feel the euphoria of the battle subside and had to remind himself that he had to prepare lest the third conroi attack them while unformed.

"Brothers," he called, "to me! Form up on me!"

And Fitz Alan's remaining dozen-and-a-half fighters began to assemble around their leader in the shadow of the Holy Lance and *Beauseant*.

"What d'ye reckon, William?"

"At least two score of the bastards left, my lord. If we stand here much longer, they'll charge and it'll be over before it starts. There are just too many of them."

"And you, Arnaldus?"

"If William is correct, and I fear he is, we should strike now. I'd rather die attacking than defending. And perhaps we might yet carry the day. What was it Saint Bernard once said? 'Rejoice, brave warrior, if you live and conquer in the Lord; but glory and exult even more if you die and join your Lord.' Always been good enough for me."

"Agreed. Brother de Fonte, call the charge."

And sixteen Templars charged forty men-at-arms.

At first, Fitz Alan thought his eyes were playing tricks on him. Rather than roweling their warhorses forward into a furious countercharge, the enemy horsemen seemed to be desperately trying to rein their horses about and ride away from the fast-approaching Templars. Being unpracticed, the maneuver produced great confusion in the enemy line as horses and lances and all the appurtenances of mounted men-at-arms became snagged and tangled. Men shoved each other; horses bit and kicked in every direction. Order gave way to chaos as the *conroi* disintegrated into a hopeless jumble of panicked men and spooked horses.

Then he saw the cause of the panic. A column of horsemen was coming up out of the valley and forming up in a long semi-circle behind the enemy *conroi*. The newcomers were clad in white-hooded surcoats fastened at the waist by a broad red sash. For a moment he thought his prayers had been answered, that the warrior saints of old had come down from heaven festooned in the colors of blood and holiness, to save them. But as their numbers swelled – and as he saw the round shields, small bows and diminutive mounts – he realized that these were not saints, but Saracens.

Fitz Alan's blood was up and the banner was almost upon the panicked throng of red-coated horsemen that moments before had seemed to him unbeatable. But he knew that charging into that vulnerable mass now, with Saracen horse-archers waiting for them on the other side, would be to sound his own death knell. He checked his horse and wheeled it back out of range of the Saracen bows, the remainder of the banner in tight formation behind him.

"What the devil is happening?" panted de Fonte, as he curbed his warhorse beside Fitz Alan's. "And who in Christ's name are they?"

Fitz Alan could see the horse-archers loosing their arrows now, see the shafts slicing through the air, see the broadheads and bodkins slashing into man and beast alike. For a heartbeat, he thought the puny arrows were having no effect. But then a horse staggered and collapsed in a great flurry of legs and lance. The horse screamed as it fell, crushing its rider. Its lashing legs then struck the beast behind it and sent another horse and rider tumbling to the ground. He saw another arrow bury itself in a man's chest, driving him back onto the high cantle of his saddle as if he had been yanked by rope. And then the *conroi* began to die quickly, arrows slicing arteries, puncturing lungs and stabbing hearts as quickly as the skilled Saracen horse-archers could put arrows to staves. Within moments it was reduced to a bloody mass of still and still-twitching bodies, man and horse entwined in death as they had been in life.

"You tell me, Arnaldus. Who are they?" Fitz Alan replied, gasping for breath.

The Gascon prided himself on knowing the dress and habits of all the many types of Saracen warrior, from the Bedouin to the Tawashi, but he couldn't place these white-coated warriors. "Don't know, Michael. Never seen the likes of them before."

Fitz Alan looked back across the field as the last surviving man-at-arms somehow managed to steer his mount clear of the bleeding and dying *conroi*. His sword held before him, he spurred his warhorse and charged the mass of murdering Saracens. By some miracle he had thus far been untouched by the archers' arrow, and just as miraculously he remained as he cut the distance to his attackers in half. For half a heartbeat, Fitz Alan found himself hoping he would ride down just one of the hooded horsemen and cut him down, that he would rid the world of just one more of these demons. He nearly made it, but then an arrow ripped into his *destrier*'s belly. The beast screamed, twisted away and charged back in the direction of Fitz Alan and his men. Saracen arrows followed the beast and its rider, arcing higher and higher as the range between hunter and prey opened up. Must be the man's saint's day, Fitz Alan thought, for no one should have been able to survive that steady shower of bolts without some kind of divine intervention.

"Brother Enyon."

"My lord."

"Prepare your bow. If either that rider or those Saracens do anything untoward...."

"Not to worry, my lord. Anyone misbehaves and I'll send 'im straight to hell." The Welshman then proceeded to sheathe his sword and unsling the horsehide case that held his warbow. He uncased the weapon, placed its butt end in his left stirrup and hooked the loop over the upper nock. He then drew an arrow from the arrow-case hanging from his saddle, smoothed the fletching and placed it across the great stave.

The survivor had somehow managed to dismount his pain-maddened warhorse and was now running in the direction of the Templars. Enyon took aim, prepared to put a bodkin through him at the first sign of trouble.

The man staggered the last few steps. "I seek your protection," he gasped, then doubled over, struggling to catch his breath.

"You what?" de Fonte exclaimed. "Was it not you who but a moment ago tried to kill us? Indeed, did you not actually kill more than a few of us?"

The survivor coughed something up from the depths of his lungs, then straightened himself and spat it back toward the Saracens. "That was before these wraiths arrived. Now, as a Christian and a pilgrim, I seek the protection of the Templars. Is it not the sworn duty of the members of your order to offer such protection to Christians like me?"

"My lord," de Fonte said to Fitz Alan, "let me kill this dog where he stands. Whatever else he might be, this man is no pilgrim. We are obliged to offer him nothing, save perhaps a quick death and a Christian burial."

Before Fitz Alan could respond, Turcault raised his hand and pointed back toward the Saracens. "My lord."

The Templars and the survivor all looked to where Turcault was pointing. There, a hundred paces or so in front of the line of Saracen horsemen was a white-hooded figure waving a white flag of parley.

"Bind him for now," Fitz Alan instructed de Fonte, gesturing toward the survivor. "We'll decide his fate later." He then turned his attention quickly back to the man with the flag. "Master Turcault, what do you make of this?" he said.

"Only the obvious, my lord. It would seem that they wish to talk."

"Then I suppose talk we must. Brother Enyon."

"Already marked him, my lord. Anything untoward...."

"Good man."

And with that he sheathed his sword and set off to parley with the hooded man carrying the flag.

The Templars watched as Fitz Alan approached the hooded man. They stood together, about half-way between the two bodies of fighting men, evidently exchanging greetings. After only a few heartbeats, however, they saw Fitz Alan draw his sword and gesture menacingly at his interlocutor. The line of Saracen horse archers appeared to quiver in response, but neither they nor the hooded man made any threatening movements. Brother Enyon made a few unconscious adjustments to his aim, but before the situation worsened and he was required to shoot, Fitz Alan resheathed his sword and continued the conversation.

"What do you make of all that?" de Fonte said to no one in particular. No one responded because no one had any idea what to make of it.

After what seemed like an eternity, both men returned to their respective formations.

"Well?" de Fonte said, as Fitz Alan rejoined the Templars, "what the devil's going on?"

"You'll not believe it when I tell you." Fitz Alan replied. "It's de Ramla. The man with the flag of parley was Father bloody Raimundus de Ramla."

It was more than a few moments before anyone spoke. When the silence was broken, it was de Fonte who did the breaking. "So the bastard did betray us. He was working for the Saracens. Why did you not kill him, Michael? Surely not because of a white rag on stick."

"I don't like the man, Arnaldus, and there have been times when I have been sorely tempted to wipe the self-satisfied look off his face with the back of a mailed hand. But he didn't betray us, at least not in the sense you mean. He lied to us and kept things from us, and there can be little doubt that he used us. But he didn't betray us. In fact, he probably saved us. I'll tell you more later, for his tale is complicated and we haven't time at the moment. And I'm not certain I understand all of it myself. For now it seems we are to join our new friends over there and do them a service."

"A service?" de Fonte sputtered, barely trying to conceal his dismay. "What kind of service?"

"A very old Templar service. We are to provide them with an escort through dangerous lands."

"An escort? And just who are these people that we must provide them an escort?"

"Assassins," Fitz Alan responded. "They are Assassins."

Epilogue

The quest for the Holy Lance had been in deadly earnest, de Ramla assured Fitz Alan, but it was not the only reason that he had accompanied the Templars to Valsainte. He had another, no less important, objective: to rendezvous with an Assassin caravan – this Assassin caravan – and escort it back to Acre.

Fitz Alan was staggered by the Hospitaller's words. "An Assassin caravan?" he said. "Carrying what?"

"Gold. Some silver as well, I believe, but mostly gold."

"Gold?" Fitz Alan exclaimed. "We came all this way, lost all these good men, for gold?" He spat a small measure of his disgust into the parched grass at his feet.

"Things are not as they appear…," de Ramla began to explain.

"I hope not, Hospitaller," Fitz Alan cut him off abruptly, "for the appearance is you've led us on a fool's errand across half of heathendom just so your bloody lord and master the Angevin could throw a few more coins on his mountain of filthy lucre. Good men, better men than you or that bastard Richard, have died so that we could retrieve the Lance, so that we could unleash its power and set Jerusalem free. They died believing they were serving Christ and His Church. And now you're telling me that their sacrifice was not in God's cause, but in Richard's? That they died in the service of nothing more than the Angevin's boundless appetite for power, wealth and pleasure?"

"That's not what I'm telling you, Brother Michael – and if you'd but hold your tongue for a moment I'd explain everything."

Fitz Alan seethed, but remained silent, almost daring de Ramla to speak his peace.

"We're not here in Richard's service," the Hospitaller said. "We're here in the cause of Christendom. We're here to serve God – nothing else."

"Go on, you lying bastard, spin your tale."

"It's no tale, simply the truth. Your mission was to recover the Lance; mine was to seal our arrangement with the Nizari. As I tried to tell you on the trail, they need us to counterbalance Saladin. And in that cause they have been willing to provide us with silver and gold – lots of silver and gold. All we needed was a way to get it from the Nizari lands to Acre. An escort – a capable escort – that's all that we needed. But none was available. And then you showed up. And Bishop Walter commanded you to recover the relic from Valsainte. And Valsainte was so close to the Nizari lands. And you were so motivated. It seemed as if Christ himself had brought all the threads together. So I was commanded to work with you to recover both the Lance and the Assassin gold."

"Commanded by whom?"

"Not who you think. It was the Hospitaller Grand Master who bade me treat with the Assassins, to find a way to get the gold from them to us – the relic was mean to be nothing more than his gift to the Temple."

"His gift?" Fitz Alan sputtered.

"Yes, his gift. You Templars may put great stock in relics and such things, but the Hospital is much more interested in material resources – those things that can actually help us best the Saracens and drive them from these lands. Gold, to put not too fine a point on it. You seek relics; we seek gold. Both are necessary if we are to liberate Jerusalem."

Fitz Alan was stunned. He fumbled for something to say, for some response to the evil he had just heard spoken, but no words came.

"I wanted to tell you the truth, Michael. Indeed, I nearly did so when you asked me about the Nizari. Do you remember? But I knew from your Bishop Walter that you'd be far more motivated by the prospect of recovering an important relic than by the prospect of acquiring some – what did you call it? – filthy lucre. So I kept my mouth shut and let you do what you do best."

"He's not my bloody bishop," was all Fitz Alan managed to say in response. Beyond that, words failed him so he simply turned his back on de Ramla and walked off in the direction of the priory. The bastard-priest, he thought, could stew in the bitter juices of his own deceitfulness. Working his way back to the main gate, he stumbled upon a small grotto carved into a limestone outcropping. In need of comfort, he went down on one knee before the Blessed Virgin. *Ave Maria, gratia plena, Dominus tecum. Benedicta tu in mulieribus, et benedictus fructus ventris tui, Iesus,* he prayed. His shoulder ached as if he'd been kicked by the devil's own warhorse, as did his ribs where the Saracen arrow had slammed into his mail only a few days before. *Hail Mary, full of grace, the Lord is with thee; blessed art thou amongst women, and blessed is the fruit of thy womb, Jesus,* he prayed again. He was bone weary, both spirit and flesh suborned by fatigue. He desperately wanted to sleep, to partake of the deep sleep that he imagined were the wages of the righteous, though he knew that for him the prospect of any real sleep was many days distant. And he wondered yet again if he even deserved such respite, if he had earned the wages of righteousness, if by his good works he had finally gained for himself a proper night's sleep – a sleep free of the night-terrors that had plagued him once and seemed to have returned. He wondered once more if he had finally been redeemed, finally been forgiven for all the monstrous evils of his life before the Order. *Mother of Mercy,* he pleaded, *pray for me. Strength and comfort, send me. Intercede with your beloved Son for the remission of my sins. Lead me home to dwell eternally in the presence of the Lord. Queen and Mother blest, pray for me.* His mind drifted back over the last few weeks, gauzy shadows of memories passing before his mind's eye. He sensed he had been tested, but he was not certain that he had been proven. He had killed, and that counted against him. But he had killed neither out of anger nor vengeance. Neither had he killed for earthly wealth or glory. No, he had killed, but he had done so solely in furtherance of the cause of justice, the cause of Christ. And he had done so with a pure heart. Had not the Holy Father himself declared that killing thus was not a sin, but an act of penance on the same plane as prayer, works of mercy, and fasting; had he not promised that killing in the name of Christ and His Church would not condemn the killer, but redeem him?

Ave Maria, gratia plena, Dominus tecum. Benedicta tu in mulieribus, et benedictus fructus ventris tui, Iesus, he prayed again, looking deeply into the brightly-colored eyes of the image of the Madonna as if he might find there the answers to his questions.

He could not deny that he had been sorely tempted to kill the hostages taken in assurance of their safe passage through that Saracen town; that he had been tempted by anger and wrath and the lust for vengeance to kill the infidels in his custody. And that also counted against him. But neither could anyone gainsay the fact that in the end he had resisted that temptation. To be sure, he thought, the credit for that belonged not to him, but to God; for had not He, in his boundless love, sent the night-terror to chastise Fitz Alan in his hour of temptation? Had not He used the Hospitaller priest to call the Templar back from the precipice? Ultimately, though, it was he, Michael Fitz Alan, knight of the Temple, who had decided to resist the blandishments of the earthly city; it was he who had decided to turn away from the Evil One; it was he who had decided to resist the powerful tug of his own sinful nature. Finally, it was *he* who had chosen the path of righteousness over the path of wickedness. In the world God had brought forth, a world in which men were created free to decide between good and evil, surely that counted in his favor.

Non nobis, Domine, sed nomini tuo da gloriam, he prayed, not wanting to take too much credit for simply doing what was right and just. *Not unto us, O Lord, but unto thy name give glory.*

He was tired now, barely able to maintain his vigil, and despite his firm resolve to remain focused on his prayer to the Holy Mother, his mind drifted where it would. He found himself now by Father Arkwright's deathbed, conversing with the old priest as if his friend had not yet returned to his eternal home.

"Well, my son, it seems as though you've succeeded in your great quest."

"I have father," came his half-dreamt response. "My men and I have recovered the Holy Spear."

"Indeed you have. And God help us all now that it is back in Christian hands. But that is not the quest of which I speak."

"I'm afraid I don't understand, father. Of what quest do you speak?"

"The only quest that truly matters to you, Michael. The quest to prove yourself – to prove yourself a true Templar, a genuine warrior-monk, one of Saint Bernard's new knights."

"I'm not so certain, Father. I made many mistakes along the way."

In his mind's eye, Fitz Alan saw the Templar chaplain laughing as heartily as he once had, back when they were at home in England, at Temple Ewell.

"Of course you made mistakes. I am aware of only one man in all of human history who made none, and He was crucified for it. But you learned the lessons you needed to learn along the way."

"Lessons? What lessons?"

"You learned to put God and his plan ahead of your petty wants and desires; to order yourself, body, soul and spirit, to the service of our Lord and Savior, Jesus Christ. You learned to wage war on vice and sin with the same skill with which you wage war on sinner and Saracen. You learned that the worldly knight within you cannot be killed, only submerged. And not too deeply, at that – at least not if you wish to be of any use to the Christ and His Church. And you have learned, my son, that there is no royal road to the new knighthood, only the hard disciplines of the Rule – disciplines that are intended to press from a man all pride and self-love, all hatred and vengeance, so that all that is left is humility before God and a selfless love of Mother Church. And, of course, a hardened and disciplined warrior. So you see, Michael, if you think about it for but a moment, you'll realize that you have indeed learned a great deal on this pilgrimage – a very great deal, indeed. You have learned to be the Templar I always knew you would become."

"Perhaps, Father. But all those sins; all those deaths at my hand; all those wrongs I committed before I joined the Order...."

"As I have said many times before, Michael, stay the course. Place your sword ever more faithfully at the service of the Church; apply your talents ever more selflessly in her defense.... That is the path to the remission of sin, Michael.... That is the path to salvation.... That is your path to freedom, should you but cleave to it..."

Then, suddenly, Fitz Alan was startled back to wakefulness by a long, rumbling peal of thunder. In an instant, Father Arkwright was gone, replaced in the Templar's field of vision by the statue of the Blessed Virgin. Rain started to fall and he turned his gaze from the Mother of Mercy toward the heavens. Warm drops of water began to fall on his face, gently washing away the layers of blood and grime that had accumulated there since departing Acre. After a while, he wiped away the remaining filth with the bloodied sleeve of his *cappa*. Then he stood up and looked back down the slope to where de Fonte and Turcault were assembling what was left of the banner. Thanks be to God, he thought, for God's mercy. And thanks be to God for the gift of these Templar warriors – the finest fighting men in all the world. God had blessed him with command of this superb band of killers – these Poor Fellow-Soldiers of Christ, these Templars. And together they had recovered the Holy Lance from deep in the bowels of heathendom. What else, he wondered, might these holy warriors accomplish in the service of Christ? What was it that the armorer had called them outside of Acre? The English Templars? They hailed from England and Wales and Gascony in the west to Tyre and Tripoli and Tortosa in the east – only a handful would have thought of themselves as English. But they were Fitz Alan's men, and he was out of the heart of England; so yes, he supposed, that was as good a description as any. They were the English Templars, the elect, the best warriors the world had ever known. And they were his to command.

𝕳istorical 𝕹ote

The story of Peter Bartholemew and the Holy Lance at the siege of Antioch is a true one, at least inasmuch as there was a monk by that name who brandished something he claimed was the Holy Lance and thereby rallied the defenders to sally forth and defeat the besieging Muslim army. Despite its rallying effect, however, there were many, including the papal legate Adhemar of Le Puy, who doubted the authenticity of relic and considered Peter a charlatan. Indeed, so pervasive were contemporary suspicions regarding Peter's claims that he ultimately volunteered to subject himself to trial by fire in order to prove himself. Unfortunately for him, the ordeal did not go well for Peter. He was badly burned during the trial and died a few weeks later of his injuries. Despite this, the belief that relics in general, and the Holy Lance in particular, had miraculous powers remained widespread throughout Christendom. It is far from fanciful, then, that King Richard – always looking for an advantage over both his Muslim enemies and Christian rivals – would seek to acquire the relic. In today's language, the Lance – like the relic of the True Cross Richard also wanted so earnestly to recover – would have been considered a very powerful "force multiplier".

There was an Order of Saint Lazarus. It was founded in the Kingdom of Jerusalem in 1098 to provide aid and succor to those who had contracted the disease of leprosy, especially Templars and Hospitallers. Dependent houses – called "Lazar houses" or *lazarettes* – were subsequently established throughout Latin Christendom. Alas, there was no Lazar house at Valsainte – that is an entirely fictional priory. But there was, and is, a Holy Valley (*Wadi Qadisha* in Arabic). Located in what is today northern Lebanon, not far from the Forest of the Cedars of God, this steep-sided gorge has been the site of monastic communities continuously since the early years of Christianity. It is thus a fitting site for the fictional Valsainte.

Although there was no Priory of Valsainte there was a monastery at

Belmont. Founded by Cistercian monks in 1157, it was known variously as *Balamand, Bellus-Mons* and *Bellimonte ultra Mare*. The Cistercians abandoned the monastery in the late-thirteenth century and it subsequently came under the authority of the Greek Orthodox Church. Situated about eighty kilometers north of Beirut, the monastery is now part of one of the campuses of the University of Balamand.

If I have taken any liberties with the historical record, it is with respect to Saladin. At least since the time of Sir Walter Scott and his great work of historical fiction *The Talisman*, the Kurdish leader of the campaign to extinguish the crusader kingdoms has been viewed in the West as a wise, gracious and chivalrous warrior. During his own time, however, Saladin was often depicted in a far more negative light. To be sure, there were those among his contemporaries who thought him a great commander and a wise ruler. Many other accounts, however, picture him as a devious, self-serving and/or incompetent leader who was extremely fortunate in his choice of both family and enemies. The truth, I suppose, can never be fully known. I do believe, though, that my portrayal of Saladin, while at odds with the picture painted by his modern hagiographers, is an at least plausible interpretation of the historical record.

That a band of Assassins should rescue Fitz Alan from Christian attackers is not terribly far-fetched. The Christian-Muslim religious and civilizational divide, while always in the background, was not always the dominating feature of the geopolitics of the region. Inter-Christian and inter-Muslim conflicts, coupled with alliances of convenience that spanned that divide, were endemic to the "international system" of what we today call the Middle East. Overlay that with sectarian divisions within both civilizational camps (Latin, Greek, Armenian, Nestorian and other sects in the Christian camp; Sunni, Shia, Nizari and other sects within the Muslim), dynastic disputes, and all the other political byproducts of feudalism and coalition politics and some idea of the complexity of the geopolitics of the region quickly becomes apparent. Only when Christian and Muslim leaders were able to mobilize "coalitions of the willing" behind a crusade or jihad respectively did the religious divide emerge as the most conspicuous and consequential. At other times, Christians fought Christians (sometimes with Muslim allies) and Muslims fought Muslims (sometimes Christian allies). Given that the Nizari – whom the Sunni majority considered to be dangerous heretics – feared that Saladin would come after them once he had eliminated the crusader kingdoms, it is entirely plausible that at least some of them would have thrown their lot in with the Christians.

A few minor terminological notes: throughout the novel, I have used the term "Father" as the honorific used when addressing a Catholic priest. This is anachronistic, of course: Catholic priests have only been referred to as Father since the restoration of the Church hierarchy in England in the mid-nineteenth century. In the late medieval era, priests were called "Dom" (from the Latin *dominus* or lord) or Sir or, in some cases, Doctor. But as all writers of historical fiction are aware, sometimes it is necessary to sacrifice a little authenticity in order to gain a lot of readability. This, I think, is one of those cases. Similarly, I have referred to Bishop Walter as King Richard's "chancellor". Again, a somewhat anachronistic term, but a useful descriptor of the bishop's political office and one that makes sense to contemporary audiences.

So, even though Fitz Alan and his men have recovered the Holy Lance, and even though Acre has finally been taken and the Christian host is on the move, there is no guaranty that King Richard's campaign to liberate Jerusalem will end in success. Saladin is still at large with a considerable and menacing field army, and Richard's army cannot safely march inland to liberate the Holy City until Richard decisively defeats the infidel horde. There is much fighting still to be done, so Fitz Alan, de Fonte and the rest of the English Templars must ride into action yet again. *Deus Vult*!

CPSIA information can be obtained at www.ICGtesting.com
Printed in the USA
LVOW12*0151170315

430828LV00004B/4/P